The Scarred Rancher's Unforgettable Bride

STAND-ALONE NOVEL

A Western Historical Romance Novel

by

Ava Winters

Copyright© 2020 by Ava Winters

All Rights Reserved.

This book may not be reproduced or transmitted in any form without the written permission of the publisher.

In no way is it legal to reproduce, duplicate, or transmit any part of this document in either electronic means or in printed format. Recording of this publication is strictly prohibited and any storage of this document is not allowed unless with written permission from the publisher

Table of Contents

The Scarred Rancher's Unforgettable Bride 1
   Table of Contents 3
   Let's connect! 5
   Letter from Ava Winters 6
Prologue 7
Chapter 1 10
Chapter 2 20
Chapter 3 32
Chapter 4 41
Chapter 5 46
Chapter 6 55
Chapter 7 67
Chapter 8 81
Chapter 9 93
Chapter 10 101
Chapter 11 113
Chapter 12 121
Chapter 13 131
Chapter 14 142
Chapter 15 157
Chapter 16 167
Chapter17 174
Chapter 18 188
Chapter 19 203

Chapter 20 216
Chapter 21 225
Chapter 22 241
Chapter 23 249
Chapter 24 258
Chapter 25 264
Chapter 26 269
Chapter 27 276
Chapter 28 287
Chapter 29 294
Chapter 30 302
Chapter 31 310
Chapter 32 321
Epilogue 326
   Also by Ava Winters 332

Let's connect!

Impact my upcoming stories!

My passionate readers influenced the core soul of the book you are holding in your hands! The title, the cover, the essence of the book as a whole was affected by them!

Their support on my publishing journey is paramount! I devote this book to them!

If you are not a member yet, join now! As an added BONUS, you will receive my Novella **"The Cowboys' Wounded Lady"**:

**FREE EXCLUSIVE GIFT
(available only to my subscribers)**

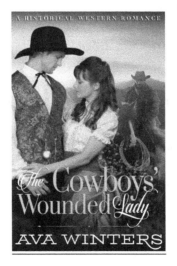

**Go to the link:
https://avawinters.com/novella-amazon**

Letter from Ava Winters

"Here is a lifelong bookworm, a devoted teacher and a mother of two boys. I also make mean sandwiches."

If someone wanted to describe me in one sentence, that would be it. There has never been a greater joy in my life than spending time with children and seeing them grow up - all my children, including the 23 little 9-year-olds that I currently teach. And I have not known such bliss than that of reading a good book.

As a Western Historical Romance writer, my passion has always been reading and writing romance novels. The historical part came after my studies as a teacher - I was mesmerized by the stories I heard, so much that I wanted to visit every place I learned about. And so, I did, finding the love of my life along the way as I walked the paths of my characters.

Now, I'm a full-time elementary school teacher, a full-time mother of two wonderful boys and a full-time writer. Wondering how I manage all of them? I did too, at first, but then I realized it's because everything I do I love, and I have the chance to share it with all of you.

And I would love to see you again in this small adventure of mine!

Until next time,

Ava Winters

Prologue

The rustling of the leaves behind her, quickened Sophie's heart as she sat on her horse in the middle of nowhere. The sound shifted her eyes to the growing shadows that stretched out towards her. Sweat moistened the palms of her hands despite the sun barely inching over the horizon. She held fast to the reins and breathed in deep to calm her rattled nerves. Her heart felt like stones in her chest as her eyes narrowed to see through the dark skies.

"Stay calm," she said more to herself than to the horse as she rubbed her hand over the steed's thick neck. The beast under her huffed and snorted as it stomped its feet to the ground, unruly and defiant.

Sophie swallowed the lump forming in her throat as she waited. Every second that ticked by only caused the fear to grow within her. The terror sank its claws into her and squeezed the courage from her veins. For a second, Sophie wondered what had possessed her to come out here alone. Chewing on her bottom lip, she tightened her grip around the reins for some security and stability. Her heart pounded in her chest as she felt exposed, but she knew she had to stay despite every fiber in her being screaming at her to run.

"No," she said defiantly as she straightened her shoulders and back. "You can't back down now. This was your idea."

She kept her eyes locked on the horizon, waiting nervously for any signs of life to come over the hill. The lonely cry of a hawk startled her as her eyes flickered to the dark blue skies. Clashing against the navy blue was a single speck of black and white. She squinted her eyes as the sun's early light kissed the horizon and scattered the shadows about her.

"Easy there," she said as her horse stomped and grunted. She could feel the tension in the morning air. There was an uncertainty about the morning that she knew her horse could feel. Neither one knew what was coming over the hills, but they understood the significance of it.

Tiny specks emerged on the horizon as the sunlight kissed the hills. Sophie gasped and clung to her saddle. Her heart pounded and rolled around in her chest as she watched the specks grow and come into view.

"Here we go. Remember the plan. Just stay calm, this will work," she said to herself as she tried to keep her hands from trembling. It all came down to this single moment and she knew it. The pressure in her chest tightened as she counted three men galloping at breakneck speeds over the hills.

"Well, what do we have here?" one of the men shouted as he rushed towards Sophie. The crackle in his eyes and the shimmer of his rifle caught her off guard. She knew these men were dangerous, but until that very moment she had no clue what she was really up against.

"Ah gotta say, I'm impressed. Here I thought you weren't going to come alone." The man's lip curled up at one corner as his eyes shimmied about. Sophie knew what he was looking for; it was the same thing she wanted, a way out, an escape.

"So, do you know what I asked for?" he said, as his men came up around her blocking off all avenues of escape. Sophie tried to keep her eyes locked on the man before her. Afraid her fear would seep through her voice, all she could do was nod.

"And? What say you?" The man glared at Sophie stealing the very warmth of her blood. She closed her eyes for a split second and mustered all the courage that sank into the depths of her being.

"You'd better kill me," Sophie said as she opened her eyes and stared down the villain before her. "Kill me now, because if you don't I promise you, you'll regret it."

"Well now, there's something that I think I can manage," the man said as his companions laughed, their horses kicking up dust around her. Sophie's eyes widened as the dark-haired man held her gaze. The rifle at his side slipped from its holster and shimmered in the light of the sun.

"Go on then," Sophie said. She exhaled sharply as her hands trembled. A slight whimper escaped her lips as the man pulled back the hammer of his rifle with a twisted smile itching at the corner of his lips.

Sophie jumped as the crack of gunfire filled her ears.

Chapter 1

One Year Earlier

The white envelope weighed heavily in Sophie's hands as her timid eyes lingered on the swift flowing letters. Although she had received several letters before, the flow of the black ink scratching through the white stunned her. As she finished reading the last line, she exhaled unaware she had been holding her breath the whole time.

Carefully, she folded up the white sheet of paper and stuffed the letter neatly back into the envelope from which it came. Swallowing hard she glanced at the open window where the summer breeze drifted through, kicking up the lace curtains her stepmother insisted on having.

"What is it?" Lenore asked pulling Sophie out of her daydream. Sophie glanced at the letter in her hands that seemed to burn hotter with every passing moment. Panic swept through her as she tried to peel her eyes off the neatly scribbled letters that addressed the note to her.

"Well? Out with it child!" Lenore snapped as she sat her embroidery circle on her lap. Sophie's attention drifted from her stepmother's irritated face to her father's.

"Who sent you the letter? And who could you possibly know from Tennessee?" Lenore pursed her lips together as her eyebrow rose up. The glare sent chills coursing through Sophie's arms.

"Father," Sophie's voice cracked as she swallowed the lump forming in her throat. She watched as her father lifted his head up from his morning paper and stared casually at her. There was a kindness in his gaze that reminded Sophie so much of Nadine.

"I have to tell you something."

"Whatever you have to say to your father," Lenore chided as she lifted her head and drew back her shoulders. "You can say to me as well. Your father and I don't keep secrets from one another."

Pulling in a long deep breath, Sophie tried to concoct a lie that would explain the letter she was absentmindedly rubbing with her thumb. Her eyes flickered to the black ink that spelled out her name and she smiled.

"I've been corresponding with a gentleman in Tennessee," Sophie blurted out. The instant the words escaped her lips she wished she could retract them.

"Excuse me," Lenore's voice dropped as her eyes popped. For a split second Sophie wondered if Lenore was having a stroke. The veins in her stepmother's forehead bulged as her neck strained.

"You have been doing what?"

Sophie tried to hold onto her courage but with each passing moment it faded from her.

"I've been writing to a rancher in Tennessee," Sophie's voice was barely a whisper as she tried not to meet Lenore's eyes. Yet, there was no escaping the wrath of her father's wife.

"Are you out of your mind, child? What on God's green earth possessed you to do such a thing? William? Are you listening to this? Do you hear what your daughter is doing? This is unacceptable. You will stop this at once," Lenore said as she lunged for Sophie.

The absence of the letter from her hands was immediate. It was as if the letter weighed a bundle of bricks, and suddenly it was just gone. Sophie could feel a piece of her very soul being ripped away and tossed aside like it was nothing as her stepmother ripped the letter from her hands. With a quivering lip, Sophie nodded and stared at the cracks in the wood floor.

"You're right," Sophie said as doubt swam about her mind. Each beat of her heart felt like a bull ramming the insides of her. Sophie tried to hold back the tears as she wrestled with the doubt.

"Of course, I was foolish to do this," Sophie said as she pulled in her lower lip trying to stifle the sobs that were bound to seep out of her.

"Yes," Lenore said as she turned the letter over in her hand. "How could you even think about leaving? Did you even think about what this would do to your father? And what about the chores that you have to do around here?" Lenore snorted as she straightened her back.

"I won't allow you to continue this," Lenore said as Sophie ground her teeth together.

"He wants me to marry him," Sophie blurted out. "He wants me to come to Tennessee and help him out there."

"And what makes you think you could do such a thing?" Lenore's voice dropped as she spoke. "You barely get your chores done around here. And you want to go gallivanting on a ranch. Ha!"

"I could do it," Sophie said, finding the willpower to talk back. William's eyebrows drew up as he stared at his daughter in awe. Sophie's heart drummed in her ears as her body tingled with fright and excitement. The adrenaline coursed through her veins like a wild river giving her the courage to speak.

"How dare you use that tone of voice with me," Lenore said as she carefully placed the embroidery circle on the table beside her. Sophie cautiously stole a glimpse at Lenore before quickly turning her attention back to her father's shocked face.

"You don't understand," Sophie said shaking her head.

"Oh, I understand completely. You thought you could just spring this on us and think we would be okay with it. Well I hate to be the bearer of bad news, but there is no way you are going anywhere young lady."

"Lenore," William's voice was deep but soothing. It was an unexpected tone, one that Sophie hadn't heard in years.

"Sit down and calm yourself," he said setting his paper aside and leaning forward in his chair.

"You can't possibly be considering this?" Lenore gasped as her eyes darted from Sophie to William.

"I said enough," William stated in a clear tone that caused Sophie's stepmother to slam her mouth shut.

"Sophie." She glanced at him doe-eyed looking for validation, but afraid of his reaction. It had been forever since kindness and understanding graced his face, yet there it was plain as day for Sophie to see. Shock stabbed her as she sat up and rolled her shoulders back.

"Who is this rancher you've been talking with?" A hint of a smile played at the corner of her father's lips as he spoke. Sophie's heart fluttered as hope sprang a leak within the depths of her being.

"Arthur, Arthur Soul."

"And you say he is a rancher huh?"

"Yes Papa, and he's not much older than I," Sophie said as she watched her father extend his hand to Lenore. The gesture startled her. She watched as their fingers entwined with one another's like they had done so many times before.

This is it, Sophie thought. *Just like every other time. He'll side with her and that will be that.* Sophie glanced at Lenore as a wicked and smug grin stretched across the woman's face.

"And just how old is he?" William asked, staring at Sophie with concern.

"According to his letter, he's 25," Sophie answered, swallowing the lump forming in her throat.

"Is this what you really want to do? Do you absolutely want to go out west and live on a ranch?"

Sophie paused as she played with the dirt under her nails. It had been forever since she thought about what she wanted. All this time she had been living for other people. Even now, it was her sister's idea to become a mail order bride. As thoughts of Nadine faded in and out of her mind, Sophie nodded.

"It is Papa," she said, drawing her eyes to meet her father's.

"Then go."

"What? You must be joking. You can't send your daughter west to go live with a stranger. Have you lost your mind?"

"Enough Lenore," William said as his brow rose up and his face turned to stone. This was enough to silence her stepmother.

"Papa?"

"I know you think I want to keep you here, and a part of me does. But you have your own path to go down and I can't stop you." William turned to face his wife as the cold stone expression faded away.

"If we try to keep her from going she may resent us for it. If we lock her down, one day she will run away. Change is inevitable, Lenore. It's time she goes out and finds her own way in this world." As William spoke, he pulled the neatly addressed letter out of Lenore's grasp and handed it back to Sophie.

"But," Lenore started but quickly grew quiet as William shook his head and pressed his lips into a tight line daring her to say another word.

Sophie jolted to her feet as she stared at her father. She couldn't believe he had sided with her. Never did she believe that she would be free to find her own path. Things had always been planned out for her all her life. Yet, here she stood looking past the wrought iron fence that surrounded her father's home and beyond the brick walls that trapped her. For a moment, she wondered and dreamed about what she was capable of outside her family home. Fear, purpose, hope, panic, all the emotions swirled inside of her as she contemplated her future and what lay before her.

Every nerve in her body fired off as she tried to contain her glee. Shaking her head she threw out her arms and rushed to her father. The instant her arms curled around his neck she felt exhilarated.

"I need to pack then," she said pressing her lips to his cheek as she pulled away from him. A prick of uncertainty jabbed a hole through her glee. She stared at her father for a moment as terror seeped in to ruin her moment.

"Go," her father said as she watched tears swell in his eyes. Sophie nodded once and released her grip. Brushing out the wrinkles of her dress, she made her way through the house and up the stairs to her room. The instant she closed the door a frosty breeze zapped her excitement. Her eyes shifted to the leather-bound book resting on her nightstand. She rushed to the small little table and opened the book.

Dear Diary,

What if you're making a mistake by moving to Tennessee? What if this is wrong and the only reason you're going through with it is because of Nadine? I loved my sister, I did. And I know she would have wanted this for me. She would have wanted to see me open my wings and fly. But she never expressed how scary it all is stepping out on that limb.

I sit here knowing fully well she would be thrilled by this opportunity. After all, she was the one who pushed for this. But is it what I want? I know I want to be rid of my stepmother. I want to see and experience things that are beyond the brick walls. But still, there is a fear that stabs me. A fear that holds me in place. But I know what Nadine would say if she were still here. She'd tell me to ride out and greet that fear, take it by the horns, and shape it into something beautiful.

But I'm not Nadine, I know that. All I can be is me, and I can't help but wonder, is it enough?

Sophie turned her attention to the open window and gazed out at the bright blue skies spotted with fluffy clouds.

"Sophie." She jumped and slammed her journal shut as the knock on her door pulled her out of her self-doubt. "Can I come in?"

"Of course, Papa," she said, turning on her heels as the door creaked open. William's eyes scanned the room before falling on her. Sophie stood in the center of her room trying to make herself taller than she already was.

"Come, sit with me," William said moving to the bed and plopping down on it. Sophie moved swiftly to his side and stared up at him with eager eyes.

"Are you okay, Papa?" Sophie asked as tears swelled in his eyes. The last time she had ever seen her father cry was the day they lost Nadine from consumption. They had all seen it coming, but still the wound cut deeper than any of them could anticipate.

"I must apologize to you my dear," he said as he cleared his throat and grabbed Sophie's hands.

"I don't understand," Sophie said as her father squeezed her hands only to find the letter clutched in her hand. Panic swept through her as she opened her hand, allowing the letter to slip into his palm.

"I should have been a better father to you and Nadine. I should have been there for you, but I wasn't and now..." he paused as Sophie watched his eyes scan the tiny envelope.

"You don't have to explain anything," Sophie said. "You did the best you could with what you had."

"I could have done more," he said as he stared up at her. "And now it's too late. I wasn't there for you and Nadine when your mother passed..." William choked as he spoke. Sophie knew each word was a struggle for him to release. She shook her head and opened her mouth to protest but was stopped.

"And after Nadine, I seemed to have left you alone when you needed me the most. Now look at you," William said and cupped his hand around Sophie's face. "You're all grown up and making choices for yourself."

"Papa," Sophie gasped as she placed her hand on his and grimaced. She swallowed hard, forcing the fear and insecurity down her throat. "If you don't want me to go, I won't."

"Oh honey," William forced a smile as he stared at his daughter. "You can't do that. You can't live your life for other people. You'll be miserable if you do."

"But Lenore is right. I have responsibilities here with you and her."

"No, the chores were to help shape you into the woman you are trying to be. I won't get in your way. You have to go out there and blaze your own trail."

"What if I'm wrong about this? What if this is a huge mistake and I go out there and hate it?"

"Sweetie, you can't 'what if' your life away. There will always be something holding you back or an excuse not to do something. But you can't let those moments define who you are. You have to push through and live."

Sophie glanced at her hands before bringing her eyes back to her father. The gray in his beard seemed to stand out a bit more now and she couldn't help but smile at it. "Is that why you sent for Lenore? Was it your way of pushing through and living again?"

Silence filled the room as William's shoulders dropped. Sophie could see the struggle in his eyes as he tried to answer. But his silence was enough. She bobbed her head and chewed at her inner cheek.

"I wondered why you sent for Lenore, but now I see. I'm on the other side of that coin."

"You make this decision for you. This is one that you have to make all on your own. But know this,"

William cupped her face bringing her eyes to meet his. Tears swelled in her eyes as she stared at her father.

"Whatever decision you make, I will back you up a hundred percent. Do you hear me? I love you always and whatever you want to do, I'm here for you."

Swallowing the lump in her throat, Sophie nodded and forced a smile, *I hope I can live up to this trust.*

Chapter 2

"You've got to be kidding me. This can't be happening right now." Arthur Soul plucked at the frayed barbed wire coiling around the wooden post. He threw his head back in frustration as a rusty bit of the wire stuck to the wooden post cut into his thumb.

Arthur glanced over at Sheriff Noonen standing beside him as he drew his thumb to his lips to clean the wound. The sheriff knelt as he wiped the sweat from his brow before snatching the coiled wire to his eyes to inspect it further.

"This looks cut," Noonen said turning his attention to Arthur. The sheriff rose as he dropped the wire and shook his head. "Don't know what to tell ya. This could be malicious, or it could be just some kids having some fun."

Arthur pressed his lips into a tight line as he gazed off towards the horizon. White fluffy clouds billowed around the low rolling hills as the morning sun kissed his face.

"The cattle drive is coming up, you know that right?" Arthur said keeping his eyes locked on the horizon. Fear squeezed his heart as he stared on. For a split second, Arthur couldn't help but think of Randal Munger. It was just like him to do something like this and Arthur knew it.

"Yep," Noonen said scratching his head. Arthur glanced over his shoulder at the heavy-set man. The sheriff's peppered scruff on his face reminded Arthur of Randal.

"I wouldn't worry too much about it," Noonen said as Arthur pulled in a deep breath to steady his nerves. "It's not like you got enemies right? After all, you've only been here for three years. A man can't really have that kind of influence on people in such a short amount of time."

Arthur's hand trembled slightly at his side. His mind raced back to Randal. Yet, there was no way it could be him, no matter if the circumstances seemed to fit. Randal after all was locked away in the state penitentiary. He was nowhere near Arthur. Still, Arthur's hand rattled to the point he clenched it into a tight fist to stop the shaking.

"You'd be surprised," Arthur said through his teeth praying he could control the fear bubbling in his gut.

"There ain't no one who comes out this far... Of course there have been other reports."

"Reports?" Arthur's ears perked up as he glanced at the sheriff.

"Three other ranchers have come to me recently about this very same issue." Sheriff Noonen rubbed the bristles on his chin as he spoke. Arthur noticed the sheriff's eyes glazing over as if he was lost in some kind of thought that he couldn't catch.

"Maybe we got cattle rustlers coming into the area."

Arthur shook his head as he slammed his fist down onto the single wooden post. Pain shot through his hand to his elbow as he grunted, "No."

"What?" Noonen asked when he snapped out of his trance.

"Nothing," Arthur said as a nagging feeling in the pit of his gut rattled him to his core. There was something all too familiar about this that didn't settle with him. Quickly, Arthur puffed out his chest and waved his hand at the sheriff.

"It don't matter I guess. As long as there isn't any cattle gone missing. I've got the men looking into it now," Arthur said as he watched the sheriff pull a bandanna from his back pocket to wipe the sweat dripping down the back of his neck.

"Well, keep me posted and I'll do what I can. You know that. Us folks got to stick together." The sheriff tipped his hat and reached for the reins wrapped around the post. His horse grunted and whined as the heavyset man mounted the steed.

"Sure thing," Arthur said as he swallowed hard and tried not to let his mind become too consumed with Randal.

Standing still and leaning against the wooden post, Arthur glanced at the clouds rolling in on the horizon. He shook his head despite the unnerving feeling in his gut. Randal Munger plagued his thoughts as the sheriff rode back to town leaving Arthur alone.

That vile and evil brute isn't here- Arthur repeated like a mantra in his head as he scanned the length of the barbed wire fence. Yet, there were signs. Signs that crept up Arthur's spine and made his blood run cold.

"Nope," Arthur said trying to mask his lie.

Surely Randal can't be here doing this to me. This is a coincidence, that's all. There is no way he has escaped. Marshal Lew Bergen promised me he will never see the light of day again. Still ...no. It isn't possible ...those men ... Randal... they're all locked up. No way they're behind this. Arthur tried convincing himself as he swallowed hard. The air became clogged in his throat when Randal's face flashed into his mind. His heart skipped in his chest as he looked grimly at the clean-cut coiled wire wrapped around the post.

Arthur pulled in a deep breath and shook his head. Pausing for a moment, he occupied himself with stroking his horse's neck. Memories flashed before him as he looked at the buckskin gelding that reminded him of one he once had. But that was a long time ago and in a different area. As far as

Arthur was concerned, it was a different life as well. Dust swirled around him as he patted the horse's neck.

Mounting his steed, Arthur reined its neck to get the horse to turn. He looked out at the tall grass that swayed and flowed in the breeze.

"I'm a different man now," Arthur told himself as he rolled his shoulders back and lifted his head high. "There's no evidence that Randal would know I was the one to sell him out. He isn't here and he's not coming for me."

Arthur tried to cling to this sliver of hope, but still, the nagging sensation was all too real.

"It's just nerves," Arthur said bobbing his head up and down. "Yeah, nerves. You got Sophie coming soon and it's a new change," he told himself as he made his way back to town. Only the birds, his horse, and the critters of the fields of Oakbury were listening to him, but he didn't mind one bit.

"Maybe I should call it off?" he said to his horse. "You know, have Sophie come later in the year?"

"No," Arthur shook his head as he trotted along. "It's too late to be turning back now. Miss Sophie will arrive in two days. But I gotta tell you, I'm not ready."

The horse grunted and neighed as they moved through the empty fields. On any other day, Arthur would have loved being so far away from everyone. However, the heaviness of uncertainty weighed him down. He knew there was no way he was going to enjoy the ride or the solitude, not with a rustling gang moving into area.

"Don't give me that," Arthur said to the horse as he leaned down to catch the horse's eye. "You don't have to tell me what I got myself into. Don't you think I know? But maybe Garner is right, maybe it is time for me to settle down. It's not like I'm getting any younger. But I'm telling you, now isn't the time. It just doesn't feel right."

Arthur's horse bobbed its head up and down as it moved carefully down the rocky terrain. Glancing out over his ranch, Arthur couldn't help but feel a sense of urgency swelling in him. He had more land than what he had three years ago, and he knew that with all that space, things were bound to happen. He gently tugged the reins and veered the horse to the babbling creek that cut through his land. Pulling in a deep breath, he let the sweet aroma of wildflowers and wet grass fill his nose. The sky opened up for him as he rubbed his neck and tried to push out Randal from his mind. Not even the speckled colored rocks gleaming in the creek could soothe his weary mind or erase Randal's face. The memory of the man was staked into him and there was nothing he could do to pull it out.

Pulling his eyes from the water, he slipped off the saddle, knelt beside the creek, and scooped the fresh water into his parched mouth. As if on cue, the horse lowered its head to also savor the free-flowing water.

"People forget things, right?" Arthur said keeping his eyes locked on the horizon. The horse dipped down once more to take in the cool water.

"Maybe Randal's forgotten all about me. Maybe I should just let this go... And just because Sophie's coming out to marry me, doesn't mean it has to be love right? She could just be a helping hand that I need around the homestead... Yeah, a helper. Someone to keep things clean."

Arthur shook his head, along with his horse, as his resolve to leave the past behind solidified. He closed his eyes and jerked his head in a final nod of approval. No matter what came his way, he'd see it through one way or another.

* * *

The wild terrain passed by the window as Sophie rubbed her thumb over the black splotches of ink on the crinkled envelope. She sighed heavily, keeping her eyes locked on the patches of trees and open plains. Her heart fluttered in her chest as she shook her head.

"I'm doing it, Nadine," she whispered to the window and tried to smile. It was, after all, her sister's idea to marry a man she'd never met. She couldn't help but flush at the thought that the only way she'd met Arthur was through letters they exchanged in the mail. Yet here she was, on her way to meet that very man, but not just meet, marry.

"Can you believe it?" she whispered as she held fast to the picture of her sister, Nadine. Sophie didn't care who was sitting around her. All she cared about was fulfilling a promise she had made to her sister. A smile played at her lips as tears threatened to spill down her cheeks. She chewed on her lower lips and fought back the urge to cry as the train moved over the tracks, bringing her closer to her new life.

"I wonder if he is as handsome in person as he is in the photo. It would seem foolish to hope for it, but I have to admit I do." Sophie blushed as she envisioned Arthur standing on the train platform, flowers in hand, waiting for her. A smile played at the corner of her lips as her cheeks burned at the thought of seeing him. Her eyes drifted to the window as the fantasy played out. Although Sophie knew it was Nadine's idea to go out west and marry a rancher to be free from their strict stepmother, Sophie still found some piece of that dream to be hers as well.

For the past three months, she had been corresponding with Arthur and dreaming of what would happen when they met. Now, here she was on the train living the life Nadine had wanted her to live. Sophie struggled with the smile as her heart trembled in her chest. She never anticipated her life to be so adventurous, but she knew she couldn't grow into the strong and self-assertive woman she wanted to be if she stayed at home. The tears Sophie tried so hard to contain spilled over and raced down her cheeks. Through blurry eyes she caught sight of Nadine's smiling face.

It was Nadine who pushed Sophie to continue writing the man she never knew. In all reality, Sophie couldn't help but wonder if it was because her older sister wanted to see her happy, or if it was a matter of security. Either way, it was Sophie on the train heading into Tennessee and Nadine was gone.

She could feel the cool liquid soothe her burning cheeks, but she didn't care who noticed. Pulling in a deep breath, she held it as she wiped the tears away. The whistle from the train startled her as she scrunched the letter in her hand and her eyes flickered to the window.

The majestic mountains reached up to the sky as the varying green trees stretched out before her. Through a small clearing of trees, Sophie noticed a speck of a town growing bigger. Sophie's hands felt clammy despite being in gloves. Her insides felt as if they were being twisted and were pulling her in different directions. The anticipation of pulling up to the small town of Oakbury drove her mad.

Quickly, she tucked the letter into her bag and straightened the wrinkles out from her dress as a second blow of the whistle rang out. A smile seeped over her lips as the other passengers on the train fumbled about the cabin making ready to disembark. But Sophie remained locked to her seat trying not to hyperventilate.

"Here we go," Sophie said as the metal brakes protested against the rails causing the train to come to a stop. Steam drifted by her window blocking out the view of the station. All her hope of catching a glimpse of Arthur before he saw her was gone. But she knew she couldn't stay in her seat forever.

Slowly she rose and rubbed her hands over her linen flounced skirt. She shifted her trimmed bonnet before reaching to the seat to grab her parasol. Swallowing the fear that lumped in her throat, she put one foot in front of the other until she found her way out of the box car and onto the train platform. She propped open her small parcel umbrella as men from the train dropped her trunk by her side.

"Thank you," she said glancing at her only belongings. She knew it wasn't' much, but it was her whole world.

"Do you have someone meeting you miss?" the man asked tipping his hat to her.

Sophie nodded as she choked out, "Yes."

"Very well Miss," the train attendant said. Sophie stood still keeping her eyes locked on him as he moved back to the train. For a moment, she wondered if Arthur had forgotten about her.

Turning slowly she scanned the platform and exhaled sharply when her eyes fell on a man standing straight as a board. Steam from the train curled around his body and stretched out about him like tentacles. Sophie squinted her eyes as the smoke and steam cleared to reveal a well-dressed man standing before her.

Her mouth parted as she suddenly forgot how to breathe. She could feel every fiber of her being tingling as she stared at him. There he stood, no more than a few feet from her with his broad, strapping shoulders pulled back. His marble gray eyes bore into her making her feel a bit uncomfortable. There was no telling if he wanted to ask her something or was sizing her up. Her face grew hotter as her eyes darted to the ground and shifted to everything else other than him.

Clearing his throat, he moved towards her. Sophie's knees weakened with each step he took. "Excuse me."

Sophie found the air had escaped her lungs as she clung to her umbrella and stared at him. There was no telling when her voice would return, but she prayed he didn't think her deaf or dumb.

"Are you Miss Sophie Fallon?" His voice was like walking on rocks, gravely and deep. It reminded her of how her father sounded. She nodded as she moved the umbrella to the other shoulder and lifted her hand.

"And you are Arthur," she said, finally finding her voice.

"Is this all you brought?" Arthur asked, glancing at the single trunk at her ankles. Sophie nodded as insecurities stabbed at her. She wished she could read his mind, at least, that would give her an idea of what he thought of her. She couldn't help but feel inadequate with her single trunk.

"Well," he said leaning down and grabbing the handles of the trunk. He glanced up at her and with a wink said, "At least you packed light."

Sophie swallowed hard trying to quench her dry mouth as she watched Arthur hoist her trunk up to his chest. He wasn't built, but was strong, that much she could see. After all, the man from the train could barely drag it to her and here was this strapping man carrying it like it was filled with air.

"I trust your trip was well," Arthur said trying to fill the silence. Sophie nodded as she studied him. He was much younger than she expected. A rush of heat rose up her neck when he glanced at her. Quickly she adverted her eyes as it dawned on her that this was the man she was about to marry.

"Suppose you don't mind getting the formalities over with now, do you?" Arthur asked as he put her trunk into the back of a wooden wagon and dusted his hands on his pants.

"No, that's fine," Sophie intoned, trying to control her breathing. She knew this day was coming, yet now that it was here, she didn't know how to feel. The anticipation was more than she could handle.

"Good, because the church is this way," he said pointing down the long dusty road. Sophie glanced around the small town and noticed the brownish church at the end of the row of buildings.

"How lovely," she said trying not to judge the buildings by their dusty appearance. She knew very well that the church was whitewashed, but with the dust rolling through the little town, it couldn't stay that way forever.

"Are you alright?" Arthur asked as he stopped and turned. Sophie tried to keep her wits upon realizing she was on the verge of marriage. When she was younger, she had envisioned a wedding where her family gave her a proper send off to a man she had given her heart to. Reality though, was much different. Here she was giving herself to a man she barely knew. She swallowed hard trying to ease the dryness in her throat. Arthur stared at her with one eyebrow raised.

"Yes, of course," Sophie said, noticing a small group of people coming out of the church. For a moment she wondered why the town had service so late in the day and then it dawned on her. The people were there for her.

"I'm sorry," Arthur said as he turned to see his friends coming out of the church's doors. "I told them we were going to have a small ceremony, but they insisted on being here... I can send them away if you want."

Sophie blinked as she counted the smiling faces around them. Seeing how well-liked he was by the community eased her mind of doubts. "You have a lot of friends here don't you?"

"You could say," Arthur said, his cheeks turning a bright red. "You could say they are my family."

"And where is..." Sophie paused, trying to find Arthur's father and mother in the crowd. But she stopped because not one person stepped forward to greet her the way family usually did.

"Never mind," she continued, dropping her gaze. Sophie shook her head and exhaled. Her legs wobbled a bit as she took a step closer to Arthur and then another. It surprised her to see so many of the community supporting their marriage. The only person really missing was Nadine, but Sophie knew she would be there if she could.

"I'm sorry my parents couldn't come," Sophie said. "They weren't very supportive of this decision. I mean, my father was, but my stepmother saw it differently."

"It's fine," Arthur said. He took Sophie's arm and curled her hand over his which caused her heart to quicken. His touch was gentle but firm. With her cheeks flushed, she couldn't help but notice Arthur's family wasn't there either. Sophie wanted to know where his family was, but didn't dare pull that thread, not on her wedding day. Still, she couldn't help but wonder if they had passed away or if Arthur's family had disowned him.

As they drew closer to the church, Sophie's hands clammed up. She could feel the beads of sweat on her neck race down her spine. Doubt seeped into her mind as they climbed the steps to the church. The wooden steps protested under their weight causing Sophie to question their integrity.

"Do you want to freshen up first?" Arthur asked as he held the door open for her. She collapsed her umbrella and stepped over the threshold.

"That won't be necessary, unless you need to," Sophie said, noticing the same hesitation in Arthur's eyes that surely mimicked her own.

He shook his head, "No."

"Then shall we?" Sophie tried to flash a smile at her new husband but could feel the awkwardness of it on her lips. Arthur replied by turning his attention to the man at the end of the altar.

Sophie straightened her shoulders as she also glanced at the man. The old withered man nodded at them with a warm smile on his face. Her heart raced despite how slowly she moved towards the minister.

If I want to back out, this is my very last chance, right now, this moment. After this, there will be no going back.

Chapter 3

Arthur's eyes flickered between Sophie and the minister as they stood at the end of the aisle. Arthur could feel the eyes of the town folk he called friends boring into the back of his head. He didn't need to turn to know exactly what each person was doing.

Mae Davidson, the wife of Garner who happened to be his closest neighbor, would have tears in her eyes. Sure enough, Arthur glanced over his shoulder to find her sitting in the second row, watching him place the ring on his mail order bride. Garner, however, wouldn't be so emotional. He'd be sitting with his arms crossed looking at Sophie and contemplating how long their relationship would last.

"Do you, Arthur Soul, take Sophie Fallon to be your lawfully wedded wife? To have and to hold from this day forward, till death do you part?" The minister stared at Arthur, but Arthur didn't mind. He knew he had to marry the girl. Not only did he need the help around his ranch, but he couldn't very well send the poor girl on her way, not when she'd come so far to marry him.

Arthur cleared his throat and swallowed hard to keep his mouth from drying out. He didn't understand why he was so nervous, but he was. Sophie, after all, was a stunning girl. It was her long neck and high arched eyebrows that set her apart. But Arthur knew better than to just see her as the oval-faced beauty, she needed to have skills to help in with his ranch.

The preacher stared at him in silence. Arthur blinked several times before glancing at Sophie. Her expression was just as blank and silent as the preacher's. But there was the glimpse of shock and confusion in her stare that startled him.

For the life of him, he couldn't remember what he was to say or where he was.

"This is the part where you say, 'I do'," the preacher whispered as he leaned in closer to Arthur.

"Oh, right... I do." Arthur's words felt scratchy in his throat. He tried swallowing but found no spit to quench his parched tongue. The collar around his neck seemed to be tightening as he stood there holding his breath.

"And do you," the preacher said turning his attention to the eighteen-year-old standing before Arthur. He could tell she was uncomfortable. She stood with too much tension in her shoulders; her close set, honey brown eyes didn't flinch as she said, "I do."

"I now pronounce you," the minister said as he stepped back to allow Arthur and Sophie to take center stage, "Husband and wife. Do you have the rings?"

Sniffles came from Sophie that caught Arthur off guard. He knew women cried at weddings, but he never imagined his own bride would be the one to cry. Slipping his hand into his pocket, he pulled out a small metal ring and glanced at her apologetically as he struggled to slip it on her finger.

"Are you alright?" Arthur asked leaning in closer to her as he slipped the small ring onto her finger. Her head bobbed up and down as she forced a smile. For a moment, Arthur didn't know what he should do. They both expected a kiss would suffice, but he didn't know how to kiss a woman he just met.

The idea of kissing a stranger seemed odd. Yet, he had to if he was to seal the deal. He cleared his throat as he watched Sophie's cheeks redden. She stood remarkably still waiting for him to make the move.

Leaning in slowly, Arthur shifted his head as Sophie craned her neck in the opposite direction. His lips grazed her upper lip as she crushed half a lip to his. For the first time in a long time, uncertainty plagued him. Awkwardly he lifted his arms up and curled them around Sophie's small frame of a body.

Sophie glanced at him as he led her down the three tiny steps before greeting the band of ranchers who called Oakbury, Tennessee their home. Although he knew the smiling faces that surrounded them, he couldn't help but feel a pinch of sadness for Sophie. She did after all come all this way alone. None of her family or friends took the trek out to this small little town.

"You don't look fine," Arthur said.

"I'll be fine," Sophie said as the small group of Arthur's friends rushed to congratulate them.

"Can't believe ya did it," Noonen said slapping Arthur's back. The force knocked Arthur away from Sophie and nearly toppled him. With quick reflexes, Arthur composed himself and nodded.

"Little Miss," Noonen said, "You got yourself a fine fellow here."

"Actually," Garner said. "It's Mrs. Soul now."

"Sophie," Arthur turned to his new wife and lifted his hand. "This here is Sheriff Noonen. I've known him and all these fine people for three years."

"Pleasure," Sophie said dipping her head as Arthur turned to his other friends.

"And this is Mae-"

"Oh, I know we're going to be the best of friends," Mae said taking Sophie's hand to shake it. Mae and Sophie stared at each other a moment before Mae released Sophie's hands. Arthur couldn't tell if it was a sign of respect or a challenge. Women were a completely different species and had their own set of rules, that much he knew for certain.

"I'm Garner," the older man said, stealing a hug from Sophie that squeezed the air from her lungs, making her cough.

"That's enough now," Arthur said tapping Garner on the shoulder. "We have to get back to the ranch."

"Right," Mae said as she slipped her hand into Garner's arm and pulled him away from Sophie and Arthur. "I suppose you two have some acquainting to do."

Mae winked at Arthur as she waved to Sophie. "If you need anything at all you give me a holler, you hear? We townsfolk stick together and help each other out. Even if it's just someone to talk to."

"Mae," Garner scolded. His eyes narrowed on his wife as he shook his head. "You leave them be. They'll be just fine."

"I was only—"

"We all know what you were doing," Garner said, moving towards the door with his wife on his arm.

"Thank you," Sophie called out to them as they stepped out of the small church leaving Arthur and Sophie.

"Well, I best be getting as well," Noonen said patting his stomach. "Dinner don't make itself now does it," he said, bumping his elbow into Arthur's rib.

"See you around Sheriff."

"You two take care," he said as he too left. Arthur glanced over his shoulder at Sophie before he moved towards the church doors.

He knew he should say something to his new bride, but he couldn't find the right things to say. Everything that went through his head seemed out of place considering he had just married the girl.

A crooked smile tickled the corner of his lips as he held the door open for Sophie. She moved gracefully and collected her small umbrella. The instant she stepped outside, she opened it up and gazed out towards the small town he called home. Arthur hoped she would see his town as the quaint little home he'd grown to love. There were only a handful of building lining the street, but the town offered the necessities.

"This certainly is a small town," Sophie said.

"Perhaps, but it does offer everything you need," Arthur replied. "To the right, the grocer, and the apothecary side by side, and then of course the barbershop. The blacksmith's shop is just around the corner and then you have the tailor and a doctor's office."

Sophie flashed a delicate smile before dropping her head. In the pit of his stomach he wished she would come to love this place as much as he did, but he knew only time would tell.

* * *

Sophie sat beside Arthur as their wagon rocked on the dirt trail. She tried hard not to press her leg against her new husband, but the seat was tight.

"Sorry," she said when her leg bumped against his once again. She shifted her weight as Arthur placed one foot on the buckboard.

"It's alright," he said, trying to give her a bit more space. Sophie fought with her umbrella as a breeze kicked up, causing it to flail around her.

Quickly, she pulled down the umbrella and tucked it behind her. She couldn't help but notice the gifts that filled the back of the carriage. A small, frail smile pulled at the corners of her lips as she stared at them. Never in all her life had she ever received so many gifts; her stepmother often kept them from her. Even during her birthday or Christmas, Sophie's gifts always seemed scarce. Her chest swelled when she realized that there would be a handful of packages in there for her.

Sophie turned in her seat and glanced at Arthur, studying him as they drove on. With her eyes locked on him, she noticed his masculine shoulders that drew her eyes to his neck. From there she found her eyes trailing to his dark, brown hair. She pulled in a deep breath when she met his deep set, marble gray eyes.

Her heart fluttered as she turned quickly to stare down the dirt road. A flame burned deep within her, tingling every ounce of her. She glanced at Arthur only to notice he had turned quickly away. His face flushed a deep crimson as his lips curled up at the corners.

"So," Sophie said, rubbing her hands over her legs. "This is strange isn't it?"

"What's that?" Arthur asked as his eyes flickered to her.

"This," she said looking up at the canopy of green leaves that covered the dirt road. "I don't think I've ever seen something so beautiful. Or been so far from home."

"Is that why you were crying earlier? All this happening too fast for you?" Arthur asked.

"No," Sophie said without hesitation. The last thing she wanted was for her new husband to think she was too soft.

"But do you miss it?" Arthur asked. Sophie's frowned as she cocked her head in confusion.

"Your home, you miss it don't you?"

"Yes and no. I miss my father," Sophie said, looking at her hands. "But my stepmother, you could say we never really got along. But it would have been nice to see their faces today. I never expected to be married without my father. But, I guess plans change," Sophie concluded, feeling Arthur's eyes on her.

"What about you?" She asked. "Is there someone you wished was here? After all, it was our wedding."

Arthur's back straightened as he dropped his foot. Sophie could feel the tension rolling off him and sat up straighter.

"I didn't mean... I didn't think," Sophie said, pressing her lips into a tight line.

"If you must know, my parents are gone," Arthur said bluntly. "They died in Texas a while ago."

"I'm so sorry," Sophie said, keeping her eyes locked on him. Pain shot through her heart as she thought of Nadine.

"I didn't know," she said. "You never mentioned them in any of your letters, so I just assumed... I thought I would meet them today."

"Sorry to disappoint you," Arthur said sharply. Sophie could feel his words slicing through her like a spear. Turning her head she kept her eyes on the passing trees. The last thing she wanted to do was irritate her husband their first night together.

The hard greens and yellow leaves drifted by as Sophie kept her mouth shut. Every moment she thought of something new to say, she refrained from letting the words out. After all, she had only truly known the man for a few hours. How was she to know what would set him off and what wouldn't? She glanced at him from the corner of her eye. Thoughts of offending him swirled and tangled her words. She knew it would be best to just sit pretty and hope for the best.

Silence filled the space between them as they rode on. The carriage bounced around on the trail as the day progressed. Sophie glanced up at the canopy to find the sun's rays filtering through the boughs of the trees, sending a gold light down on the road.

"It really is lovely here," she said, hoping that she hadn't offended him too gravely and sticking to a topic less controversial. The weather was always neutral ground, or at least that was what her stepmother always told her. "I like the trees. Is this your land?"

"Almost," Arthur said as they came to a fork in the road. Sophie made a mental note to turn left on the trail in case she had to make it back to town on her own.

"This is mine," Arthur said as the trees parted. Sophie's eyes widened when she saw the grand open fields with a speckle of trees. In all the letters Arthur sent, he never once told her how big his place was. Sophie shook her head as her mouth fell open. Sure, she expected a house, but this was by far bigger than the home she had left.

"This is all yours?" she said in awe.

"Yes," he said, bobbing his head. "Well, I guess yours now too."

"And you built the house and all this by yourself?" Sophie asked, pulling her eyes away from the rolling green fields.

"Not all of it, no, I got help from a few of the townsfolk. I know it's intimidating, but it's one of the reasons I needed you to come," he said. "It's going to be busy around here. We have the spring roundup soon and I'm going to need all hands-on board."

Sophie nodded as she pressed her lips together. Arthur's eyes narrowed on her just like her father would do. It was a quick way to put her in her place and it made her feel small.

"I understand," Sophie said, swallowing her nerves.

The carriage rattled as Sophie kept her eyes locked on the horizon. She noticed a speck of a house growing bigger in the distance. Every so often, she glanced at Arthur as her heart fluttered. It didn't take long before the carriage pulled up to the well-built, log house. Sophie breathed in deep admiring the gentle hint of pine that swirled about the property. It was the same smell she had picked off Arthur as they stood so close to each other in the chapel.

"Welcome home," Arthur said, pulling the reins back to stop the carriage. Sophie sucked in a deep breath as she stared at the house.

"This is a bit bigger than you explained in your letters," Sophie said as she rose to her feet. She glanced at Arthur who was patting the horses' necks before clearing her throat.

"Oh, right," Arthur said, darting around the steed towards Sophie to stand beside the carriage. Sophie tried not to pay any attention to his strong hands around her waist as he lowered her to the ground.

"I guess we both have some adjusting to do," he said with his hands locked around her waist. Sophie could feel every breath pulling into her lungs as she stared into Arthur's marble gray eyes.

"Yes," she said breathlessly when he released her. "It would seem so."

Chapter 4

"I'm sure you'd like to freshen up now," Arthur said as he rubbed his hand over his hair. The timid smile on Sophie's tender face wasn't something he was expecting, not after the way he treated her earlier.

In the pit of his gut, he knew he shouldn't have snapped at her. She was just curious about his family. Any woman would be, especially if they were marrying. Arthur sighed heavily as he averted his eyes to the floor and rubbed his toes against the polished wooden floor.

"I'm sorry about what I said on the ride here," he said as Sophie unpinned her hat and glanced around the living space.

"I shouldn't have been so hasty. It's just," he paused as he slipped his fingers into his side vest pocket and played with the watch.

"I wouldn't worry about it too much," Sophie said in hushed tones. "You aren't the only one who has lost someone. It's clear we both had hopes of loved ones around us today."

"Can I ask you something?" Arthur said looking up at her. "Are you always this forgiving?"

"Suppose it's in my nature," Sophie said. "I don't know about you, but I did go to church and was taught to forgive."

Arthur nodded his head as he leaned against the door frame and stared at Sophie. He was impressed by her sleek, slender figure. The dress she had chosen to get married in wasn't all that flattering on the girl; it showcased Sophie's strong, broad shoulders and tiny waist. As Arthur looked her over, he couldn't help but notice her honey brown eyes staring at him before quickly darting to the ground. All in all she stunned him and made him realized that if he let himself go, he could get lost in her eyes.

Shaking his head as if she entranced him, Arthur pushed off the door frame and cleared his throat. "You can get cleaned up around back. I'll bring in your trunk."

"Thank you," Sophie said.

Arthur nodded and spun on his heels. Pulling in a deep breath he moved swiftly down the hall towards the front door. Deep within him he could feel pressure squeezing his heart. It was a rough feeling stealing the breath from him. He glanced over his shoulder only to find Sophie walking down the hallway and headed towards the kitchen.

Finding the house stifling, he quickly pushed through the front door and sucked in deeply. The blue sky with its white puffy clouds shifted colors as the sun drifted towards the horizon. He moved swiftly around his horse and brushed his fingertips over the horse's neck.

"Times they are a changing," he said to the horse as he held the bridle, forcing the horse to look at him. "I don't know what it is about this woman, but…" Arthur paused, letting go, and moved around the steed. He exhaled sharply as his eyes drifted to his house knowing she was in there, somewhere, getting acquainted with her new belongings.

"This is going to be an adjustment for sure. Not just for me, but her too. You and I both know I ain't the easiest person to live with."

The horse tossed its head up as Arthur stopped at the back of the carriage. He reached in and pulled out the only luggage Sophie brought with her. A stab of pity nagged him as he pulled the trunk out of the back. He had met woman from all walks of life, but he had never met one that wasn't equipped with an overabundance of stuff. Yet, here was one who fell into his life and only carried this single trunk with her.

He ran his hand over the old chest and gasped. Flashes of his parents' faces came into his view. The crushing sensation in his chest tightened as he looked at the etching around the edges of the chest. Granted the chest was from a catalog and there were probably a hundred other people with the same trunk, still, the coincidence that she would bring one here stunned him.

"This can't be," he said as a tidal wave of guilt and love plowed over him and knocked him back.

Arthur stumbled backwards shaking his head. His eyes were locked on the trunk as his heel rammed against a rock causing him to lose his balance. Arthur stretched his arms out and snagged the back of the carriage before he fell back.

Trying to catch his breath, he clung to the wagon with one hand and grabbed his chest with the other. He shook his head as he pushed down the thoughts of his parents. Swallowing down the lump of emotion clogging his throat, he tried to compose himself.

In the house he heard the clapping of Sophie's shoes on the wooden floor. He knew she would be expecting her trunk soon. With trembling hands, he reached for the trunk and slid it out of the back.

"Arthur?" Sophie's voice rang out as he moved up the stairs.

"Sorry," he answered as he propped the trunk against the wall and his knee to grab the door. Carefully he pried the door open and maneuvered the trunk back into his hands when his foot caught the door.

"Oh my," Sophie said. "Here, let me help."

Sophie rushed to the door and held it open for him with a wide-eyed stare. Curiosity and concern were etched on her face as he moved past her. He didn't stop to answer her unspoken questions but drifted down the hallway towards the back bedroom and sat the trunk at the foot of the bed.

"Everything okay?"

"Yes," Arthur said stretching out his back when Sophie stepped into the room.

"Is there anything else I can do for you?" Arthur asked as he moved out of the room to give Sophie some space.

"No," Sophie said, shaking her head. Arthur pressed his lips into a tight line and glanced over his shoulder. "I will start making dinner momentarily."

"You don't have to do that."

"It's the reason you married me, isn't it? To help around here? I am a good cook if I do say so myself," Sophie said taking a step closer to Arthur. He moved back once more trying to keep the space between them. With each step Sophie took, Arthur stole back from her, always keeping her at arm's length.

"I know the marriage was rushed and all," he said, stepping back once more. "But perhaps we shouldn't rush the rest. After all, we'll be married for some time, God willing."

Air whistled through Sophie's clenched teeth. Judging from the relief that washed over her face and the hint of a smile, he realized she wasn't ready to consummate the marriage either.

"If you don't like the room," Arthur said glancing around the room.

"No, it's fine really," Sophie said, stealing a step closer to him. "Thank you."

"Then I'll let you change and get settled."

"And then I'll make dinner," Sophie insisted. Arthur's head twitched a bit as he consented to her cooking against his better judgment. But if he was going to get used to this new life, he had to start somewhere.

"Looking forward to it," he said leaving the room.

Chapter 5

"Mr. Soul, Mr. Soul," Sam Goodrich plowed through the barn doors panting and heaving. His sandy blonde hair was messy and tossed about while his broad, square shoulders were tense as he pushed through the barn doors. Arthur glanced up from a saddle he was mending and moved around the stall to get a better glimpse of his ranch hand. Sam looked disheveled. His brow creased and a small 'v' appeared at the bridge of his nose.

"What's wrong?" Arthur asked as he moved swiftly to the water pump and filled a bucket up. Sam clung to the post of the barn trying desperately to regain his breathing as Arthur handed him the bucket of fresh water.

"We have a problem," Sam said between gulps of water.

"I can see that, what is it? Is it Sophie?"

"No, it's the ranch hands, they are..." Sam inhaled deeply and let out the air in his lungs slowly. Arthur pulled up a stool for Sam and forced him to sit.

"What?" Arthur said quickly as his eyes darted to the open barn door wondering if they were about to charge through.

"Staging a sit in. They are demanding more pay."

"You aren't serious, I just gave them a raise," Arthur said, his shoulders dropping. "This cannot be happening right now. There is no way I can afford to shell out more money right now. Not with the barn roof that needs to be patched up, more wire for the property fence, and supplies for the roundup. The boys know I need all hands ready for the spring roundup. Why would they do this to me? Haven't I treated them decent in the past?"

"Of course you have," Sam said setting the bucket down. "I've tried to keep this under wraps, but today was too much."

"Who started it? Who is it that has them riled up?" Arthur asked as he moved to the stall to lean against the post.

"I'm not sure. The only one I can think of is the two new cowboys I hired a few weeks ago. It seems before they came everyone was content. Now," Sam threw up his hand towards the door and shrugged.

"What are you going to do?" Sam asked, glancing over his shoulder to look at Arthur.

"What can I do but pay them more money. They have me over a barrel. I can't afford to go into the roundup with men short. Everyone is needed. Damn it," Arthur said as he stood up and stomped to the bucket. In one swing of his foot, he sent the bucket flying into the air spilling the rest of the water.

Arthur grunted as he pressed his lips into a tight line and grounded his teeth. He shook his head and clenched his fists into a tight ball.

"What's going on in here?" Sophie's voice startled him. Arthur shifted around to find her lovely ace staring at him with confusion written all over it. He knew he had lost his temper, but he had every right to. Still, that didn't excuse him from his bad manners.

"Nothing," Arthur said shortly as he glared at Sam daring him to say a word. The last thing Arthur wanted was to get Sophie involved in his troubles.

"Well, I was just going to do the laundry," Sophie said, moving to fetch water from the pump. Sam dipped his hat to her as she moved off to the watering pump to fill her bucket.

Silence filled the space between the three of them as Arthur tried to get his temper under control.

"All right then," Sophie said, picking up the bucket and leaving the barn without a second glance at Arthur.

"Why didn't you tell her?" Sam asked.

"No. She doesn't need to get involved in this. She hasn't been here more than two weeks. Doesn't even have her bearings yet. I can't bring her into this mess."

"Well, if you ask me," Sam said.

"I didn't," Arthur said, cutting him off.

"She should know. It's not a good idea to keep things from wives. They have a way of finding things out eventually."

Arthur glanced at the open barn doors and his shoulders dropped. He could only imagine what Sophie thought of him now. He shook his head feeling remorse as he moved towards the doors and leaned against the door frame.

"If you don't mind me saying there, boss," Sam said as he moved to Arthur's side. "It seems to me that you have a bit of a crush on your wife."

"What makes you think that?" Arthur asked, his eyes remaining locked on the petite beauty near the wash tub.

"I've seen how you've been looking at her," Sam said resting his arm on Arthur's shoulder. "There's no hiding those feelings either. Women can see right through us. She'll interpret it as you are pushing her away and that's not your intention is it?"

"Sam," Arthur pulled his attention off Sophie and glared at Sam with one eyebrow raised. "What makes you such an expert on these things?"

"Ah, you know," Sam said slipping his hat on his head and shrugging. "But I'll tell you this much, that woman there. She likes you too."

"There is no way to know that." Arthur said glancing back at Sophie. Hope swelled in his chest as he thought of their recent interaction.

"She could have gotten water by going around the barn. Instead, she came in to check on you. That's showing interest. She worries about you."

Arthur slowly exhaled as he watched Sophie. She moved leisurely, the loose strands of her hair ruffling in the breeze on the nap of her neck and shining in the sunlight entranced him. Although she wasn't as full figured as other girls, she had a beauty to her that was uniquely her own. Deep inside him, Arthur couldn't deny his attraction to her.

"Maybe I'll…" Arthur said as he thought of picking her flowers before shaking his head and ruling that gesture out. "Or perhaps…"

"Looks to me like you got a lot on your mind right now," Sam said patting his friend on the shoulder. "I'll leave you be with this one."

Sam waved Arthur goodbye as Arthur remained propped against the barn door frame. The hard shell surrounding his heart seemed to crack as Sophie wiped the sweat from her brow and stared up into the sky. In the distance he could hear the lonely whistle of the train. The sound seeped into him and chipped away at the wall he built around his heart.

"I know," he said with a smile and pushed off the frame of the barn.

* * *

A warm breeze kissed Sophie's face as she plunged her hands into the wooden bucket and pulled up Arthur's pants. She wrung out the clothes tightly trying to take out her frustration on the clothes. Grunting she kept her eyes locked on the soapy water as it fell back into the bucket. As she watched the waters, her ears perked as the whistle of the train caught her attention.

Despite her irritation, a smile pulled up at the corners of her lips as she realized it had been nearly two weeks since she stepped off the platform. Her life had done a complete turnabout since that day, but in all honesty she was relieved not to have her stepmother hounding her day in and day out.

The lonely whistle faded as Sophie drew the rest of the laundry out of the bucket and hung them out on the rope. It was a strenuous job, but it was hers now and she was going to do it to the best of her ability.

"Hello there," Mae said coming around the corner of the house. Sophie lifted her hand up to shield her eyes as she noticed the middle-aged woman with light brown hair.

"Hey Mae," Sophie said, popping the plug in the bucket to let the water spill out into the grass.

"I see you've started your chores early today," Mae said as she gave Sophie a little hug. It was always a pleasure to see Mae.

"Did you milk the cow yet?" Mae asked as Sophie put the last set of socks on the rope and stepped back.

"No," Sophie huffed. "But I'll get to it."

"You know that cow is on a schedule and needs to be milked twice a day."

Sophie wiped her brow with the back of her hand and shook her head. Exhaling, she stared at Mae in disbelief.

"I'm never going to get the hang of all this," Sophie said. "This is getting to be so much."

"Don't you worry, you'll get used to it soon enough. You just got to find your flow is all."

"Sometimes I feel like I might not ever figure things out. There's just so much to learn. And it's not like I'm not used to hard work, I am. It's just so much more here to do."

Mae laughed as she walked over to Sophie and put her arms around her shoulders. The middle-aged woman squeezed her tightly making her feel as if she belonged there, despite all her insecurities.

"Tell me something," Mae said, releasing Sophie. "Do you regret coming out here?"

"No," Sophie smiled wryly. "Not one bit. But I've never ran a household before."

"Well, you're doing a great job. I'm sure if you keep at it, you'll find your place. Now, I'm going to milk the cow if you get water for the garden."

"Are you sure you want to help me? I feel so bad. You're neglecting your own ranch aren't you?"

Mae shook her head as she swatted at the air. "Naw, my mother-in-law has things taken care of there. You don't worry your pretty little head about that."

"It's just... I want to be the best wife I can be, you know? I don't want Arthur to think he's made a mistake marrying me."

Mae crossed her arms over her chest and stared at Sophie. A big laugh escaped Mae's lips as she slapped her hand on her hip.

"Oh darling," Mae said. "Don't you worry about that either. You just be yourself and the rest will fall into place, you'll see. Arthur's a good man, no doubt about that. He wouldn't have married you if he didn't want to."

"I know he wants me to be happy," Sophie said as she pushed her arm into Mae's. The women walked around to the side of the house where Sophie gasped the instant she noticed Arthur. "But I'm still not sure if I'm cut out for this."

"Try running a house with two young kids, then talk to me about being overwhelmed," Mae said patting Sophie's hand.

Sophie sighed and stared compassionately at Mae. One thing was certain; Sophie didn't know what she would do without her new friend. Life on the ranch was harder than she expected, and she knew she had a lot to learn.

"Mae," Arthur said dipping his hat as he moved closer to them with one hand behind his back. Mae's face lit up as she gave Sophie one more squeeze.

"I'll be going to milk that cow now," Mae said winking at Arthur.

"Arthur," Sophie said lifting her head up. Her nerves were shot as Arthur stared at her with tight lips.

"There's something I need you to do," Arthur said stealing a step closer. Sophie's eyes lit up as she tucked the loose strand of hair behind her ear.

"Certainly, what do you need from me?"

Arthur pulled his hand from behind his back and opened it. For a moment Sophie stared dumbstruck at his empty hand before slowly looking up at him.

"Forgive me," Arthur said. "I shouldn't have lost my temper and I shouldn't have been so short with you."

"I..." Sophie tried to think of something to say, but she couldn't believe her ears. It wasn't very often someone asked her to forgive them. Yet, here her husband was, doing just that. He leaned down and plucked the wildflower at her feet and presented it to her.

"Yes," she finally said taking the flower from his hand. "I forgive you."

"Thank you," Arthur replied, stepping towards her, still with his hand out. Sophie slipped her hand into his and studied him as he lifted her hand to his lips.

"No," he said pressing his lips to her knuckles. "Thank you."

Arthur stood up as Sophie's cheeks burned and her lips curled up at the corners. She pulled her hand to her chest as she watched him walk back to the barn. Mae stood around the corner with a smile stretching from ear to ear causing Sophie to blush even more.

"Maybe there is hope for us," Sophie whispered glancing at her knuckles. She pushed her hair behind her ear as her heart fluttered when she caught Arthur looking over his shoulder to steal one more glimpse at her.

She grabbed the basket of laundry and walked up the steps to the house still feeling her cheeks burning. With her heart quickening, she walked down the hallway and pushed through her bedroom. Setting the basket on her bed, she rushed to the small desk by the window and pulled out the journal. Glancing over her shoulder to the door, she opened the book and sat down.

Dear Diary,

Today, I must admit was different. I have been struggling to please Arthur for weeks now, and today he approached me. He handed me wildflowers and kissed my hand. It has been the first encounter he's had with me since I've come here. My heart is still frantically beating within my chest as I think of his lips on my knuckles. How strange to be feeling a tenderness towards him. I don't know if I should take this to heart as something more, or if it was simply a kind gesture on his part.

This is all so new for me. I know Nadine would laugh at my presumption that Arthur likes me. But then again, what if he does? What if something has changed over these past weeks? Is it wrong of me to hope for more than a marriage of convenience? Is it wrong to hope for love? Oh if only I had my sister to write to, she would know what to do. Perhaps I should simply wait to see what other things transpire between us. I would hate to jump to conclusions only to be rejected. I can hear my stepmother's voice in my head calling me a foolish girl and it saddens me. But maybe, just maybe, there is something there between us that simply wasn't there before.

Chapter 6

The sun dipped into the tree turning the bright blue-sky orange. Sophie looked up to see the array of colors dancing on the clouds as she stepped out onto the porch.

"Dinner," she called, her eyes lingered on the sky as Arthur charged out of the barn. Sophie pulled in a deep breath and lowered her head as her husband passed by without a word. She wanted to reach out to him, find some way to comfort him but she didn't know where to begin.

"Everything alright?" She asked as she followed him into the house.

"Fine." Arthur's voice was sharp and to the point. Swallowing hard she nodded and clamped her lips shut as she watched him move through the kitchen like a bull.

"I'll have the food on the table in just a moment," she said. "If you wanted to clean yourself up."

"Good," Arthur grunted, pushing through the back door. The tender moment they shared just a few hours before seemed to have vanished in Arthur's mind. Worry and stress had replaced the tender gaze.

Sophie's heart rattled nervously in her chest as she pulled the bird from the Dutch oven. She couldn't help but smile at her handy work. If there was one thing she was great at, it was cooking. Not even her daddy could resist her meals. Plus, it was the one thing her stepmother couldn't complain about.

The aroma of rosemary swirled about the kitchen and filled the whole house with its homey fragrance. For a moment Sophie wondered if she had seasoned the duck too much, but as she slipped the knife into the breast and stole a sample, she couldn't help but roll her eyes. The juices of the meat exploded in her mouth as the meat of the bird melted.

With a smile plastered to her face, she moved the duck to the center of the table in the dining room and set it down gingerly. Stepping back she admired her handy work as Arthur barged in again through the back door.

Sophie paused to steal a glance at him. Arthur's eyes were down with his shoulders back. For a moment she wondered if he was too absorbed in his thoughts to even smell the meal. The moment his head snapped up and he closed his eyes; Sophie knew she had got to him. There was no way anyone could resist her cooking.

"Is that rosemary?" Arthur asked as he stormed into the dining room and pulled out a chair.

"Yes," Sophie said delightfully. "Roasted stuff duck with rosemary. There are potatoes inside and some carrots too."

Arthur huffed as Sophie scurried to the kitchen and scrambled to grab the plates. She moved back to the living room with everything in hand for a nice meal and stopped short. Arthur's chin was dropped to his chest and his eyes were closed. Panic shot through her as she rushed to his side.

"Arthur?" Sophie said, placing one hand on his shoulder. He jumped up in his seat and whipped his head about searching for some unknown threat before his eyes fell on Sophie. She stepped back unsure of what he would do only to notice that his scared and fierce expression had melted.

"Are you alright?" she asked setting the plate down in front of him.

"Tired."

"I can see that."

"It's been a rough day." Arthur's gravel voice sounded grainier than ever. She nodded as she turned her attention to the bird on the table.

"Well, nothing like a decent meal to make things right as rain."

Arthur didn't say a word as Sophie filled his plate up with food and handed it to him before serving herself. She took her plate and sat at the far end of the table, giving him as much space as she could. Every so often, she glanced at him wondering if the hard wrinkles in his forehead would ever go away. Somehow over the last few hours, the smooth faced man she married, who had presented her with the wildflower, had vanished and was replaced by a hard-distant man she didn't even know.

"Beside rough, how else did things go for you today?" Sophie said as she pulled a fork full of meat into her mouth.

"Well, if you must know," Arthur set his fork on the table and leaned back in his seat. "The fence needs mending and I've got a goat that doesn't seem to want to give milk anymore. Not to mention my wife forgot to milk the cow this evening which will cause the cow to dry up eventually but not before it suffers from some other aliment."

Sophie gasped as her eyes shot to the front door. She knew, in the back of her mind, that she had forgotten to do something. Her lower lip quivered as she looked at the duck on her plate. All she wanted was to give him a fancy meal, she completely forgot about the cow.

"I'm sorry," Sophie said, trying to keep her tears under wraps.

"Why are you crying over milk?" Arthur asked, his eyes boring into hers.

"I'm trying, I promise I am."

"I know, and that's fine," Arthur said, reaching across the table. His wrinkled face smoothened for a moment as he stared at her. "But the cow is the one thing on the farm you cannot neglect," Arthur said as he leaned over the table.

"I understand," Sophie said, nodding and fighting the tears swelling in her eyes.

Arthur leaned back and stabbed his fork into the meat. He pushed the meat into his mouth. With wide eyes and a slow moan of approval, Arthur flashed a crooked little smile.

"And just so you know," he said. Sophie noticed his head was cocked down as he tried to catch her eye. "The meal is delicious. I can honestly say, I've never tasted anything so good. Where did you learn to cook like this?"

Sophie lifted her head up and puffed out her chest as her tears dried up. Sniffling, she smiled, proud of her work.

"It's just a gift," she said, sitting up taller.

"Well, I like it." Arthur lifted his fork up as if to toast to her before the food found its way into his belly. Sophie giggled as the deep lines in Arthur's forehead seemed to vanish.

"Thank you," she said, putting the food into her mouth and savoring every bite.

"So," Sophie set her fork down and pushed her plate away from her. "I hope things are better for you tomorrow."

It was as if her words had stabbed him. The comfort he felt in her presence vanished and the worry lines seeped into his brow once more.

"I really need to learn to keep my mouth shut," Sophie said, rising from the table. She grabbed the dirty dishes and moved into the kitchen. The tension in the dining room seemed to expand to her as she turned to gather the rest of the plates from the table. Arthur had one arm crossed over his chest as the other stroked the bristles on his chin. Sophie opened her mouth but then shut it quickly once again.

She slipped to his side and grabbed his dish as he stared at the cracks in the dining room table. A mumble slipped from Arthur's lips causing Sophie to stop and turn. But his eyes remained locked on that one spot and she knew he wasn't talking to her.

"I'm going to just go and milk the cow now," Sophie said, setting the plates in the sink.

"Mmm." Arthur grunted as Sophie snagged the lantern from the side of the door and stepped out into the night.

The cool night air drifted around her and washed all scent of rosemary off her. She glanced up to see the twinkling lights of the stars shining down on her.

"I can't believe I forgot to milk the cow," she grumbled as she moved through the dark open space. The grass crunched under her weight as she moved. The soft pale light from the lantern only illuminated so much and for a moment, Sophie wondered what else lurked in the shadows out here at night.

Sure, she had heard the coyotes howling in the distance the last few nights. Their song even put her to sleep. But being out in the darkness exposed her; she wished she would have taken the rifle with her to the barn.

"Serves you right," she mumbled to the blackness trying to keep her fears under control. "If you hadn't forgotten to do this, then maybe you wouldn't be out here after dark with god knows what watching you."

The neighing of the horse startled her as she reached the barn and threw open the doors. The animals in their stalls each cried out in a harmonious chorus of moos and neighs at the sight of her. Lifting her lantern up, Sophie couldn't help but laugh as each of the animals stared at her.

"Silly girl," she said as she grabbed the milking stool and the pail from the corner of the barn. "I really can work myself up. Looks like you can too," she said to the animals in the stalls.

Sophie opened the stall with the cow and moved around the animal. She placed the stool like Mae showed her and sat down.

"Alright now," Sophie said, looking at the udders. "You're going to work for me right?"

Reaching under the cow, Sophie started milking. The sound of the milk hitting the metal pail bounced off the walls of the barn. Exhaling, she glanced up at the cow as it turned its head to stare at her.

"At least I have you to talk to," Sophie said to the cow. *Even if it's only a one-sided conversation, but hey, us girls gotta stick together.*

*   *   *

Arthur sat back in his seat letting the food settle when the rapping on the door pulled him from his thoughts. His head whipped around as he moved with haste to the door. Swiftly he pulled the rifle from the corner and held it ready.

You're jumping to conclusions.

Sucking in a deep breath, he reached for the door and pulled it open with the end of the barrel pointed into the darkness. With his finger inching towards the trigger he waited. Only the sound of his frantic heartbeat filled the silence. His blood ran cold as he dared to step past the threshold.

Carefully Arthur shifted his weight, allowing the small orange light of the living room to flood the porch. His eyes narrowed as he tried to see through the gray veil of shadows.

"Whoa, easy there." The barrel of Arthur's gun shimmied to the left as a hand reached out and grabbed the end of it. In a single thrust, Arthur's aim was ruined. Before he could get his finger on the trigger to fire, a man stepped into the light.

No. Arthur dropped the gun and stumbled back. His eyes widened as the butt of the gun rammed the wooden porch. Fear stabbed at Arthur like a dull blade trying to twist in his side.

"What on God's green earth are you doing here?" Arthur said holding the gun to his side. A tall man pulled his hat from his head as the light caused the golden badge on it to shimmer. Arthur didn't need an introduction; he had seen the marshal before. It was a long time ago, but he knew he would never forget the man's face.

"I could have killed you Bergen," Arthur said through clenched teeth. Arthur glanced over his shoulder into the house. He quickly scanned the area before stepping out onto the porch and closing the door behind him.

"What are you doing here?" Arthur asked even though he already knew the answer.

"You know why I've come," the marshal said, playing with his wide brim hat. "He's escaped."

The words slapped Arthur hard. He knew what the marshal was going to say, but for some sick reason he needed to hear it. He shook his head, allowing his mind to wrap around the reality that Randal Munger was on the loose.

"You sure?" Arthur asked trying to keep his cool.

"Positive," Bergen said refusing to look Arthur in the eyes. "We've been looking for him for nearly two months now."

"I see and only now you come to me?" Arthur hissed as he stepped forward. His eyes lingered on the shadows as his body tensed.

"At least I came."

"How did it happen?" Arthur asked crossing his arms against his chest in a vain attempt to keep from beating the marshal to a pulp.

"Honestly, we aren't sure. It could have been a bribe when he was being transferred from the state penitentiary. Or just dumb luck."

Pressing his lips into a tight line, Arthur stared down the marshal. In the pit of his stomach he could feel a turning. Sophie's delicious meal was on the verge of coming back up. All Arthur could do was to keep breathing deeply to settle his nerves.

"You're telling me, one of your men may have been bribed to let that man go? What kind of game are you running there?"

"Look you weren't there, you don't know what happened. You don't have a clue the guilt I've felt over the years. But I got news that I'm not doing so hot and I want to make things right, which is why I'm here to settle up with you."

"You're right," Arthur said dropping his arms and moving closer to the marshal. "I wasn't there. I was trying to keep my past where it belongs, in the past. But now you're saying Randal is on the loose?"

"Randal was never supposed to get out of that cell, but he can be persuasive." Beads of sweat formed on Bergen's forehead as he pulled his hat from his head and fiddled with it.

"When you have a family to care for, and a daughter that's battling consumption, a man will do anything, even sell his soul if he has to."

"So you sold your soul to the devil to save your daughter?"

Bergen didn't say a word. His eyes shifted around Arthur as if Arthur was a snake. The sinking sensation in Arthur's stomach grew progressively worse as he studied the man before him.

"Look, Arthur," Bergen glanced up at him as he raised his hands in the air. "It was a different time. I was a different person back then."

"What did you do?" Arthur growled.

"Randal offered me five thousand dollars to tell him who ratted him out."

Arthur's body trembled as he listened to the marshal. Then, as if a great wind swept through the plain and sucked out all the air, Arthur's body went numb. He could feel the anger rising in him. The terror that swirled about his stomach causing his heart to race was gone. Even the air that he pulled into his lungs seemed to vanish.

"You... Told him?" Arthur stood incredibly still as his hands balled into tight little fists.

"My family needed that money," Bergen said, lifting his hands up. His voice broke as he spoke.

"You have three seconds to get off my land or I shoot you for trespassing."

"I didn't tell him where you were going," Bergen said trembling.

"Three..."

"He doesn't know where to even start looking."

"Two..."

Arthur snagged the gun and cocked it. The loud snapping caused the critters in the trees to go spark up before falling silent. An eeriness filled the void around them as Arthur pulled the gun up to his chin and aimed at the marshal.

"You aren't going to shoot a man of the law are you?" Bergen asked, quickly stepping down the steps.

"You ain't a man of the law. Not anymore. Right now you're a trespasser and I got every right to pull this trigger."

Arthur's eyes darted to the shadows as he wondered if Randal was out there right now, watching them. His stomach tied in knots as he watched Bergen stumble back towards his horse.

"I came here to warn you," the marshal said. "That single moment has caused me more harm than it ever did me good. I know now that it was the biggest mistake of my life."

"Save the speech for your wife," Arthur said as he raised the gun up and pulled the trigger. The shot rang out, scattering the critters in the trees who took to the sky in droves.

"I don't expect I'll be seeing you again," Arthur said, lowering the barrel. The marshal's eyes were wide and full of fear. Swallowing the lump in his throat Arthur watched the marshal struggle with his horse.

"You best be getting on your way before I decide to put you out of your misery," Arthur snarled as his heart skipped and jumped. He wanted to look for Sophie inside, but he didn't dare take his eyes off the marshal.

Bergen bit his lower lip and slipped his hat back on his head before mounting his steed.

"Arthur?" Sophie's voice called out in the darkness. Terror struck him. The last thing he wanted was for Sophie to be involved in all this. She was just an innocent bystander, unfortunate and unlucky. He exhaled as he spied her shadow stretching out on the grass as she came around the corner.

"Arthur?"

"Get now," Arthur ordered. Bergen nodded and pulled the reins, turning his horse about. Panic and adrenaline coursed through Arthur's veins as Sophie came around the corner.

"Was that a gun shot?" she asked, holding a metal pail in her arms.

"Thought I saw a snake," Arthur said through his teeth as the marshal disappeared into the night.

"A snake?" Sophie's voice dropped as she scanned the area.

"You aren't in the city anymore," Arthur snapped. "There are things out here that could kill you."

He knew those words were truer now than ever before. With Randal out there somewhere hunting him down, Arthur knew Sophie wasn't safe with him. Out of all the things that could have happened, he had to bring her into this. Guilt racked his nerves as he spun on his heels and moved towards the door.

"You best be getting inside," Arthur said. "Wouldn't want the wolves to descend."

"There are wolves out here too?" she asked. Arthur's eyebrow pulled up as he watched her move up the stairs. The wooden planks on the porch creaked and moaned as her heels clacked against them.

"I knew there were coyotes," Sophie said as she passed him. Any other time, Arthur would have laughed at her naivety. But tonight, he knew he would be sleeping with one eye open.

"Who would have thought they'd be so close to town," Sophie said as the milk sloshed in the pail.

"You'd be surprised where they show up," Arthur said, looking over his shoulder to steal one more glance outside. *And some even walk about in human skin. They're the worst danger of all, especially to a timid city girl and a newly married man.*

Chapter 7

"Is everything okay?" Sophie asked popping her head around the corner. With her eyebrow raised and head cocked she waited a moment. Hearing no answer, she stepped back into the kitchen and sat the pail of milk on the counter. Her hands trembled as different scenarios played out in her mind.

Stand your ground. Be confident.

Slowly she turned, straightened her shoulders, and walked back into the living room. She stared at Arthur as he pulled the curtains back and stared out into the night.

"Arthur?"

"I'm Fine." His voice wavered as he spoke to the window.

"You don't look fine. You look like a man that has the world weighing him down." Sophie moved next to Arthur and placed her hand on his shoulder. The simple touched caused him to jump. His head whipped around, and the stark, wild gaze chilled her. Gasping, Sophie stepped back.

"You... You don't want me here anymore, do you?" The air around Sophie felt like it was being sucked away. She found it harder and harder to breath as Arthur stared at her in silence.

"I can do better," she started as she dropped her gaze. "I know it's taken me longer to catch on, but I swear I can do better. I will do better. I'll get up earlier to milk the cow and stay up later to make sure the house is in order before -" Tears pooled in her eyes as she dropped her head.

"Sophie," Arthur's voice was stern and short. He lifted her head up by her chin forcing her to look at him. "This has nothing to do with you."

"But... I know there is something going on with you." Sophie stepped back as she fiddled with her nails.

"There is nothing going on with me. You're reading into things," Arthur said flatly as he struggled with keeping his eyes on her.

"Something is going on. You're not acting like yourself." Sophie moved to the window and pulled the curtain back. Only darkness greeted her. She couldn't see anything lingering in the front yard that would cause Arthur so much stress.

"What are you doing?" Arthur asked, yanking the curtain from her, and covering the window once more.

"Tell me what's out there that you don't want me to see. I know you're hiding something. This sketchy behavior isn't like you."

"How would you know what I'm like?" Arthur snapped. "You haven't known me long enough to know who I am."

Sophie's mouth snapped shut. "You're right. But this behavior isn't like you. It's like... Well, I don't know what it's like. Either you don't like my cooking and it's made you crazy or you're scared of something out there." Sophie pointed to the window and reached out towards the curtain to pull it back. Arthur's hand was on hers instantly stopping her.

"I don't get scared," Arthur snapped.

"No. You just get closed off and distant." Sophie folded her arms over her chest. Her body trembled as she spoke. Never in all her life had she the nerve to speak this way. But she knew she had to say something. Her throat went dry as Arthur glared daggers at her.

"One minute you're kissing my hand and apologizing to me and the next you're like this. You know your mood swings are making my head spin."

Arthur's shoulders dropped and he exhaled. "You're right. I haven't been fair to you. I don't mean to be this way. But you don't understand."

"Then help me to understand," Sophie moved to the sofa and sat down. She straightened her back as she smoothed the wrinkles out of her dress.

"I can't," Arthur shook his head as he paced the length of the living room.

"You can't? Or you won't?"

"Does it matter?" Arthur stopped by the couch and stared at her as he dug his fingers into the cushions of the sofa.

"It does to me. I made a vow to you Arthur Soul. To honor and obey you, and to stay by your side no matter what. But how can I help you and help this marriage if you won't tell me what is really going on. Isn't that what marriage is all about? Helping and relying on one another? But how can I do that when you push me away every chance you get?"

"Sophie..." Arthur's voice dropped with his eyes. His entire body deflated as he moved around the couch and sat down. "There's just... I am..."

"Start from the beginning," Sophie said reaching her hand out to his. Arthur stared at her hand on his for what seemed like eternity before he cleared his throat.

"I'm not proud of my past," he said in barely a whisper. "There are things I've done... Things that could destroy me."

Sophie followed Arthur as he rose from the couch and headed back to the window. She couldn't help but feel a sinking feeling as he propped himself against the wall with one arm and peered out into the night.

"I grew up on a ranch similar to this one," Arthur said as Sophie shifted in her seat to face him. Her heart drummed as her hands turned clammy, but she didn't dare interrupt him.

"I lived in El Paso, Texas with my parents and my brother. I thought life couldn't get better. I was set to lead the cattle drive that year with my father at my side to ensure I did everything right. It was a test you see," Arthur glanced over his shoulder to Sophie, his eyebrows hid his eyes as he looked at her.

"If I did good, Father would let me make the run the following year with a crew of my own."

"So what happened?"

"Randal Munger happened," Arthur said the name like an expletive.

"Who?" Sophie's brows rose. Her breathing came in bursts as she sat there listening.

"Randal Munger was… is an outlaw. He…" Sophie rose to her feet and swiftly moved to Arthur's side as his voice broke. She moved him to the couch and let him fall into the cushions.

"Arthur, you don't have to go any further. I'm sorry I brought it up."

"No," Arthur cleared his throat and lifted his head high. "You need to hear this. It's because of what I've done that your life might be in danger."

"What are you going on about?" Sophie rubbed her hands on his arms as if he was cold as winter. But she couldn't deny the fear bubbling in her stomach.

Arthur grabbed Sophie's hands and drew them to his lap. Sucking in a deep breath, he played with the creases between her fingers. Sophie's heart fluttered as he touched her so delicately that she didn't know how to react.

"Randal Munger killed my family in Texas. He raided the ranch. I..." Arthur's fingers trembled as he continued to trace the lines of her palm.

"If I hadn't gone into town, I would have been able to stop him."

"It wasn't your fault," Sophie said, pulling her hand out of his and wrapping her arms around Arthur's shoulders. Resting her head on his shoulder, Sophie held him.

"But I wasn't there."

"How were you supposed to know what was going to happen? Could you predict the future? And say you were there, who's to say this Randal guy wouldn't have killed you as well?"

Arthur pushed Sophie off him and rose to his feet. She could see his eyes burning as he shook his head. Sadness and grief were etched in the lines of his brow as he stumbled away from her.

"Don't," Arthur said, turning his back to her. "Don't say this is all okay. It's not. Randal deserves the gallows for what he did."

"I'm not saying he doesn't," Sophie said, rising and moving to Arthur with her arms out. Arthur twisted his head and with pursed lips glared at her. Sophie stopped and dropped her arms defeated.

"I want to help you, please. Just let me help you," she said in a small voice.

"You can't. If Randal knew I had a wife, he'd kill you just like he did my family."

"There is no way for you to know that."

Arthur reached out and grabbed Sophie's arms. A whimper escaped her lips as he pulled her to him. The fear in her stomach twisted into knots as Sophie dreaded the worse.

"Randal Munger is a killer. I thought…" Arthur dropped Sophie as her lower lip trembled and side stepped around her.

"Don't do that," Sophie said turning on her heels. "Don't push me away when you've opened up so much already."

"You shouldn't be married to me Sophie. I'm not a good person."

"Why are you saying these things? Do you really want me to leave?"

"Yes." Arthur dropped his head and reached for the chair as his body wobbled. The crack in Sophie's heart split as the word struck her harder than any fist could have.

"You're lying."

"I want you gone Sophie," Arthur said through gritted teeth. "You need to pack your things and go. Tonight."

"I'm not leaving you."

"You have to," Arthur twisted around and pulled her to him. His embrace squeezed the air from Sophie's lungs as he held her.

"I can't put you in danger." Sophie tapped Arthur's shoulder frantically as the last bit of air escaped her lips. Immediately Arthur released her. Sophie coughed and hacked, pulling in fresh air as she reached for the chair before falling.

"Why do you keep saying I'm in danger?" She asked between gulps of fresh air.

"Randal Munger is on the loose. He knows it was me. He's coming for me I know it. You can't be here when he does."

"You're talking in riddles," Sophie said. "What did you do to make him come after you?"

Arthur's face turned white. Sophie rubbed her chest as she regained herself and stood before her husband. His eyes twitched as the life drained from him.

"Arthur, what did you do?"

Arthur reached out for Sophie, wrapping his strong arms around her tiny frame. His hot breath tickled the top of her head as he held her close. She could feel his heart beating frantically as his fingers dug into the fabric of her dress. He scooped his arm around the base of Sophie's neck and held her as she clung to him.

*   *   *

"What would you think of me if I told you I ran with him and his gang for a few years?" Arthur kept his eyes on Sophie. He wanted to see every detailed reaction as she sat on the couch.

"Is that the truth?"

Arthur nodded without saying a word. His heart pounded in his chest as Sophie mulled over the information. She pulled in a deep breath and stared him right in the eyes.

"It doesn't matter," she said. Shock, horror, relief, Arthur's body trembled with so many emotions rushing through him.

"It doesn't matter?" he said slowly letting the words sink in. He stared at her a moment and pulled in a long deep breath. "You have to know why though. You need to hear the truth."

"I'll listen," Sophie said, bobbing her head as she kept her eyes locked on him. His body tensed a moment as he exhaled.

"It was the 13th of May. A summer storm rolled in and turned the blue sky to gray. It was the kind of storm that sends even a strong man to look for shelter. The air was charged as streaks of lightning crashed between the clouds," Arthur said as the memory slapped him like cold water on a chilly day.

"A clap of thunder rattled my feet. Not sure if you ever been to Texas, but the sky there is bigger and the storms that come are meaner than anything you'll find anywhere else. I rode five miles to get to town. It was meant to be a simple stop. All I needed to do was pick up a few last minute supplies for the run and return home." Arthur swallowed hard.

"The grocer, Mr. Robert stood on his porch checking his pocket watch as I loaded up the last bit. He wished me well and lifted his hand up to say goodbye," Arthur's chest felt heavy as he closed his eyes.

"I figured I had all the time in the world to get back home. There was no urgency. Sure, the storm was coming, but that's what it did during those months. So, I'd get a bit wet. I didn't care. The rains would make a nice reprieve from the obsessive heat that beat down on everything and turned the grass yellow."

Sophie's hand flinched as Arthur spied her reaching for him when he opened his eyes. Pain rippled through him like a million bees stinging him all at once. But the way Sophie stared at him, so heartbroken, so injured made him want to crumble.

"When I got to the ranch, the barbed wire had been cut. It coiled around the post like a noose. I figured the herd had tried to make a break for the greener pastures and got spooked by the rumbling.

"I figured Johnny would be coming out to see me like he always did when I went to town. He'd always wanted to be the first to know the news and what was going on outside our little space. When he didn't show, my stomach sank.

"It wasn't a coincidence that the wire was cut. Or my younger brother wasn't out there to greet me."

"Arthur," Sophie's voice was hardly audible as she reached for him. The warmth of her hand on his soothed some of the fears that dug into his soul like hooks.

"You don't have to... I didn't..."

"But you need to know, I want you to know. That way it will be you making the decision to go. Don't you see? I have enough on my conscious. I can't afford to have you on there too."

Sophie dropped her eyes and sat on the couch in silence. The weight of her not speaking filled Arthur with dread as he waited on her to make the choice. Slowly, she drew her eyes back to him and nodded.

"I told you," she said very clearly as she wiped the tears from her cheeks. "I promised you I'd stick by you. You're not going to be able to get rid of me so easily."

"Maybe," Arthur said as he stared at the thin cracks in the wooden door. "But you haven't heard everything."

"You don't have to," Sophie said quickly. "Not if it means that it will hurt you."

A sliver of a smile tickled Arthur's lip. Sophie was the kindest, most understanding person he ever met. Not in a lifetime did he believe he could meet someone as pure as her.

"I hunted him, Sophie. I hunted him with the intent of killing him. I wanted him to pay for what he did to my family. Don't you understand that? I'm not a good guy." Arthur's words came gushing out as he moved closer to Sophie and snatched her hand from off her lap.

"But you didn't kill him, you took the higher road."

She thinks of me as a coward. Arthur jerked his head away sharply as Sophie cupped her hand to his face drawing his eyes back to her.

"You're too kind to be killer," Sophie said. "I see it in the way you treat the animals in the barn. I see it in the way you carry yourself. You have honor and you would be justified in killing him. But that kind of act does something to a man. It hardens them, makes them callous. A callous man wouldn't kiss a girl's hand. Or pick her wildflowers to brighten her room. No, Arthur Soul, you are no killer."

Weak, soft, it's no wonder he's coming after me.

"Arthur, you asked me to sit here and listen to you. And I have. But there isn't anything you are going to be able to tell me that's going to make me want to run away from you. I'm with you for life."

"Tell me," Arthur said, chewing his lip. "Did you see that man at the door earlier?"

Sophie pursed her lips and nodded sharply.

"I thought you did. That was a marshal. His name is Lew Bergen. At the peak of Randal's terror I got together with Lew and ratted Randal out. I told the marshal everything he needed to know about Randal and what he was planning."

"See, you aren't so bad. You wanted to do what was right and you did. You didn't take matters into your own hands even though you had the opportunity."

"I had several," Arthur growled. "There were so many nights I'd slip into his room with a gun in hand ready to pull that trigger."

"But you didn't."

Arthur shook his head and dug his nails into the palm of his hands. "But I wanted to. If I had, we wouldn't be in the situation we are in now."

"And what's that?" Sophie asked.

"The marshal was kind enough to inform me that Randal is out and most likely looking for me," malice leaked from every word Arthur said. "For all I know, the marshal led Randal right to me by showing up at my front door."

"Why do you say that?"

"Randal offered that marshal lots of money to be released. That's why he came here tonight. To warn me Randal was coming for me. Now do you see why your life is in danger? Why you shouldn't be with me? Randal will kill you in front of me to prove that he is invisible and that I can't do anything to stop him."

"Randal knows you live here?" Sophie's eyes glanced to the window. Understanding fluttered across her face as she realized the dangers lurking in the dark.

"It's possible," Arthur said, plopping down on the seat next to Sophie. He rubbed his temples with his fingers trying to work out the headache throbbing and pounding his brain.

"Then he could already be here?" Sophie asked, as she balled her hands into small little fists and lifted her head up.

A flash of light flickered in Arthur's mind. He sat up and cocked his head as if he heard something in the distance. The wheels began spinning as he shook his head.

"What?" Sophie said, reaching for him.

"I didn't think it was related. I assumed it was…"

"What?"

"Before you came out here, the fencing to my property was cut. The wire curled around the post reminded me of when I came home to find my family…" Arthur couldn't bring himself to finish his thoughts as he rose and paced the living room floor.

"Then the men revolting," Arthur said more to himself than to Sophie.

"When did your men do that? I thought they loved you? Is that what you and Sam were talking about in the barn earlier today?"

Arthur nodded. "I think Randal is already here. I've put you in so much danger."

"Don't you do that. Don't dismiss me or underestimate me Arthur Soul, I'm stronger than you think I am."

"Sophie this is bigger than us."

"No. This is all about us. Don't you see? You can't run from Randal forever. You'll never be able to live if you do. You have to stand up to him and face this fear or it will ruin your life. You'll be constantly looking over your shoulder every second of every day and I won't let you do that."

Arthur cupped his hands around Sophie's face and stared at her. Her eyes were red from the tears that she fought against. Her tender face broke his heart as she nudged her head into his hand. A single tear raced down her cheek as she gazed into his eyes. He couldn't help but find her absolutely irresistible. She was so much braver than he ever gave her credit for. He no longer saw a slender eighteen-year-old girl sitting before him, but a well-rounded and intelligent woman. She had a spirit within her that mimicked his own. Carefully, he brushed his thumb over her cheek wiping the moisture away.

"You sure about this?" he asked, staring at her. Her face was inches from his. She was so close, he could taste her breath on his tongue.

"I'm staying with you."

"Sophie, you are by far one of the most hardheaded women I have ever met," Arthur said as a smile pulled at the corner of his lips. "And one of the bravest and most sincere."

Embarrassment flushed her cheeks crimson. "You aren't running from me, so I won't run from you."

"I don't deserve you," Arthur whispered as he pressed his forehead to hers.

"You've been honest with me so far," Sophie said pulling back. "But I need to ask," she hesitated and exhaled as her eyes bore into his.

"Is there anything else you need to tell me?"

"Arthur Soul isn't my real name. I changed it after I spoke with the marshal. I couldn't risk Randal escaping and coming after me. Not after all that went down."

Sophie nodded slowly allowing his words to sink in. "I don't care what your previous name was. To me you're Arthur Soul, you are my husband. Do you understand? That life you once had is no more. This is who you are now. You've taken the high road and have built an amazing life for yourself here."

"I..." Arthur closed his eyes and his head dropped. Feeling the warmth of Sophie's hands on his face, he smiled. "I can't believe how lucky I am to have you."

Pulling back, Sophie dipped her head to catch Arthur's eye. She paused as she stared at him. Arthur's heart pounded as he wished he could read her thoughts.

Are you mad at me? Is there any anger that is boiling under that calm porcelain face?

Before Arthur could open his mouth to speak, Sophie leaned in and crushed her lips to his. With her hands locked around his face, Arthur had nowhere to go, but he didn't mind. The love that flowed out of her and into him filled him with hope. As their lips molded to one another's, Arthur ran his fingers through Sophie's hair and curled his hand around the nap of her neck.

A slight moan escaped her mouth, a moan that vibrated throughout Arthur as he scooped his wife into his arms and held her. Her mouth was tender and so much softer than he expected. She curled her arms around his neck as she held him to her.

Chapter 8

Sophie pulled back and stared at Arthur. The shock and awe on her face reflected in his deep-set eyes. With her heart fluttering in her chest like butterfly wings, she rose and cleared her throat.

"I..." she gasped brushing her fingertips over her lips. "I think it's time for me to retire for the night."

"Yes, of course," Arthur said rising with her. He rolled his shoulders back and dipped his head as Sophie turned her back to him and drifted down the hallway.

What was that? Did that really just happen?

Sophie glanced over her shoulder to find Arthur plopped on the couch rubbing the back of his neck. Wonder and curiosity filled her as she pulled open her bedroom door and stepped inside. Sophie smiled as her skin tingled. Every fiber of her body tingled as her heart quickened.

Turning, she pressed her palms to the door and leaned in. Hope swirled about her as her ears perked to hear if Arthur would be coming to the door. The sparks firing off within her rattled her nerves.

What a strange thing to have happened? But why do I want to do it again? Why do I want Arthur to come to me? What is this?

The clacking of Arthur's boots echoing in the house filled her with excitement. She pressed her ear to the door straining to listen.

What if I didn't kiss him the right way? What if he was repulsed by me? ... No, he liked it. He wouldn't have held me so tightly if he was put off. But still...

Sophie's mind whirled with conflicting emotions as she swallowed the lump in her throat. The footsteps grew closer causing her heart to race frantically. Chewing on her lower lip, she held her breath as the steps stopped at her door.

Stepping back she stared at the wooden door and waited.

He is right there.

Sophie pressed her hand to the door, half expecting the raps of his knuckles on the door. The anticipation caused her heartbeats to drag on. Each second seemed like eternity.

What if he knocks? What would I say? What would I do?

Fiddling with her fingers she forced herself to breathe. She exhaled when her ears perked as the thudding of Arthur's boots drifted down the hallway. Sophie heard the groaning of the bedroom door before it clicked shut.

Sophie stood staring at the door as reality sunk in. Arthur wouldn't be rapping on her door. The moment had already passed.

Stupid. I should have stayed on the couch. Why did I get up and leave the living room? Why didn't I just wait for him to pull away first?

Frustration filled her as she paced the length of her room. With each pass by the door, she paused, wondering if he would come back or if she should give it up and go to him.

Too restless to sleep, Sophie glanced about her room wondering what she could do to calm her nerves. There wasn't much she had for entertainment, a few books rested on her small desk along with her leather-bound journal.

Sophie moved to her desk and pulled out the small chair. She sucked in a deep breath as she sat down. With her heart thudding in her ears, she reached for her journal and a pen. Frantically, she opened the book and cleared her throat.

Dear Diary,

You won't believe what just happened. I can hardly believe it. But Arthur kissed me. It wasn't the kind of kiss father and Lenore shared. It wasn't some peck of affection. No, he kissed me.

Although, I do have to admit I'm not quite sure how I should take it. Was it a wild and rambunctious kiss that meant nothing to him? Did he plan to kiss me when he did or did the situation just call for it?

Even now I can feel my heart trying to take flight as I think about it. This wasn't supposed to happen. I came here under the pretext that there would be no emotions between Arthur and myself. It was a marriage of convenience and nothing more. But it has become more. So much more.

The other day he picked the wildflowers and brought them to my room. I came in after lunch to find them waiting for me. It was a nice surprise and one that I must admit I liked. I'm beginning to believe there are two sides to Arthur Soul. One that is hard and disciplined and the other, kind, and carefree. It surprises me every day what I learn about the man.

Still, I can't help but think of Nadine when I see him. She, after all, was the one to encourage this union. It was her hopes and dreams to settle far away from Papa and Lenore. I can't help but wonder if I am somehow a fraud. If maybe I shouldn't be living this life.

Then again where would I be now if I hadn't followed Nadine's counsel and written Arthur back? Would I be blushing over someone else's kiss? I doubt it. There is something about this Arthur Soul, he is daring and kind.

So what if he rode with a gang? He certainly doesn't have any of the qualities that would make someone suspect. The fact that he was honest with me is more than I could have ever asked for. But is this my dream or Nadine's? I can't help but feel the stab of guilt for living the life she always wanted.

Her passing still affects me. There are times I wish she was here so that I could write to her and explain all that has happened. I believe she would be so proud of me if she were still here. I told Arthur not to live in fear. That we would face whatever comes together.

Certainly, she was with me as I pushed him to stay strong. I couldn't have said such things without her by my side. Yet, I did. There is something unusual going on inside of me. I feel stronger than before. Perhaps frontier life does that to a person. Makes them harder, but it is so much more than the lifestyle that I have become accustomed to. It is as if my sister's spirit is guiding me for something within the depths of my being is shifting.

Am I becoming a confident, self-assured woman? Is this what it feels like to finally make that leap? I can't be certain. And in all honesty, I would hate to be tested.

I can't imagine what would happen if Arthur's rival Randal Munger shows up on our doorstep. What would I be capable of doing? Would I stand up to the man? I would have to now that I have convinced Arthur I am this woman of substance.

But could I? Could I face such a person? Honestly, I don't know. I just want to be the person Nadine would be proud of. Someone I can be proud of.

Sophie stared at the words and traced her fingers over the off-white pages. She sighed as she shut the book. With the kiss still lingering on her mind, she couldn't help the burning in her cheeks as she thought of Arthur.

* * *

Did that seriously just happen? Why did I do that? What was I thinking?

Arthur stared at the door with his mouth open. His heart fluttered as he wiped his sweaty palms over his pants. Every muscle in his body trembled as he plopped down on the bed and slipped his arms out of his suspenders.

Mulling over the event, he stripped his shoes from his feet and tossed them into the corner. The shoes landed with a thud as his eyes remained unfocused. Even his head felt a bit dizzy from the experience.

But... She didn't pull away. She kissed me back... But what does this mean? Does this mean she wants more from me? Was I too brash in thinking we could be something more than what we are right now? Or was this just a one-time thing?

Arthur ran his fingers through his hair as he dropped back into the pillows and stared at the ceiling. The warm night air drifted through the open window as the humming of the cicadas in the trees sang to him.

I can't let that happen again. We made a deal. A marriage of convenience doesn't have room for emotions. Yet, why is it that I feel this way? Why did she pull me to her? I shouldn't have let my emotions run away with me. I shouldn't have told her a thing.

Arthur clenched his teeth as he drew the pillow from under his head and crushed it into his face. The ends of the feathers stuffed into the fabric poked his face as he grunted into it.

I don't have time for this. I have the spring round up coming soon, and then there's Randal, and now Sophie. What am I getting myself into? I can't be doing this. No. Come tomorrow, I'll go on like I've always done. I'll see to it that the chores are done, and life goes on.

Arthur's head jerked as if to resolve the matter just like that. He tossed the pillow to the headboard and sat up. Deep within him, he could feel his heart stirring.

I can't believe I told her those things. Why did I tell her about my past? That wasn't supposed to slip.

Frustrated, Arthur unbuttoned his shirt aggressively and jumped to his feet. The wood moaned as he walked around the bed glaring at the things around his room. Pulling in a deep breath, Arthur tried to calm his nerves, but he knew there was no way he was going to be able to rest.

With his skin tingling and his lips burning to kiss her again, Arthur pulled his suspenders back up and hunted for the boots he had carelessly tossed.

"I can't stay here tonight," he said to the lonely and empty room. Arthur walked to the door and pulled it open. He moved swiftly down the hallway taking extra care near Sophie's room.

The last thing he wanted was to see her face. He couldn't afford to see her right now, not after kissing her the way he did. Keeping his eyes lowered and tip toeing down the hall, Arthur exhaled as he reached the front door.

The warm air flowed around him as he stepped out onto the porch. With the walls gone, he could breathe easier. The night sounds filled his ears and he tried to focus on the crickets playing their haunting melody as he moved down the steps.

She believes in me.

The thought came swift and unexpectedly as he walked to the barn. It was a thought that was as sharp as a blade and as harmless as a butterfly, yet there it was in all its beauty and splendor. Arthur's chest dropped as if he had been lugging around three extra barrels of hay on his back and suddenly they were gone.

He blinked as he stood in the open space between the house and the barn. After all these years, he never knew he had been carrying such a heavy load until it was gone.

She believes in me. Supports me. No one has ever done that since...

Arthur turned his head and stared at the house with its wooden shutters and wrap around porch. He studied the building and realized he'd seen a similar one a long time ago. Shaking his head he stood there dumbstruck.

She's what I've been missing... A place to belong... A family.

Flooded with this new revelation, Arthur dropped to his knees as he fought back the tears swelling in his eyes. He had been alone for so long that he had forgotten what it was like to have someone care for him. Even though he knew Sophie was simply looking for a marriage of convenience, he couldn't help but wonder if she knew just how much she had grown on him.

I can't do that to her. I can't pressure her into a different contract or expect that she feels the same way about me.

Arthur dug his fingers into the dirt as he exhaled. His eyes scanned the house and drifted to the soft tender light in the window. The small orange glow was unexpected but there it was, lighting up the room just enough for him to catch a glimpse of her.

His heart fluttered as he spied her sitting at her desk. He wondered what she was doing or if she was even affected by the kiss they shared. With the questions swirling about his mind, he rose to his feet.

I should knock on her window and ask her to walk with me... No. I can't do that. Not after telling her Randal could be out here. Maybe I should pick some flowers and leave them on the sill... No. I need to let this go...

With a quick jerk of his head his decision was made. Arthur knew he couldn't ask her to adjust her plans because of something that was stirring in him. Pulling in a deep breath, he watched the dirt crumble through his fingers and dusted his hands on his pants.

"I shouldn't have kissed you," Arthur said in hushed tones as he stared at Sophie through the open window. "I didn't mean to confuse you or lead you astray from the path you wanted to be on. You came out here to help me, not fall in love with me and here I am mucking things up."

His heart thudded as he stared at her in the room. She seemed like she was so far away, yet right there in his home. Arthur dropped his gaze and tried to force the thoughts of her into the back of his mind. There was no way for him to turn back the clock and he knew it. All he could do now was honor his agreement.

Arthur kicked the dirt as he mozied back to the house and climbed the stairs. The door creaked as he pulled it open. Surely the sound would reach Sophie. But with his mind made up and a little fresh air, he didn't mind running into her.

Moving down the dark hallway, he paused at her door. The orange light streaked under the door like a golden welcome mat. He mustered all he had not to knock on the door and disturb her.

Let her rest. You'll see her tomorrow.

Arthur moved past her door and slipped into his room. He pulled off his shoes once more and readied himself for bed. As he slipped between the covers and stared up at the ceiling, the box he tucked the kiss away in the back of his mind rattled as he closed his eyes.

The first rays of the morning light drifted in through the window as Arthur stirred to the sound of the crow. Rubbing his eyes he glanced at the empty space in his bed. For a brief moment he thought he spied Sophie resting beside him.

Jumping up, his heart raced.

When did she sneak into the room? And why didn't I hear her?

Rubbing the sleep from his eyes, Arthur looked back at the bed. The pillow with its flower embroidery was mangled and tucked into the sheets. Arthur sighed heavily and shook his head as his nerves calmed.

A sharp pain of longing stabbed him as he scanned the room. His heart sank as he realized he was alone with nothing but the pillow.

You got to get over this.

Throwing his feet over the side of the bed, Arthur rose and stretched his arms towards the ceiling. Closing his eyes he steadied himself.

She'll be getting up soon. You can't ignore her. Just pretend like last night meant nothing to you. The kiss was a mistake and if she brings it up, you'll say it to her face.

Still, Arthur knew he wasn't ready for what the day had in store for him. He wiped the back of his hand over his brow as he pulled in a deep breath. Never in all his life had he been so nervous. Not even when he knew she was coming. Not even when he walked down the aisle. Yet, for some reason this day seemed to weigh heavily on him as he dressed.

After pulling the suspender up his shoulder, he stopped at the door. With a trembling hand he reached for the knob.

Get a grip.

Clearing his throat, he twisted the knob and pulled open the door. Immediately, his eyes drifted towards the last door on the right. He knew it was her room. With a dry throat and racked nerves he moved down the hallway.

The clicking of metal perked his ears. His heart thudded in his ears as his palms grew sweaty. Any minute now, he knew she would step out of her room and he would have to see her. His nerves rattled as he contemplated what he would say to her. Uncertain if he should bring up the kiss or not, panic shot up his spine. Before Sophie could pull open the door, Arthur took off down the hallway and out the front door.

His heart raced as his throat closed off all air. He knew it was rude to bolt from the house so quickly. Yet, he wasn't ready to see her especially since it was so early.

The dawn's early light rose over the horizon as the birds whistled and chattered to the new morning. The dew on the grass lingered on his lawn. Arthur swallowed the lump in his throat as he kept his eyes locked on the barn door.

The instant he stepped into the barn, relief washed through him. He dropped his head and exhaled surprised by how much air came out of his open mouth.

"Good morning."

Arthur froze. Her voice was like a soft bell that chimed at church. Slowly he lifted his eyes to find her beside the cow pulling on the teats. The lump he thought he'd swallowed cut off his air supply as he stared at her dumbstruck.

"Morning," he managed to choke out.

"Did you sleep well?" Sophie's eyes remained locked on him as he bobbed his head.

"You?"

"I've had better," she said with a smile. Arthur couldn't take his eyes off her as the milk splattered into the pail.

"Is there anything I can do to help with that?" Arthur asked. He pressed his lips into a tight line and closed his eyes as his face flushed a brighter red.

"No," Sophie said. Arthur watched as the soft rays of light hit her face. He sucked in a quick shallow breath as if she had stolen the last one from him.

"What are you doing up so early? Normally you don't come out here till midmorning. I must say though, I'm pleased to see you here so early," Arthur said, moving to the stall beside Sophie's.

"I thought you might like fresh milk with breakfast."

Arthur nodded as he spied Sophie smiling from the corner of his eye. It was but a whisper of a smile, but it was there. His heart fluttered unexpectedly as she rose from the stool.

"Give me about thirty minutes or so and I'll have food on the table for you."

"You don't have to rush," Arthur said, trying not to make eye contact.

"Oh," Sophie said with a concerned look on her face. "Are you not hungry?"

She stood with the pail in her arms as the sun's rays kissed her face. Arthur's eyes widened as he stared at her in the morning light. Despite the dirt smudge on her forehead, her skin was flawless, her hair was in a loose bun allowing the tresses to flow down her neck and frame her face.

Wow.

"If you're cooking," Arthur said, daring to make eye contact. "I'll be there."

The hint of a smile that had been teasing the corners of Sophie's lips exploded. Her face beamed as her eyes sparkled.

"I'll call you when it's ready then."

Chapter 9

The aroma of bacon filled the house as Arthur pushed through the back door and stepped into the kitchen. He pulled in a deep breath as his stomach grumbled. Moving swiftly through the kitchen, he stopped short. Placing the last fork on the table, Sophie flashed a quick smile as she sat the fork down beside the plate. Her cheeks glowed a brighter red making her look stunning.

"Smells wonderful," Arthur said as he swallowed hard. He wasn't sure if it was the food that made his stomach turn or his nerves.

"Thank you," Sophie said as she pulled out his chair at the head of the table. Arthur salivated as he took in all the food Sophie had placed on the table. She had certainly gone all out with the fresh biscuits, grits, scrambled eggs, and a heaping pile of bacon. He licked his lips as he moved around the table to his open seat.

With his stomach yearning for food, he reached out to the pile of bacon in the center of the table. He gasped as his fingers brushed something warm and found he'd brushed against Sophie's fingers reaching for the plate as well.

"Sorry," he said, leaning back to give her space.

"Did you sleep well?" she asked as she served him the bacon first.

"Actually, I did," Arthur answered, reaching for the pitcher of milk. As the white creamy liquid flowed into his cup he struggled to find something to say.

The sound of Sophie's chair scraping the wooden floor as she pulled it out filled the silence. She glanced at him and nodded as she brushed her hands over her apron and held her hand out.

"Care to say the blessing?" Sophie asked in a small voice that made it difficult for Arthur to hear what she was saying. If it weren't for her open palm resting on the table, waiting for his, he wouldn't have known what she had asked.

With his heart fluttering in his chest, he placed his hand in hers and lowered his head. As he prayed over the food he couldn't help but think of last night and all that had happened. He could still taste her on his lips and smell her in his clothes. But he didn't know if she thought of him the same way he was thinking about her.

"Amen," Sophie said, lifting her head as she looked at him. Arthur couldn't help but notice the golden specks in her eyes. Almost as if they were made from honey. The morning light drifted through the window making her look even more radiant than before.

"Is everything okay?" Sophie asked as she paused to take her first bite.

"Of course," Arthur said, clearing his throat and trying to keep his eyes on his plate of food.

"You seem distracted today," Sophie noticed, finally taking the bite. She stared at him as if waiting for him to say something.

"Just got a lot on my mind," Arthur said.

"Of course," Sophie answered, shaking her head. She pushed the eggs around on her plate before exhaling heavily.

"I'm sorry," she finally said.

Arthur dropped his fork and pulled the napkin from the side of his plate to clear the corner of his lips. "What could you possibly be sorry for?"

"Last night," Sophie said. "The kiss. I know we had agreed for this to be a marriage of convenience... it was something that shouldn't have happened. For that I'm sorry."

"No," Arthur said as his hand instinctively darted to hers. "I shouldn't have assumed that you wanted me to kiss you. Unless?" His eyebrows rose as he cocked his head to look at her.

"Was it something you did want?"

Sophie straightened her shoulders back as she dropped her gaze. Arthur noticed the way she chewed on her lower lip as if holding in her thoughts. A crinkle in her brow creased her eyes as she pursed her lips and turned to face him.

"Honestly, yes. I wanted the kiss," she said. "But that doesn't matter. We agreed to a marriage without love. I can't ask you to go back on that now. As for me, I'll pretend it didn't happen."

"If that is what you want," Arthur's voice dropped as he moved his hand off Sophie's.

"It is. It'll be simpler that way," she said as her eyes focused on something across the room.

"A moment of weakness then," Arthur agreed.

"Precisely," Sophie bobbed her head once and went back to eating her food on her plate.

A pang in Arthur's heart seemed to splinter as he wrapped his head around what she was asking him to do. For so long he'd been alone, without any real family and he had started to believe that Sophie could fill that gaping hole. But by the look of determination on her face, and the conviction in her tone of voice, Arthur wasn't so sure it was the right thing to do. He knew he couldn't put the kiss behind him so easily.

"The Davidson's are coming for dinner tonight," Sophie said. Arthur glanced at her for a brief moment. There was a sadness in her voice that he couldn't quite explain. He realized that she was struggling to put last night behind her too.

"Is it Tuesday already?" Arthur asked. Sophie nodded her head as she finished the last bites of food from her plate.

"I was going to roast a duck," Sophie said. Her eyes shifted to him and then fell back to her empty plate. "If that's alright."

"Duck sounds great," Arthur said, wiping his mouth and setting the napkin down on his plate.

"Is there anything in particular you need me to do today?" Sophie asked.

"Wow," Arthur said, leaning back in his chair. He stared at her until she turned to look at him.

"What?" Panic washed over her expression as she held her breath.

"You're really starting to fit in here, you know that?" Arthur said with a hint of a smile. "It's nice to see you adjusting so well. I was worried about that when you first arrived."

"I made you a promise," Sophie said, allowing the fear to subside. "I'm just trying to make good on it."

Slowly Arthur sat up and leaned across the table. He kept his eyes locked on her as if she were a wild creature in the woods ready to dart away any moment and curled his fingers over hers. The warmth of her hand under his seemed to radiate throughout his body.

"You're doing fine," Arthur said. "Really, you are."

"Still haven't gotten the hang of plowing the garden," Sophie blushed as her eyes dropped to their hands on the table. Arthur noticed she didn't pull away. Her hand remained still under his. Carefully he curled his fingers between hers and held it there.

"Thank you," Arthur said, catching her attention.

"I'll get to the dishes," Sophie said.

"I'm not talking about breakfast," Arthur said. "I'm talking about you being here. Thank you for sticking by me."

A hint of a smile played at the corners of Sophie's lips as their eyes met each other's.

"I can't tell you what it means to me to have you here."

"Like I said before," Sophie squeezed her fingers tightly around his. "I made you a promise."

"This is more than just a promise," Arthur said.

"You're right, this is our life," Sophie said.

Arthur stared at Sophie as their hands molded together between the two empty dinner plates. His heart pounded in his chest as every ounce of him wanted to pull her to him and hold her once again. He fought the instinct to caress her right then and there.

"Well," Sophie said just as someone rapped on the door. "I have to get to my chores."

"Right," Arthur said, feeling the cold air as she pulled her hand away from his. "Chores. The ranch won't run itself will it?"

Arthur remained in his chair a moment longer as the rapping on the door continued. Grunting, he rose to his feet. Stealing one last glimpse at Sophie, he could feel his heart swelling as she collected the plates from the table.

"Arthur," Sam's voice called from the other side of the door. Rolling his eyes, Arthur turned to the door and pulled it open.

"Howdy Sam," Arthur said as he reached for his boots by the door.

"You ready?" Sam asked as he poked his head through the open door.

"Morning Sophie," Sam called out, catching Sophie's eye. She waved as she glanced at Arthur.

"Morning Sam," she answered still keeping her gaze on Arthur.

"Ma'am," Sam dipped his head before turning his attention back to Arthur.

"Did you get the wood for the barn roof?" Arthur promptly asked while slipping on his boots.

"Yep. Ready to go boss," Sam said. Arthur glanced over his shoulder hoping to catch one more glimpse of Sophie before stepping out. All he could see was her back as she scrubbed the dished.

"Come on then," Arthur said, turning to Sam. "Let's get started."

"You sure nothing is going on between you two?" Sam asked as he nudged his elbow into Arthur's arm.

"No," Arthur lied as his heart ached to be closer to Sophie.

"Well, I got the ladder set up already, and the supplies are on the roof ready to go," Sam said.

"Thanks Sam," Arthur said as he climbed the ladder. He paused at the top and tried not to look at the ground. His heart fluttered to think of the height of the roof. To get his mind off the dizzying height, he allowed the sounds of the leaves rustling in the wind to soothe his nerves. He pulled in a deep breath and pulled himself up to the top of the roof.

Don't look down. Keep your mind on the job and get this done.

He gazed over the top of the barn to find Sophie in the backyard banging a stick against the rugs. The breeze played with the loose strands of her hair distracting him from his height problem momentarily.

"What's going on up there?" Sam called from the ground. Arthur quickly shook his head and noticed the distance to the ground. With his heart pounding in his ears, he swallowed the lump in his throat.

Stay focused. He moved swiftly to the supplies and began working.

"I see," Sam said with a playfulness to his voice as he reached the top and walked over to Arthur.

"Stop gawking at my wife," Arthur scolded. "And get to work."

"Yes sir," Sam said with a chuckle as Arthur glanced over his shoulder to steal one more glimpse of Sophie. She brushed her hand over her brow and turned. For a brief moment their eyes met, and the box Arthur shoved in the back of his mind rattled.

It took all he had to concentrate on the task at hand. Each chance he got, he tried to find Sophie in the yard. It seemed as if she too wanted him to find her out there. No matter where she was, he spotted her, and they'd lock eyes briefly before quickly getting back to work.

By the time the sun had crossed the sky, Arthur wished the Davidson's weren't coming over. He didn't know how much strength he had left trying to keep his distance from Sophie. For a split second he found his thoughts wandering back to last night and how her lips felt on his.

"Well boss," Sam said interrupting his daydream. "Quitting time. I'll see you tomorrow."

"Bright and early," Sam continued as he climbed down the ladder. Arthur double checked the repairs before carefully climbing down the ladder and moving towards the house. A sweet floral fragrance drifted through the air reminding Arthur of Sophie. The faint aroma of lavender caused his heart to skip as he found himself moving quickly to the house.

Chapter 10

"I prepared a bath for you," Sophie said coming around the corner with a pot of boiling water. He followed her to the washroom where a single wooden barrel rested in the center of the room. Steam rose up from its center as Arthur pulled his straps off his shoulders. Sophie smiled at him while she poured the last bit of hot water into the tub.

"Thank you," Arthur said as he was assailed by a strange sensation. With his eyes locked on her, he couldn't believe how long it had been since someone prepared his bath. A chip around his heart crumbled as Sophie dipped her head and walked out of the room, leaving him to his business.

Slowly he undressed as his mind swirled with thoughts of Sophie. It was strange the effect she was having on him. He couldn't understand why his emotions seemed to be all over the place.

What is going on here? She isn't interested in me. So why is she doing these things?

Arthur slipped into the bath, letting the warm waters flowing around his body soothe his aching bones. The heat from the water seemed to wash out all his doubts and insecurities about Sophie. He realized he was overthinking things.

Any loyal and honorable wife would do these things. Nothing is special about this bath. Nothing special about the kiss. So why do I feel so... off balanced?

His thoughts continued to plague him as he washed up. Not even the soap and warm waters could help him get out of his head. He pulled himself out of the tub and dried off. Wrapping the towel around his waist, he moved to the washroom door and pulled it open.

"OH," Sophie said, quickly averting her eyes to the ground. Arthur could see the red in her cheeks as he stepped out into the hallway without his shirt on.

"I'm so sorry, I thought you'd be in your room by now," Sophie said, covering one hand over her eyes to keep from peeking at him.

"My apologies," Arthur said as he moved swiftly down the hallway and slipped into his room. His heart raced as he pressed the palm of his hand to the door and rested his head on the door frame.

Idiot. I should have been more careful. Now what will she think of me?

Arthur pressed his lips together and closed his eyes as he pushed off the door. He knew there was no turning back the clock, what was done, was done. All he could do now was try not to embarrass himself further.

He turned on his heels and opened his eyes. There, lying on the bed was his cleanest wool pants that Sophie clearly had pressed for him. A white buttoned shirt rested on top of it alongside a pale blue vest. His mouth dropped as he noticed Sophie must have laid them out for him while he was bathing. Shaking his head, he couldn't understand why she was doing these things. It was new. But the more he thought about it, the more he realized that she was finding little things to do to show him she cared for him. A smile played on the corners of his lips as he dressed.

"Arthur," Sophie's voice was muffled and soft coming through the door as she rapped her knuckles on the wood.

"Our guests have arrived," she said.

"I'll be right out," Arthur said, stealing one last moment. He took a deep breath and adjusted his tie once more.

He pulled open the bedroom door and stopped. Sophie stood before him with her hair pulled back into a loose bun. Small curls framed her face. He noticed her slender neckline as the floral dress hung on her shoulders before tapering off to her waistline. A crooked little smile played with his lips as he noticed the way her skirt billowed out from her hips to the floor.

"You look amazing," Arthur said as a lump formed in his throat. He couldn't believe how nervous he was staring at her. It was as if a veil was pulled up from his eyes and he was seeing her for the first time.

"You look very handsome tonight as well," she said smiling.

Her cheeks turned crimson as she looked away from him. The rattling on the front door startled them, causing them both to jump.

"I'll get it," Sophie said the same time Arthur stated, "Allow me."

Sophie moved to the side giving Arthur room to pass. She kept her eyes down as he moved past her. Heat flushed his face as her fingertips brushed his as he walked by her.

Clearing his throat, Arthur pulled open the front door.

"Garner," Arthur greeted the man at the door. Garner chuckled as he stepped over the threshold with his arms stretched out. Arthur took Garner's hand and shook it aggressively with a huge smile. Garner grabbed Arthur's arm and nodded.

"Good to see ya again," Garner said, squeezing the air from Arthur's lungs.

"And you," he choked as Garner hoisted him a bit off the ground before setting him down.

"And look what we have here," Garner commented, glancing over his shoulder to Mae. "Isn't she a sight for sore eyes."

"Yes, yes," Mae said, trying to corral her three-year old son to get in the house while cradling their youngest daughter.

"Sophie could you help me please?" Mae pleaded as she held her daughter out to Sophie. Instinctively, Sophie reached for the child in Mae's arms and held it close.

Arthur blinked as he saw Sophie with the young child in her arms. He was impressed at how natural Sophie looked carrying the baby on her hip. The swelling in his heart caused him to exhale.

I wonder if that will be our life one of these days? Will Sophie ever want one of her own? Is it possible I'll be a dad?

"What's cooking?" Garner said, moving into the living room. "It smells wonderful."

"Duck," Sophie answered as Mae dragged Aiden into the living room by the ear.

"Now listen here, you'll be nice tonight or so help me," Mae glared at her three-year old. The little boy's lip quiver as he shook his head. The stern expression on Mae's face ceased as she stood up.

"Sophie," Mae said in such a delicate and delightful voice that Arthur couldn't believe the change. "How are you doing dear? You look amazing."

"Thank you," Sophie said. Mae reached her arms out for Abigale. The little girl clenched Sophie's neck refusing to go back to her mother.

"Now there's a sight to see," Mae laughed. "It's not every day that girl doesn't want my hip. You seeing this Arthur?" Mae asked, looking at him.

"Looks like your young wife here is a natural," Mae laughed as she pried Abigale off Sophie.

"No," Sophie said, shaking her head. "I'm not really good with children."

"Really? Could have fooled me," Mae said with a wink.

Arthur noticed the blush of embarrassment in Sophie's face. It was her back straightening and the way her shoulders stiffened that caught him by surprise.

"Sophie," Arthur said, stepping to her side. "When is the duck going to be ready?"

"Now actually," Sophie said with a hint of gratitude to her smile. "Excuse me," Sophie said to Mae as she walked around Mae.

Mae and Garner gasped as Sophie brought out the roasting pan with the bird. Arthur couldn't help but feel a sense of pride in his wife. He was certainly blessed with a mail order bride that could cook as well as she could and it made Arthur wonder what else Sophie would be great at doing.

"That wife of yours is pretty good with the young ones," Garner said, nudging Arthur in his arm.

"Yeah," Arthur said as Aiden tailed Sophie into the kitchen. His heart thudded in his chest as his mind drifted and a whole new life flashed before his eyes. In that single moment he could see it all so clearly. Sophie in the living room with the baby in her arms playing with its little fingers as she sang a soft lullaby. A second later the vision was gone but the desire for that life remained.

Maybe one of these days.

*   *   *

"Well Sophie," Garner leaned back in his chair and wiped the corners of his mouth. "That was some meal. Where'd you learn to cook like that? I'm gonna have to have Mae come over here for some lessons."

"You hush now," Mae said. "My cooking is just as good."

"You tell that to Aiden there," Garner said laughing. "I honestly can't remember the last time that boy ate everything on his plate without a struggle."

"This was my sister's favorite meal," Sophie said, glancing at the empty plate in front of her.

"And where is your sister now?" Mae asked, pushing the plate away from her with small scraps still on it.

"In heaven," Sophie answered as she tried to force a smile on her lips.

"Oh my, I'm so sorry. You never mentioned that before," Mae said. By the aghast look on her face, Sophie realized her friend truly was shocked by the news.

"It's alright," Sophie said.

"Might I ask how?" Mae leaned in with a sympathetic gaze that warmed Sophie's heart. Sophie knew her friend wasn't asking out of malice.

"Consumption," Sophie answered, looking at Arthur. She could feel his gaze on her as she answered. His marble gray eyes looked as if the world had just collapsed around him.

"Well this really isn't dinner conversation," Garner said, clearing his throat. "How about we head to the porch and enjoy the evening air?"

"That's a great idea," Arthur said, scooting back from the table. Sophie rose and leaned over to collect the empty plates.

"Sophie, don't worry about the dishes right now. We can get them later," Arthur said, reaching for her hand. Her heart raced as his fingers curled around her hand stopping her from picking the plate up. She looked up to catch his eye on her.

"Actually," Mae said, "How about you men head outside. Us women folk will get the table cleared and meet you in a few minutes."

"How's the preparations coming for the cattle drive?" Sophie overheard Garner asking as he followed Arthur out the door. Sophie looked at Mae as she reached for the plates.

"So?" Mae asked with a peculiar gaze that made Sophie's skin burn hot. "What's new with you?"

"Nothing," Sophie said as little Abigale started to scream. Instinctively, Sophie picked up the girl and coddled her. The girl felt so snug in her arms that she couldn't help but let all her stress go. As Sophie stared into the little girl's eyes, all she could see was a bright future.

"You're looking like you want one," Mae said, crossing her arms with a pleased smile stretching across her face.

"Oh, no. I don't think so," Sophie said, inhaling deeply. There was no denying the longing in her heart. Simply holding the child was enough for her to melt.

"Why not?" Mae asked as Aiden ran circles around the table. "Aiden," Mae snapped as she threw her hands on her hips and shook her head. "Go outside with your father and leave us girls to talk."

"Oh fine," the little boy said as his shoulders slumped. Sophie watched the boy race to the door. The pitter patter of his little shoes on the wooden floor struck a chord with her.

"Well?" Mae asked, turning her attention back to Sophie.

"I don't know. It's not that I haven't thought of having children. It's just... Arthur and I have an understanding... I don't think he wants them."

"Pish posh," Mae said, waving her hand at Sophie. "All men want a family. They want someone to carry on their name. Even if you don't have, boy, trust me, Arthur would be over the moon if you were to have a baby."

Sophie's cheeks burned as she thought about having a family. Although her heart fluttered with excitement, she couldn't help but feel overwhelmed by how a child is made. Sophie glanced at Mae wondering if she understood her hesitation.

"Don't you worry your pretty little head," Mae said, grabbing a dish and plunging it into the sink. "It'll happen when it happens. That much is certain."

"When did you know you wanted to have kids?" Sophie asked as she pulled a towel from the counter to dry the dishes Mae washed.

"I always wanted children," Mae said with a gleam to her eye. "And don't you think twice about the mechanics of it all. There's nothing to be scared of."

Sophie's mouth dropped as her face turned a darker shade of red. Her heart fluttered and her fingers nearly let the plate slip from her grasp. Mae chuckled and shook her head.

"Well, on to a different topic," Mae said, holding back her laughter and quickly changing the topic. "I'm headed into town tomorrow, feel like tagging along?" Mae asked as she held out her arms to claim Abigale. Sophie carefully slipped the child into her mother's arms and stepped away.

"Actually, I think I have a list around here somewhere. There were a few items we needed stocking up on."

Sophie smiled as she piled the plates into her arms and brought them into the kitchen. She sat them on the countertop as Mae sat Abigale down on the floor at their feet.

"You know," Mae grabbed a plate and scraped the food into the slop bucket. "I really am sorry to hear about your sister. I didn't mean any harm by bringing that up."

"I know," Sophie said, resting her hand on Mae's shoulder. "You couldn't have known."

"You know what I do know?" Mae asked, raising one eyebrow. "I know your husband couldn't keep his eyes off you tonight."

"Stop," Sophie said as she felt her cheeks burn. It was an odd feeling to hear Mae speak of Arthur in such a manner. For a moment, Sophie wanted to tell Mae about the kiss they had shared but she knew if she did then she would have to admit that it happened.

"I think your husband is starting to take notice of you," Mae said.

"Is that a bad thing?" Sophie asked, looking to Mae for reassurance.

"Course not dear. Just means that things are changing around here and who knows, you just might have little ones running around here before long."

Sophie's hands felt clammy as she tried not to look at Arthur through the window. Secretly, she hoped that her husband fancied her. But still, there was the fact that their marriage wasn't supposed to end up like this.

What if Arthur is simply getting used to me being around here? It doesn't mean he likes me or anything. We don't have to renegotiate our arrangement. But, what if we did? Would he be open to it?

"I don't know about that," Sophie said, focusing on the dishes. "Arthur and I... well we haven't...."

"You hush now, I don't need to know the mechanics dear. It'll happen in its own good time."

Sophie placed the last dish back into the cabinet and smiled secretly to herself. Thoughts of having a family life drifted into her mind. It was a desire she never expected to have for herself in this place, yet, the longer she thought about it, the more she wanted it.

"Mae," Garner's voice boomed through the house. "We need to get going," Garner said. "This boy of yours is more trouble that what he's worth."

Mae leaned down and scooped Abigale off the floor, "He's half yours."

"I take no responsibility for him," Garner said, turning with the boy in his arms.

"Garner, put your son down and let him walk," Mae ordered as she hugged Sophie.

"I'll pick you up tomorrow bright and early," Mae promised.

"Mae, I'm leaving with or without you," Garner threatened as the door closed behind him. Sophie couldn't help but laugh at the sight. She moved to the front door with Mae and held it open for her. Reaching towards her, Mae gave Sophie one last hug as Garner dropped the boy into the back of the wagon. With one hand covering her mouth, Sophie tried to hide her delight as she heard the thud of the boy dropping into the back of the wagon.

"I don't want to go," the boy wailed.

"We're leaving and that's that. You're tired and cranky," Garner scolded.

"You sure you don't want one?" Mae asked as she hoisted herself up onto the wagon with Abigale in her arms.

"I'll see you tomorrow Mae," Sophie said, waving goodbye. Arthur turned to look at Sophie with questions in his eyes.

"Don't ask," Sophie said, laughing as the boy in the back scrambled to climb up to the front.

"That was some dinner," Arthur sighed as he held the door for Sophie. She stepped inside and blushed.

"What did you and Garner talk about?"

"The cattle drive coming up. It seems he had some ideas to help this year."

"Were they any good?" Sophie asked looking up at him. Arthur shook his head and smiled.

"Nope."

"Well, the dishes are done, and truth be told, I'm tired," Sophie said, trying hard not to make eye contact. Yet, no matter how hard she tried, she found herself falling into his stare.

"Good night then," Arthur said as he reached for her hand. "Dinner really was delicious."

Sophie's heart fluttered as if a million butterflies took flight all at once within her. She could feel the heat rising as Arthur pressed his lips to her hand and held it longer than she expected. As she stared at her husband, she couldn't help but feel a nudging in her core. There was a fire that had been kindled within her. Although she knew she would never act on the desire, she could no longer deny it was there.

"Good night," she said as Arthur dropped her hand. She moved past him concentrating on her footing. With her head swimming, she prayed she wouldn't stumble over her own feet. The moment she reached her bedroom door, she paused and looked over her shoulder. Arthur stood by the couch watching her, a smile lingered on his lips that was tender, gentle, and completely genuine.

"Sleep well," she heard him say as she opened the door and stepped into her room.

Chapter 11

Arthur rested his arms over the corral and glared at the sunlight filtering through the gray low hanging clouds. He exhaled slowly, allowing his mind to drift to Sophie. There was no way he could have known his heart would shift when he first started writing to her. But as his eyes lingered on the clouds, he couldn't imagine his life without her.

Sophie was more than just a convenience to him. She was his companion now. Each day, she proved how resilient she was over and over again, and Arthur realized he'd need her to be even stronger in the coming days. Not only was he planning on heading out for the cattle drive and leaving her alone, but he knew Randal Munger was looking for him.

What if he comes when I'm gone? Don't be silly, Randal doesn't know where I'm at. Unless...

A chill shot up Arthur's spine as he envisioned Randal following Bergen here to Tennessee to find him. Although Arthur couldn't know for certain if Randal had tailed Bergen, it was something Randal had done before. Arthur couldn't shake the fact that he'd followed a target for Randal before when he rode with the gang.

Texas is a long way away. There's no way Randal would track Bergen over several state lines. Not unless Randal is that determined to find me. Then again, if I had time to rot in a cell as long as Randal did, I'd want to find the man who put me there.

A lump formed in Arthur's throat as he thought of all the ways Randal could ruin him. Suddenly, the life Arthur had built for himself seemed so fragile. He scanned the tree line surrounding his ranch wondering if there were eyes peering back at him as he stood there leaning against the railing.

He couldn't help but worry about Sophie. She was an innocent in all this, yet, she would be the first Randal would go after and Arthur knew it. He glanced over his shoulder to stare at the house. Although Arthur knew he could trust Sophie, he didn't know what Randal was up to, or even where he was at. Time was something that Arthur knew he was running out of.

The pounding of hooves on the dirt road startled him. Arthur whipped his head around to find Mae coming up the way. Her hair was pinned back, and it appeared the kids were at home.

"Morning Arthur," Mae called out, throwing her hand up.

"Mae, what are you doing here?" he asked, trying to steady his nerves.

"Come to pick up Sophie. We're headed into town today for supplies," Mae said pulling back the reins. The horses stopped in front of the corral and stood like sentinels before Arthur.

"You okay?" Mae asked. "You look like you've seen a ghost or something."

"I'm fine," Arthur said, running the back of his hand over his brow before turning to face the house. "Sophie shouldn't be too much longer."

"It's a fine morning, don't you think? I always did love it when the clouds lingered a bit." Mae shot Arthur a smile as her eyes drifted to the sky.

"Never been a fan of cloudy days. Don't get much done," he said, dusting his hands on his pants.

Maybe that's the reason for the uneasiness. I've never been one to be comfortable on days like this. Feels too much like it did before.

Before Arthur could stop it, his mind raced back to the fateful day he lost his parents and brother. The sky was just as dark, and the air filled with the same electrical charge making him even more uneasy.

"Mae," Sophie's voice startled him. Arthur snapped back to find Sophie on the porch, tucking her hair into the baby blue bonnet that matched her skirt.

"Wasn't expecting you for a bit," Sophie said as she kept her eyes locked on Arthur who was moving down the steps.

"It looked like rain," Mae said with her arms open. Sophie stepped into Mae's hug and squeezed her friend as Arthur cleared his throat.

"It does look like it could rain today," Arthur agreed. "Think you ladies can be back before it does?"

"You know there's no way of knowing what the weather will do," Mae said, shaking her head. "All we can do is be prepared."

"Are we ready then?" Sophie asked as she stepped up to the wagon. Arthur quickly stepped to Sophie's side and held out his hand. For a brief moment, he felt a pang of uncertainty stab him. He wanted to hold onto Sophie's hand and never let it go.

"Arthur?" Sophie looked at his hand clinging to hers as he helped her up to the seat.

"Sorry," Arthur said, reluctantly releasing his grip on her. "You two be careful today, ya hear?"

"There isn't anything to worry about," Mae said with a smirk. "And if you're worried about the weather, don't be. It'll clear up soon enough you'll see."

Arthur felt pressure tightening around his heart. He wanted to reach out and hold onto Sophie. There was an urgency to tell her to stay with him or at the very least go with them.

"You know," Arthur said as he watched Sophie straighten the wrinkles in her skirt. "Maybe I should come along."

"Nonsense," Mae said, waving one hand at him as she grabbed the reins with the other. "You don't need to be coming today. Besides, you'd just be bored with the conversation."

Arthur shook his head and stepped back from the wagon. With his eyes locked on Sophie, a dread swelled in him that he couldn't explain.

"You're probably right," he said with a faint smile. "You ladies have fun in town and take your time."

"Are you okay?" Sophie asked as Mae cracked the reins, startling the horses. "I can stay if you want me to. If you think the weather will be too bad."

"Don't be giving him any excuse to keep you on the ranch today. We get two days a month for girl talk and truth be told, I need this time. So you're going, no if's, and's or but's." Mae glared at Arthur daring him to say otherwise.

"I'll see you when you get back," Arthur said, lifting his hand up. The dread and fear poked and prodded him as he watched them moved further and further away from him.

"Be careful," he said in barely a whisper as he kept his eyes locked on Sophie as she rocked and swayed in the seat. He couldn't help but think he should be going with them. But he knew it was her chance to get away from the ranch for a bit and have quiet time with Mae.

He lifted his hand up as they reached the border of his road to wave goodbye. Sophie turned in her seat and threw her hand up, mimicking Arthur's gesture. Chewing on his lower lip he remained by the corral until the small buckboard was out of sight and he exhaled.

She'll be okay. They're just going to town. What's the worst that could happen in town? Oakbury is a quiet little place. Nothing bad ever happens around these parts, right?

*   *   *

"Are you even listening to me?" Mae asked, turning her head, and narrowing her gaze on Sophie. Sophie knew Mae was going on about something with the kids, but her mind was preoccupied with Arthur and the panic she noticed in his eyes as they left.

"Sorry," Sophie admitted, dropping her head, and focusing on the dirt under her nails.

"Where were you just now?" Mae asked with a crooked little smile.

"Nowhere really," Sophie said as her cheeks turned a darker red.

"You were thinking about Arthur, weren't you?" Mae asked, scooting closer to Sophie.

"Maybe a little," Sophie admitted as she looked up to the gray skies. The clouds looked as if they were full of water just waiting to dump on them.

"Did something happen between you two?" Mae asked, raising her eyebrows as her smile vanished.

"Nothing bad," Sophie said, shaking her head in her defense. "I don't think Arthur has a bad bone in his whole body."

Sophie's attention faded as she thought of Arthur and his dark hair. She couldn't help but feel her stomach fluttering as she thought of his marble gray eyes and sturdy shoulders. There was so much to him she still didn't know. But she knew she had the rest of her life to figure it out.

The long whistle of the train tugged on her heart string as their wagon crossed the railroad tracks. It wasn't so much the sound of the train in the distance that made her palms grow sweaty. It was more the fact that she couldn't help but wonder how many people took the train every day and did what she did.

"I wonder how many people pick up their lives and move to a new area," Sophie said more to herself than to Mae as she stared off hoping to catch a glimpse of the train.

"I'd assume there's a lot that do it especially now since the railroads connect so much of the country. Why you asking? You thinking of leaving Oakbury?"

"No," Sophie said, shaking her head quickly. "I've grown rather fond of this little town and the ranch."

"Don't you mean Arthur?" Mae winked as she pulled to the posts by the blacksmith's store and stopped the horses.

"Maybe a little," Sophie said. "This place is my home now. But I can't help but wonder how many people pick up their life and set roots down someplace completely new and different. Do they know what they are doing or just hope for the best?"

"Well," Mae said, slipping down to the ground. Sophie watched as Mae dusted her skirt and looked up at her. "I suppose they hope that where they put their feet is the best place for them. After all, if they don't like it, they could always keep going until they find a place they do like."

Sophie nodded as she scanned the small little town. She noticed the women and children hurrying down the boardwalk to the barbershop. Some folks stopped at the tailors to take in the newest fashion trends while others lingered about the grocers.

"Best get going," Mae said turning her attention to the sky. Sophie stole a moment to look up and dropped her jaw. The sky had grown darker since they left the ranch and for a moment she wondered if they were going to get caught in a storm heading home.

"I'll only be a bit," Sophie said, climbing off the wagon. "I just need a few things from the grocer, and I need to place an order with the blacksmith."

"Garner ordered shoes too," Mae said, walking around the horses and tying them to the posts. "Why don't we hit the blacksmith first and then the grocers?"

Sophie nodded as Mae scooped her arm around Sophie's and led her into the blacksmith's stall. The smell of coal filled the space causing Sophie's nose to wrinkle. Various tools hung from the walls as the heat of the furnace seared Mae's face.

"Hello ladies, what can I do for you today?"

"Eddie," Mae smiled, releasing Sophie's arm. "How are you doing today?"

"Not bad. Still kicking," Eddie said with a huge grin that pearly whites.

"And your father?" Mae asked, moving around the fire pit to the donkey latched to the wheel that kept the air going on the flames.

"He's been better," Eddie said, stealing a glimpse at Sophie as she remained in the middle of the area. "Well, it's a blessing he's still around, you know?"

"No, no we can't," Mae said, winking at Sophie. "Garner wanted to know if you'd finish his order he placed last week."

"The shoes right?" Eddie asked, turning on his heels to move around the fire pit. Sophie couldn't help but wrinkle her nose at the smell that lingered in the area. It was salt and grime, but she wasn't about to say a thing about it.

"Hello miss." A strange deep voice said behind her. Sophie felt her body twitch as the man stepped around her. She couldn't help but notice his wiry mustache and thin physique. All she could see was how his skin clung to his bones. Even his belt hung down further than most of the men in town did. Sophie stepped closer to Mae as fear pricked her.

Chapter 12

"Sir," Sophie said trying not to choke on the fumes in the stall. She lowered her gaze and stepped back giving the stranger all the room she could.

"Have you seen the blacksmith?" he asked as he chewed on a long thin strand of tobacco.

Sophie didn't say a word. She pointed to the furnace as Eddie stepped out around it with his hammer in hand. Mae's eyes popped as she noticed the stranger lurking so close to Sophie and moved swiftly to Sophie's side.

"Mrs. Davidson, I'll have your order ready soon," Eddie said, keeping his eyes locked on the thin lanky stranger.

"Thank you Eddie," Mae said scooping her arm into Sophie's and tugging at her. "We'll be back later then."

"Can I help you stranger?" Eddie asked, stepping closer to the stranger.

"Don't suppose you can," the stranger said. Sophie glanced over her shoulder to find the man staring at her. A chill streaked down her spine as a lump of fear formed in her throat.

Mae is right here with me. No need to panic. Just because you don't trust that glare, doesn't mean you have to be rude.

Sophie pulled in a deep breath as she followed Mae out of the stall and down the road.

"Don't you look back at him. Don't give him a reason to talk to us." Mae's voice was barely audible. Sophie had to lean in closer just to hear her. But she didn't need to hear everything; clearly Mae felt the same uncertainty as the strange man followed them out of the blacksmith's shop.

"Excuse me," the man said as he cleared his throat. There was a rattle in the back of his throat that caught Sophie by surprise. The last time she heard such a scratchy rattle was from Nadine just before she passed.

"You wouldn't happen to know where I could get cleaned up a bit would you? Seems the people in this town aren't too keen on strangers," the man said.

Sophie started to turn. Mae jerked Sophie's arm, forcing Sophie to stop. Slowly Mae turned and lifted her head up and Sophie turned with her.

"You can go to the saloon," Mae said, nudging her head towards the group of men standing in front of the largest building on the strip. "I'm sure Max will get you set right up."

"Max huh?" the man said, keeping his eyes locked on Sophie as Mae spoke. The cold chill stabbing Sophie turned artic as his eyes narrowed on her. She swallowed hard and dropped her gaze.

"Come on Mae," Sophie said nudging her friend. "I want to look at the new dresses that have come in."

"And I'm certain each one will look sublime on you miss," the man said with a crooked little smile that made Sophie's skin crawl.

Sophie's nerves rattled and her hands balled into little fists as she swallowed the fear lodged in her throat, "I am married."

"My apologies ma'am. I never suspected that a flower such as yourself would be wed. And where is your strapping husband?" The stranger didn't take his eyes off Sophie as his smile grew.

"That is none of your business," Mae snapped as she jerked Sophie's arm and started walking.

"Just keep your head straight," Mae whispered. "He'll leave us alone once we get to the grocer."

That's it. Just keep your head down. Don't show fear. You can't let him know he scares you. Count the steps to the grocer. One. Two. Three.

Sophie tried not to think of the man behind her. She didn't want to let him know that she could practically feel his hot breath on her neck as they moved swiftly towards the grocer's store. How she wished the sheriff was out sitting on his chair and watching.

Of all the days Noonen had to be inside.

Sophie shook her head trying not to recoil as the man leaned in closer and pulled in a deep breath. She could smell his body odor lingering off him. For a split moment she wondered if she'd be able to slap him hard enough to make him think twice about getting closer to her.

"Why Mrs. Davidson, it's so good to see you today," Allen said, stepping out of his shop. The moment Sophie saw him her heart leapt with joy.

Maybe now the stranger will give me some space.

Allen nodded and dipped his hat to Sophie as Mae led her into the store. For a moment, Sophie wondered if the stranger would dare follow them in. From the corner of her eye, she caught a glimpse of the stranger in the reflection of the glass. His eyes lingered on her as he licked his lips and stepped back and out of the shop.

"Mrs. Soul," Allen said smiling. "It's grand to see you too."

"Thank you," Sophie said as Mae slipped her arm out of Sophie's. Judging from the way her arm throbbed, Sophie hadn't noticed the panicked grasp Mae had on her. It seemed Sophie wasn't the only one with a bad feeling of the stranger following them.

From the corner of her eye, Sophie spied two more men across the way. Quickly she tugged on Mae's arm and nodded her head. Mae's eyes shifted to the men across the road who stared at them as they walked towards the grocers.

"Mr. Wickmore," Sophie said, trying to steady her nerves. "I have a few things I'll be needing." With a trembling hand, Sophie pulled the list of items from her pouch. Allen glanced at her hand before his eyes shot to her face.

"Is everything alright Mrs. Soul?" Allen asked, standing a bit taller than usual.

"We're fine," Mae answered as her eyes flickered to the doorway. Relief washed over Sophie as she noticed the wiry mustache man was gone. The same relief smoothed out Mae's worry as well.

"Very well," Allen said, taking the list. "I'll have this ready in a jiffy."

"Mr. Wickmore," Mae turned and tried to keep her eyes off the doorway. "Do you know anything about those men across the way?" Mae tried to keep her voice down as she looked at Adam.

"Drifters. They came in last night. Max mentioned that they've been rowdy since they got here. But that's to be expected when you're out in the wilderness for any extended amount of time."

"Did they say when they plan to leave Oakbury?" The concern in Mae's voice startled Sophie. It wasn't like Mae to wonder about folks coming and going.

"No ma'am. But like most drifters, they get tired of our small little town and move on to the next. Why, I'll bet you they will be headed back out in a few days."

"Let's hope so," Mae said as Sophie glanced at the window and noticed the group of men across the way. Each looked as if they'd been on the road since birth. Their clothes were tattered and dirty, their hair disheveled and unkempt. But it was the smudges of dirt that were smeared over their noses and cheeks that caused Sophie to shudder.

"Here you go Mrs. Soul," Allen said, handing her a bag of goods. "Do you need help carrying this to your wagon?"

"Mae came with me," Sophie told him. "We'll manage."

"I have to stop off at the post," Mae said with a bit of a smile on her lips.

"Okay," Sophie said, taking the sack of items from Allen and following Mae out the door.

The instant Sophie stepped out of the store, she could feel her blood freezing. It was funny how safe she felt in the grocer's, yet, only being a foot away from it held such consequences for her.

"Keep your eyes straight ahead," Mae said, lifting her chin up and rolling her shoulders back. "Don't let them know you're scared."

Sophie nodded and followed close beside Mae as they walked towards the small little shack with the white sign that simply read "The Post".

In the back of her mind, Sophie's thoughts lingered on Arthur. She couldn't help but wonder if these were the kind of men he once rode with. Her heart raced as she thought of Randal Munger and all the things Arthur told her about him. Although she didn't know what Randal looked like, there was no doubt in her mind that he might look just as grungy as the men across the street.

Fear lodged into her throat as her eyes flickered to the side. The lanky man was following her, keeping to his side of the street but keeping pace with them.

"Mae," Sophie said as she found her voice cracking.

"I know," Mae answered as two men stepped out of the alleyway to stop Mae and Sophie.

"Excuse me," Mae said, trying to step around the bigger man with curly oily hair.

"Well you two look like you could use a bit of fun," the oily haired man said, spitting out the chew in his mouth.

"I beg your pardon?" Mae said as she stepped back. Sophie watched as Mae's hand jerked back and flew forward. The man's eyes narrowed as he grabbed Mae by the wrists and shook his head.

"That's not very nice. Do you treat strangers like that?" The other man smiled revealing his empty mouth. Sophie couldn't help but flinch as she stepped back, ready to make a run for the grocer.

"Well hello again," the tall lanky man said as Sophie stepped back into his open arms. Before she could let out a scream, the man slipped his hand over her mouth silencing her.

Get your hands off me.

Sophie wiggled and squirmed as the man carried her around the corner to the alleyway. Her eyes frantically searched for anyone willing to step up and help them. When she didn't see anyone coming to her aid, her heart sank.

"Isn't this a treat," the man with no teeth said as he dragged his fingers down Mae's cheek. Sophie watched as her friend squirmed with all her strength trying to break free from the men's grasp.

"We got two for one special going on here boys," the wiry man said as he chuckled. Sophie tried to chomp down on his fingers, but there wasn't enough flesh between her lips.

Please God. Nadine help me, give me strength.

Sophie looked to find tears streaming down Mae's red cheeks as the men groped and dragged their hands over her body. A fire exploded within Sophie as she saw the terror and panic in Mae's eyes. There wasn't anyone coming to help them, and Sophie knew it.

With all her might, she pulled back her leg and lifted her knee. The blunt force of her strike caused the toothless man to stumble back from her as she pulled her leg back once more and rammed her heel into the wiry man's shin.

Instantly his hand dropped as a stream of cursed words flew from his mouth. Sophie didn't hesitate, the scream that had been swelling in her chest exploded and bounced off the walls of the alley.

"Hush," the thin lanky man said, wrapping his fingers around her throat to cut off her scream.

Sophie tried to pull in air, but she was getting shorter and shorter breaths as the man's hand squeezed harder.

I can't die here. Not like this.

Flashes of Arthur drifted into Sophie's mind. Her life on the ranch and all the things she ever wanted flickered through her eyes. With every passing moment, there was only one thing she could hold onto. Arthur and the life she wanted with him.

I love you Arthur.

"What is going on here?"

Through blurred vision, Sophie noticed a tall man walking down the alleyway carrying something hard and shiny.

"Move along old man," Sophie heard the toothless man say as he turned his attention back to Sophie.

"EDDIE GET OUT HERE NOW!" The man's voice carried through the alleyway.

"Let's get," the lanky man said, dropping Sophie. The instant her feet hit the ground, she pulled in a sharp ragged breath. Her vision was filled with stars and specks of rainbows as she reached out for Mae.

"Mrs. Davidson?"

Mae glanced up as she rocked and cried in Sophie's arms. "James?"

"Eddie get out here now!" James shouted again. It didn't take Eddie long to come rushing around the corner. Sophie noticed the shock in his eyes as he saw the three of them.

"Get the sheriff and get a pose together. Those drifters done this, and they need to be stopped," James said pulling Mae off Sophie and helping her to her feet. Sophie could feel the panic and the terror stabbing her like sharp little blades, but she knew if she cried, she wouldn't stop.

Slowly, she pulled herself off the ground and tried not to think of the pain in her crushed throat. She glared down the end of the alleyway as Eddie rushed to get the sheriff. Eddie's voice drifted through the street as he called up for men to come and help.

Chewing on her lips, Sophie couldn't help but wonder why this happened. Out of all the women on the street, and all the people in town, why did it have to happen to her? She forced herself to swallow the regret and anger down even though she couldn't help but whimper at each and every delicate movement.

"What's going on here?" The sheriff's eyes bugged out as he spotted Sophie and Mae.

"Three men attacked them," James said.

"Do you know who they were?" Noonen asked, taking slow steps towards them. Sophie couldn't help but watch the sheriff as he lifted his hands up to the air.

"No sir, they were with them drifters that had come into town a few days ago," Eddie said as the sheriff moved to Sophie.

"Get Alex and some men together and see if you can't round them up," Noonen said, curling his arms around Sophie's shoulders.

"I'm going to get these women home safely. I'm sure their husbands will be better suited to put their minds at ease than any of us can." Noonen kept his eyes locked on Sophie as he escorted her out of the alleyway. Sophie glanced over her shoulder to Mae who seemed to be stuck on James.

"It happened so fast," Mae said between gasps of air.

"Shh, you're fine now," Noonen said over his shoulder. "Let's just get you back home okay?"

Sophie stared out at the town before her as she climbed up onto the wagon. A small drop of rain fell from the sky as the clap of thunder rolled over her head.

Don't cry. Just keep your head up. It's like Mae said, don't let them see that you're breaking.

Chapter 13

Arthur wiped the sweat from his brow as the sun beat down on him. The pile of straw seemed to get bigger and bigger every time he looked at it. Carefully, he pitched the hay into a wheel barrel and drove the barrel to the stable. The horses neighed and whinnied upon seeing him as each seemed anxious to get their new bedding.

"Come on Thunder," Arthur said, unhitching the latch to the steed's stall and luring the huge horse out with a carrot. "Your turn."

The horse snorted as Arthur led it out into the day light and into the corral. For a moment he couldn't help but wonder what was taking Sophie so long. The sun was already high in the sky and it seemed as if she'd been gone far longer than she needed to be.

Arthur turned to look to the end of his road. His heart sank as he realized no one was coming up his path.

"I hope everything is okay," he said to Thunder as the horse stole the last bit of carrot from his hand. Arthur rubbed his hands down the horse's thick neck and over its shoulders.

"You're probably right. Knowing the girls, they got caught up looking at the latest catalog or something and contemplating which pattern to buy."

Still, Arthur couldn't shake the nagging sensation in his gut or fight the urge to look down the road one more time. With no sighting of Sophie or Mae, he had no choice but to get back to work. He turned on his heels and went back into the stables to muck out Thunder's stall. Trying hard not to think too much of Sophie, he cleaned out the stall quickly, putting all his effort into it as he could. Still, every so often he found himself glancing towards the dirt road.

She's fine. Give her more credit. Besides, it's the middle of the day. She's just spending time with Mae is all. Nothing to be too paranoid about. Let her have this time and don't worry so much.

Arthur pulled in a heavy breath and released it slowly, trying to push out all the fear and insecurities that seemed to be swelling in his chest. Although he didn't have a clue what was going on, he knew there was no point in dwelling on it for too long.

After shoveling the last bit of soiled straw from the stall, Arthur dumped the fresh hay into the stall and spread it about. The dust and smell of the hay tickled his nose. Stepping out of the stall he began sneezing uncontrollably. Each sneeze shot out of him harder than the one before.

Not again.

The sneezing fit caused his stomach muscles to ache with each new sneeze. Quickly he raced to the barrel of water and dunked his head into it. The fresh cold water felt wonderful on his hot head. Pulling his head back up he sucked in a deep breath. The itchiness in his nose and eyes seemed to vanish almost instantly. As he wiped the sleeve of his shirt over his eyes, he noticed a buckboard coming down the way. For a moment, his heart fluttered knowing Sophie would soon be home. But the joy quickly sank like a ton of rocks into the pit of his gut.

Who is that riding with them? Is that? No.

Fear gripped Arthur's heart as he noticed the sheriff riding on the side of the buckboard with his rifle out. The sight of them made his blood run cold as the buckboard came to a halt by the corral. Without a second thought, Arthur raced to the corral and swooped in next to Sophie. His fingers curled around her small waist helping her down.

"What's going on?" Arthur asked as soon as Sophie's feet touched the ground.

"They were attacked in town," Noonen said bluntly.

"Sheriff," Mae scolded Noonen. "I thought we'd agree to ease him into the news. Not just blurt it out like that."

"What?" Arthur's fear stole his voice as his eyes widened. Suddenly nothing else mattered but Sophie's safety. He could feel rage boiling inside of him as he scanned every inch of her body. Gasping, he brushed his fingers ever so gently down her neck.

"It's not that bad," Sophie said with a ragged voice. Arthur's heart stopped as he heard his wife trying to speak.

"Not that bad? You can barely talk."

"That's because your wife has a set of lungs on her," Noonen said with a hint of a chuckle. "She screamed so loud that everyone in town heard her no doubt."

Arthur kept his eyes on Sophie as Noonen spoke. He noticed her cheeks burning as the sheriff went on about her sounding the alarm. But still, it didn't ease the terror spiking through his heart as he wrapped his arms around Sophie protectively.

"Who was it?" Arthur demanded as he turned to Noonen. Sliding off his horse, Noonen shrugged.

"Don't know. Some of the boys in town mentioned how they were drifters. Seeing as how no one was able to catch them after the attack, makes me think they were just looking for a good time and picked the wrong girls."

"Sophie was great," Mae said, smiling at Sophie. "She fought back and rammed her knee into one of them."

"You did that?" Arthur asked, looking at Sophie. She smiled wryly as if she was too embarrassed to take credit.

"Are you sure you don't know who did this?" Arthur asked, turning to Mae. Mae shook her head and shrugged.

"I've never seen them around town before. And you know me, I'll find every excuse in the book to head to town and I've never crossed paths with them before." Mae paused and looked down before pressing her lips into a tight line. "Your wife saved my life."

"You would have done the same for me," Sophie said through a scratchy barely audible voice.

"Shh, don't talk," Arthur said, guiding her to the house. "You need to rest and get better."

"I mean it. Those men were going to kill me," Mae said gravely. "Your wife made sure I came back today and for that I am eternally grateful."

"Why do you say that?" Arthur asked Mae.

"One asked if they had the right girl," Mae said as her eyes darted to Sophie. "The other said he heard her talking to the grocer and that he was positive of it. That's when the order was given to get rid of me."

Instinctively, Arthur clung to Sophie, pushing her body closer to his. All he wanted was to have her attached to him at all times. There was no way he was going to let her out of his sight again. Breathing in deeply, Sophie tapped his hand and stared at him with a pleading gaze. He shook his head 'no' refusing to release her. But her tender gaze stole his resolve and he slowly pried his hands off her, allowing Sophie to comfort her friend.

"I'm going to escort Mrs. Davidson back to her ranch just to be on the safe side. But I doubt we will be seeing those men around again. Chances are they are long gone," Noonen said propping his rifle on his shoulder

"Right," Arthur said as he kept his eyes locked on Sophie.

I shouldn't have let you go alone today. I knew I should have gone with you. Stupid. Why didn't I listen to my gut?

"Come Mae, let's get you home," Noonen said, mounting his horse. "I got other business back in town and I can't get to it until I know you're safe at home."

"I'll be back to check on you later," Mae promised, cupping Sophie's face as a mother would do. Smiling weakly, Sophie nodded.

Arthur opened his arms up for Sophie and kept her close as they watched Mae climb back on the buckboard.

"Let's get you inside. I'll draw you a bath and we can put this day behind us," Arthur said.

"Don't you worry Mrs. Sophie, I'll be keeping an eye out for those men. The moment they step foot back into town we'll arrest them for assault. You have my word," Noonen said turning his horse.

"Thank you Sheriff," Arthur said as they climbed the steps to their front door.

Pulling open the front door, Arthur stepped aside allowing Sophie to enter first. He glanced over his shoulder and scanned the area before stepping into the house. There was no way he was going to let anything happen to her ever again.

"Arthur," Sophie's voice was barely a whisper, but it was loud enough to catch his attention. Instantly, Arthur was at Sophie's side.

"This wasn't your fault, you know that right?" Sophie said, cupping her hand to his face and holding his gaze. "There was no way we could have known this was going to happen today. I'm just sorry about the supplies."

"Don't you worry about that," Arthur said, shaking his head.

Unbelievable. After all that happened to you, you're worried about the groceries?

Arthur fought the urge to press his lips to hers. He stared at her for a moment before his eyes drifted to the black and blue marks on her neck and face.

"This wasn't your fault," Sophie reiterated, drawing Arthur's eyes to hers. In the depths of her steely gaze, Arthur noticed the determination and authority.

"I'm fine, I promise. Don't beat yourself up for this. It was my mistake."

"How is any of this your fault?" Arthur asked as he brushed his fingertips ever so lightly over the bruises.

"I should have been more vigilant and cautious," Sophie said.

"And I should have followed my gut and came with you today."

"No," Sophie said, shaking her head. Reaching out for him, she held him by the shoulders and kept his eyes on her. "You can't do that. You can't hold yourself responsible for anything that happened in town today. I'm going to rest for a bit and pretend this never happened. The sheriff and Mae are right. They were drifters and won't be coming back."

Arthur nodded, pressing his lips into a tight line as she released him. He stood still, trying to control the tremors of his hands. All he could think of was finding those men who did this to his wife. He wanted revenge. As his thoughts twisted and turned, a calm came over him. His jaw dropped as he glanced over his shoulder towards the window.

First the cut barbed wire, then Bergen showing up, now my wife gets assaulted in town. This isn't random acts. These are attacks. Deliberate and focused attacks... Randal Munger.

His heart fluttered as the sound thundered in his ears. Panic shot through him like an arrow striking its target dead center. With his eyes locked on the hallway, he knew what he had to do.

I will not allow him to hurt you Sophie. That is a promise.

* * *

Sophie shot out of bed, sweat dripping down her face as the dark sinister eyes of her assault lingered before her. Quickly she threw her hands up to rub the sleep from them and to ensure that what she was seeing wasn't there. All she could think of was his hands on her mouth and wrists. Even now, she could feel his clammy fingers curled around her skin, pinning her down. With her throat dry, no cries or screams could escape her chapped lips. For once she was pleased the scream didn't escape. The last thing she wanted was to worry Arthur or let him know how much that day still tormented her.

Scanning the room, she held her breath expecting to see someone lurking in the shadows.

Just a dream.

Sucking in a deep breath through her nose, she tried to steady herself and muster the courage to pull the covers off her. Peeling her fingers out of her sheets, she removed them carefully. Each moan of the house caused her to jump. She knew if she was in any real danger Arthur was down the hallway and would be there in a heartbeat. Still, she didn't want to give notice to her fears.

It took several minutes for the panic and fear to subside enough for Sophie think about moving. If she stayed still, she thought, she'd be able to blend into the shadows of the room. With her eyes peeled on the darkness engulfing her, she wished the lamp wasn't so far away. Only when her heart returned to its normal rhythm did she slip her feet off the edge of the bed and stand. With wobbly legs, she made her way to her desk and sat down in the small chair.

It was just a dream, get a hold of yourself. There is nothing to worry about. He's not here, there is no one here. It's only the wind you hear.

Sophie tried to swallow the lump in her throat and quench her parched tongue, but the terror stole every drop from her. Chewing on her lower lip, she pulled out her journal and ran her fingers over the binding. For some reason, that small book seemed to be her lifeline. It was the light she needed in her dark world.

Fumbling with the knickknacks on her desk, she finally found the small box of matches near her lamp. As she pulled one out and struck it against the box, she was relieved to see it illuminate the shadows around her. Carefully, she lit the lamp on her desk. With the fire burning and flickering between her fingers, she found herself entrance by the way the flame danced.

With a flick of her wrist, the small flame went out and a small stream of smoke drifted up from the burnt wood. She exhaled as she set it down on her window seal and focused on her journal. Steadily, she pulled out a pen and opened the book.

Dear Diary,

It has been a week since the attack in town, yet I can still see his dark eyes every night I sleep. The sinister gaze I find in my dreams haunts my waking hours too. I wish it would go away. In the pit of my core I pray for the sheriff to find those men and hang them. Granted, the punishment doesn't fit the crime, but still it is what I secretly want. The need for justice is unquenchable. I can't in good consciousness let it go, despite the fact that the bruises are gone. Sometimes I think I can still see a hint of them left behind. As if they will always be there for me to see.

Honestly, I don't know what to do. Each night I wake with sweat pouring out of me and I see his eyes glaring at me. Some nights Mae is killed, other times it's just me and him in the alley. Tonight was different. Tonight, I saw him across the street glaring at me and in a blink of an eye he had his hands on my throat, cutting off my air supply and making it difficult for me to let out the scream.

I can't let Arthur know the events are still plaguing me. He hasn't let me out of his sight since that day. It doesn't matter where I go or what I do, he's there like a shadow lingering so close. Please don't get me wrong, the attention is nice. Having him close settles my fears, but still, he won't always be around to help me. I have to face this fear alone and tackle it or it will ruin me, that much I'm sure of.

What am I to do? What would Nadine do in my shoes? I can't remember a time she'd been in such a predicament or so afraid. There was never a time I needed her more than right now. How I'd love to have her snuggle in bed with me, watching over me as I slept. At least then I'd know the shadows and nightmares wouldn't touch me.

But what do I do about Arthur? Telling him would just fuel his determination to keep me close to him. Or perhaps it would have the opposite effect and he'd find me weak and frail. How I wish this never happened. But it did, and deep within, I feel the worst is yet to come. There is a storm brewing, I can feel it in my bones. I just pray we are ready and prepared when it finally does hit.

Sophie closed her journal and stared out into the darkness. She pulled in a deep breath watching the flashes of light streak across the sky. With each crack of lightning she noticed the branches of the trees twisting and shifting like fingers. Chills ran down her spine as she turned the knob of the lamp causing the flame to go out. She sat still for a moment looking out into the nothing as the winds blew through the trees.

Rising slowly, Sophie moved back to the bed and pulled the covers over her legs. She leaned back into the pillows and listened as the house moaned and the windows rattled. Her mind drifted to Arthur in the other room. She couldn't help but wonder if he was feeling the same insecurities as she was. If maybe he could feel the winds shifting too.

Snuggling down into the bed, Sophie tried to toss out all negative thoughts. But no matter how hard she tried, the sinister eyes of her attacker were all she could see as she closed her eyes. Quickly, she shot out of bed and tried to steady herself.

You're alright. You're home. He's long gone, and you have nothing to worry about.

She allowed her mind to fill up with all the ways Arthur had changed since they married. Slowly her mind filled with Arthur's face and the tender kiss he stole on the couch. With her doubts melting away and her body relaxed, Sophie found herself drifting back to sleep. She knew the nightmares would return, but for now, she was safe and sound at home.

Chapter 14

The sun's light trickled into the bedroom pushing the shadows away. Sophie stretched as her eyes fluttered open. The horrors of last night lingered in the back of her mind, but with the rising sun, the horrors seemed all but a distant memory. She smiled at the sparrows singing by her window seal.

"Well good morning to you too," she said a bit chipper than she was the day before. For some reason she always felt good on Sunday mornings. Perhaps it was because it was the only day of the week she could sleep in and rest. During the course of the week, she'd get up before the crack of dawn to start her chores. But Sunday was her day of rest. The only thing she knew she had to do was get dressed and head to church.

Pulling the covers off her, she slipped her feet over the edge of the bed. A slight chill raced up her legs as she jumped out of bed and rushed to her closet.

A smile played at the corner of her lips as she opened the closet door and pulled out the dress she'd been working on all week. It was light green. Not the color of the leaves around the house, but more of a mossy color. As Sophie studied her creation she found her chest swelling with pride at the less frilly dress in her hands. It wasn't nearly as flashy as some of her other dresses, but it was the first one she had made on the ranch.

I hope Arthur likes this.

She glanced over her shoulder, looking to the door as the sound of Arthur's boots stomped by her bedroom door. Cupping her hand to her mouth, she contained the giggle that wanted to explode out of her. For some reason she was feeling awfully giddy despite the awful night she had. Breathing in deeply, Sophie thought of Arthur's reaction to her dress.

Here's goes nothing.

Sophie quickly shimmied out of her nightgown and into her new dress. She stood in front of the mirror for a moment fixing her hair and pinning her hat on her head. The light green complemented her honey brown eyes making the golden specks sparkle that much more. Pleased with her reflection, Sophie slipped on her shoes and made her way to the bedroom door.

Act natural.

She reached for the knob just as she heard Arthur's boots and a tap. Gasping, she paused. He was right on the other side, she could see his shadow from under the door and it made her heart skip.

"Yes?" Sophie answered, trying to make her voice muffled and further away than where she was.

"It's almost time for church. Are we going today?"

"Of course, I'll be right out," Sophie said with a smile as she stole one last glimpse at herself in the mirror. She waited a moment or two for Arthur to leave and pressed her ear against the door until she couldn't hear him any longer. She wanted to make a stunning impression and hoped to find him in the sitting room waiting for her.

Sophie twisted the knob and pulled open the door. Her shoes clacked on the wooden floor as she made her way down the hallway. The moment she turned the corner she noticed Arthur on the couch, precisely where she'd hoped he would be. Slowly he turned to look at her.

Pausing, Sophie stood in the hallway, allowing the entrance to frame her. Arthur rose and straightened his tie. The lack of interest in her outfit stunned her. Rejection washed over her as she looked down at her outfit to see if she had misplaced anything or didn't make it correctly.

"What do you think of my new dress?" Sophie asked, trying to prompt him to compliment her. Arthur's eyebrows rose for a brief moment as he scanned her from head to toe.

"You look nice," he said flatly before turning towards the kitchen.

Swallowing her pride, Sophie followed Arthur into the kitchen and grabbed the pot of beef stew she'd made the night before. Prying open the lid, she stole a quick taste hoping it hadn't lost its zing. A smile played at the corner of her lips as she nodded. If fashion didn't impress Arthur, she knew her cooking sure did.

"Are you ready?" Arthur asked, holding the back door open for her.

"What's the rush?" Sophie asked.

"Want to talk to the sheriff before service today. Maybe he's heard something about the men who -"

Arthur stopped and shook his head as his lips tightened into a sleek line. "Never mind. Let's just get there early today."

"You don't have to walk on eggshells around me. I'm not as fragile as you think I am," Sophie said, hoping her fear didn't give her away. She wondered if Arthur had heard the nightmares she'd been having over the past weeks.

All this time I thought I was keeping it under control.

Pulling in a deep breath she stared at Arthur. Nothing in his expression gave him away. He stood with his shoulders back and head held high.

"I just don't want you to have to worry about it. We will find who did that to you and Mae," Arthur said more as a promise than a statement. Sophie smiled briefly as she grabbed the lid to the pot and pulled it off the stove.

"Well, I'm not worried about it and you shouldn't either. What's done is done."

"You can really see it that way?" Arthur asked as Sophie moved past him and carefully maneuvered the steps of the back porch.

"Yes, and you should too." The determination and strength Sophie heard in her own voice thrilled her.

If only I can believe my own words.

Carefully setting the pot of stew in the back of the wagon, Sophie walked to the front. Arthur stood there with his hand out ready to help her up. The touch of his fingers on her sent a warm thrill coursing through her. She knew it was simply a gesture to help her up to the front, but still, she found herself longing for something a bit more than just light touches.

Sophie pushed the fabric of her dress down as Arthur climbed in beside her and took the reins. He flashed his eyes at her and gave her a crooked little smile that sent her heart fluttering.

"You really do look beautiful," he said with a hint of red to his cheeks. "Any man would be proud to have you sitting beside them."

"Arthur," Sophie whispered as she felt her face getting hotter.

"What?" Arthur said smiling as he cracked the reins. The horses neighed and tossed their heads as they started. The wagon wasn't nearly as bumpy as the buckboard, but still Sophie found her knees rubbing against Arthur's every so often. Each time they touched, Sophie peeked at him, wondering if he minded. By the gleam in his eyes, it was clear he didn't.

Sophie kept her eyes straight and stole glimpses of him as they made their way to town. It seemed as if everyone came out to church. Arthur pulled beside the Davidson's carriage and slipped down to tie the horses to the post. Sophie didn't wait for Arthur to get down, she slipped off and found her footing quickly as the bells of the church rang out.

"Hey Arthur." Sophie and Arthur turned to see Noonen walking down the main strip with a huge smile on his face.

"Stay here Sophie," Arthur said.

"Whatever the sheriff has to say, he can say in front of me," Sophie stated. The tone of her voice shocked both her and Arthur, causing him to stare at her.

"Are you sure you want to know?" Arthur asked as he lifted his hand up for Sophie to take.

"Yes," she nodded.

Stepping forward, Sophie grabbed Arthur's hand and made her way down the main strip to meet with Noonen.

"Beautiful day today, don't ya think?" Noonen greeted them, glancing around at the white puffy clouds that drifted through the blue sky.

"It is," Sophie answered with a smile.

"It's good to see you're in good spirits all things considered. Most women folk would be too scared to come off their lands."

"Well I'm not like most women," Sophie said, squeezing Arthur's hand and smiling.

"No, that you are not. But if you're wondering if there is any news, I'm afraid to say there's not. No one has spotted those men in town or outside of town. Chances are they were just drifters like I said before. I doubt we will see them again."

"Well, it doesn't hurt to ask right?" Arthur said, looking at Sophie. "Sometimes it isn't what we want to hear, but it's better than nothing."

"Thank you Sheriff," Sophie replied as the bells rang out a second time.

"Looks like church is calling us sinners to come on in," Noonen quipped, laughing.

"Will you be joining us today?" Sophie asked Noonen with wide hopeful eyes.

"Sorry, not today. Someone's got to keep an eye out around these parts," Noonen said, dipping his hat.

"Well thank you for the work you do." Sophie smiled brightly as a dark cloud drifted over her heart. Deep down she wanted those men captured. But since it was close to a week now, she knew they could be in a completely different state.

"Of course," Noonen said as he turned.

"Come on, let's see if the Davidson's are here already," Arthur said, nudging Sophie. She turned with him and moved back to the white church that stood out like a pillar of hope in the dusty little town.

Sophie smiled as she spotted Mae and Garner in the middle pews and quickly slipped in next to them. She reached her arms out and embraced Mae just as the music started. Although she tried to pay attention to the service, Sophie couldn't help but think about what the sheriff had said.

Drifters coming in to cause trouble. That was, after all, what Noonen said. But who would come into a town just to stir things up? Why would anyone want to do that?

Before Sophie realized it, the service was over, and Mae was pushing her knee to get her to stand. Dumbstruck, Sophie rose and looked around the nearly empty church.

"Well that was certainly something," Mae said, laughing.

"What's that?" Sophie asked as she scooted down the narrow path between the pews.

"You weren't paying any attention today, were you?" Mae asked, dragging her son behind her as Abigale clung to her neck.

"Busted," Sophie answered. "You could say my mind was elsewhere."

"Well, did you forget you're coming over for lunch today?" Mae asked as they moved down the aisle towards the door.

"No, I brought soup. It's in the wagon ready to be reheated," Sophie said with a hint of a smile.

"Good, cause I'd hate for you to have to go back to your place to pick it up," Mae said, pawning Abigale off to Garner as she picked up Aiden.

Sophie smiled as she watched Mae climb up by herself. It seemed as if Garner knew better than to coddle his wife. Mae was tough and Sophie could only wish to be that strong.

"You were a million miles away today in church," Arthur said as he helped Sophie up to the seat.

"I'm sorry," Sophie said.

"I knew I shouldn't have let you talk with Noonen. The news would just bother you."

"Actually," Sophie smiled. "I wasn't thinking about that at all."

"Then what was on your mind?"

"Nothing," Sophie said as Arthur climbed up beside her.

"You're lying," Arthur said, raising his eyebrow as he stared at her.

"Fine," Sophie exhaled and dropped her shoulders. "I was wondering about the stew and if I put enough spices in it. Garner said it was bland the last time I made it," Sophie said with a spark to her eyes. Arthur shook his head as he followed the Davidson's.

Sophie exhaled and focused on the white clouds in the sky, trying to keep her thoughts from drifting back to her attackers. There was no way she was going to let her fear control her. Although it scared her and rattled her to her core, Sophie realized she couldn't live constantly looking over her shoulder. Instead, she tried to concentrate on the way the leaves danced with the wind and wondered if it would be possible to forget about the men that attacked her.

Only time will tell. With enough time, all will be forgotten.

Arthur pulled up beside the Davidson's wagon as Sophie started to laugh. Aiden was running around like a wild child driving Mae to pull at her hair. From the crinkle in Mae's forehead, Sophie and Arthur knew Mae was about to blow.

"Aiden, will you please settle down," Mae said in the most controlled voice she could muster.

"I got him," Arthur said laughing as he took off after the three-year-old. It didn't take long for Arthur to overtake the child. With a squeal of delight, the boy flew in the air as Arthur curled his arms around Aiden's waist and tossed him into the air.

Sophie laughed as she watched Arthur play with Aiden. For each toss that sent Aiden up into the air, Arthur was right there to catch him. The boy laughed and squealed with delight that even Mae couldn't help but laugh. A pang in Sophie's chest startled her as she moved next to Mae.

"Are you sure you two don't want any kids? You know you can have mine if you want them."

"Funny," Sophie said, keeping her eyes locked on Arthur as he played in the field with the small boy. "But I don't think it's in our future."

"Why do you say things like that? You and I both know that man there is head over heels for you. If you asked him to give you a child, I'll bet you he would in a heartbeat."

"I'm not so sure about that. We got married for the convenience of it, not out of love and family."

"Sometimes things change," Mae said with a wink. "Like how I doubt we'll be having any of that soup you made for us."

"Why?" Sophie asked as she looked at the wagon to find the birds swooping down around it.

"Oh get, scat," Sophie shouted as she rushed towards the wagon sending the birds flying high.

"Mommy look," Aiden said, pointing to the sky as the birds took flight. Sophie's face turned a darker shade of red as she glanced at Arthur. He stood laughing with the boy on his shoulders. The embarrassment and anger vanished as she looked at them.

Maybe a family wouldn't be so bad if Arthur wanted it too.

* * *

"Thank you so much for having us," Arthur said, lifting his hand up to wave goodbye.

I don't know how she does it. The resiliency of this woman is astounding. Even Sophie seems unshaken and undisturbed by the attack from last week. Maybe there is hope for us to have a family and be just as happy as the Davidson's. But Randal... he's still out there and no doubt will find his way to me one of these days. Can't think of a family right now, not when Sophie's attack has me on edge like it does. But maybe one day I'll have what Garner has.

The Davidson's stood on their front lawn, Mae held Abigale as Aiden clung to her leg and paddled his little hand in the air. Garner stood with his suspenders and belly out as if he had no worries at all. The sight of them made Arthur's heart swell.

"Till next time," Sophie said, waving goodbye. Arthur wondered if her heart was still dead set on not having the family life. But by the way she kept her eyes on Abigale, Arthur wasn't so sure. He wished with all his might that he could give her the life she wanted.

"Penny for your thoughts?" Sophie turned her head and stared at him with such concern in her eyes it nearly broke him.

"I'm fine," Arthur said as they moved down the road between their house and the Davidson's.

"Sure you are," she retorted. "What's wrong? You had a smile on your face a few hours ago and now it's gone. Clearly you're lost in thought."

"Seems we both have had our moments today, you at church and me now."

"Is that what you want then? For me to be quiet so you can think, or did you want to share?"

Arthur pulled in a long deep breath and held it. He looked at Sophie for a moment before turning his attention back to the dusty road ahead of them.

"I know you may be over the event in town," Arthur said, dropping his shoulders. "But I'm not. It kills me to think about it. To know that some man had his hands on you."

"Then don't think about it," Sophie said, reaching for him. She placed her hand on his shoulder and looked at him with her pleadingly.

"I don't know how to stop. When I close my eyes I think about it and what you went through. I should have been there."

"Should have, could have, would have, but that is not how it went down. I'm just grateful that we are alive and safe. I'm with you and Mae was able to go back to her children and husband."

"But it shouldn't have happened in the first place. You shouldn't have had to endure that. Mae shouldn't have to live with the fear that she does. Did you know Garner told me she wakes up every night screaming? It's been a solid week of

Mae waking up in the dead of night covered in sweat because of what happened."

Sophie dropped her gaze and stared at the footrest. Arthur pressed his lips together and shook his head.

"Is that what's happening with you too?" he asked, scooting a bit closer to Sophie. She didn't budge or flinch as his knee brushed against hers.

"No. I'm not having the terrors that Mae has," she said in a stone-cold voice that felt wrong.

"Sophie," Arthur turned his head towards her and shifted his weight. He wanted to pull her to him and hold her. He wanted to make all the demons she faced flee from her, but he knew that he couldn't do it alone. She would have to let him in.

"I'm here for you. You know that right? No matter what. I know we had our moment in the living room where you stood up for me. I've never done that for you but now I'm telling you, I'm here."

"I know that," Sophie nodded as she kept her gaze on the wooden plank at their feet.

"Are you sure?"

"Of course," Sophie said, whipping her head up. Her eyes were red and a bit swollen, but no tears trickled down her cheeks.

"What if all this is because of Randal?" Arthur blurted out as he dropped his gaze. Sophie's expression shifted from sad to confused.

"I don't' see how. It doesn't make any sense. You can't try and point blame where there is none. We don't know where Randal is."

"That's just it, we don't know. He could be three states away or three miles. But everything that's happened just seems to fit so neatly."

"How so?" Sophie asked, placing her hand on Arthur's, and causing him to shift the reins to one hand.

"Before you came out, I had issues with my barbed wire fences getting cut. Other ranchers also reported the same problem to Noonen. Then my men started acting out and causing issues, complaining of how they weren't getting paid enough when that was never an issue before. Now you and Mae get attacked by some strangers. It just doesn't make sense."

"It's like they are minor distractions to keep us on our toes?"

"Exactly," Arthur said. "Think about it. If they were one after another and all focused on one thing, then anyone with half a brain would see what was being attacked and why. But the fences, the men, and you. It all seems linked back to me. These are things that are mine. My property, my livelihood, my family life. Please tell me I'm being paranoid."

Arthur's heart sank as Sophie squeezed his hand and stared at him. Her small shoulders lifted up in a shrug as she shook her head.

"I don't know what to tell you," she said. "I don't know this man. But the chances of him being here now, don't you think it is kind of slim? How would the Randal even know where to look for you? Didn't you say you knew him in El Paso, Texas? That's a long way away from Oakbury, Tennessee."

"You're right," Arthur said, shaking his head. "It was also a long time ago. But still, there's this nagging feeling I just can't shake."

"Like a storm is coming?" Sophie asked, turning her attention to the trees.

"Exactly, a storm. And I don't know if we're ready for it."

"Neither do I," she said as their homestead came into view. "But I do know, whatever happens, we are going to face it together."

"I can't let you fight my battles," Arthur said. "I don't know what I'd do if you got hurt. There's no way I would put the lives of our friends and neighbors in danger because of what I did in my past. I'd never forgive myself if anything happened to this place or to you." Arthur looked at Sophie as the horses drew up to the corral and stopped without being prompted.

"It'll be okay," Sophie said, forcing a smile. "But you can't face them alone either. I won't let you."

"This isn't your battle, or your problem."

"You're my husband," Sophie said in a stern voice. "No matter which way the winds blow, that won't change. Do you understand? I made you a promise Arthur Soul, and I'm not going to let you break that promise."

Arthur glanced around the ranch, searching the shadows for intruders. His heart was heavy with the burden, but in the darkness a small insignificant light shined. It was that hope that he clung to as he slipped off the wagon and moved around to help Sophie down.

He curled his fingers around her waist he sat her on the ground. She looked up at him with a loving gaze with her hands on his shoulders. Arthur could easily slip into this moment and hold onto it forever.

"I need to get out of this dress," Sophie said, pulling her hands away and stepping out of his grasp.

"Of course," Arthur said, clearing his throat. Sophie moved around him and headed towards the steps. He could hear her tiny footsteps as she ascended the stairs and then silence. Fear stabbed him. He turned around quickly. Sophie stood at the top of the steps looking over her shoulder with a wide smile on her face.

"I really do like that dress," Arthur said, turning to face her. Sophie's face lit up with pride as if his words were the best thing she had ever heard. It was these moments that Arthur cherished the most. They were small and fragile and the one thing he never wanted to give up.

Chapter 15

Arthur pulled back the curtain as he took a sip from his black coffee. The sky was gray as the limbs of the trees on his property whipped about. He couldn't help but feel as if the morning was a mirror image of the turmoil he felt inside.

Can't do this. I can't leave her here alone. What if something happens when I'm gone?

Arthur struggled with his thoughts as time ticked by, drawing him closer and closer to the cattle drive. Never before had he had to worry about such things. It felt strange for him to contemplate caring for another person, yet he felt complete in doing so.

He turned to find Sophie on the couch, book in hand. Her feet were propped beside her as she quietly turned the pages. The sight of her there filled his heart with a light that he never wanted extinguished.

You can't stay here. The boys are counting on you to help them... but I've never had to leave someone before. I don't know if I want to.

Arthur grunted as he turned back in frustration unable to make up his mind. He kept his eyes to the dark sky as the steam rose from his cup.

"Sophie," he finally said. She looked up from her book and cocked her head. Arthur's mouth opened and closed several times before he moved around the couch and sat in the armchair next to her.

"You look over worked and tired," Sophie said. "Should I make you some chamomile tea to soothe you nerves instead?"

Arthur glanced at the mug in his hand and shook his head. "It's not the coffee."

"But there is something troubling you," Sophie insisted, placing a marker in her book, and closing it. He watched how delicately she placed the book in her lap to give him her undivided attention.

"You know the cattle drive is coming up in a few days," Arthur finally managed to say. Sophie's eyebrows rose as she nodded her head. "I'm just worried about you."

"Arthur Soul," Sophie's lips pulled up at the corners as she stared at him. "You don't have to be."

"Well I am. I'm worried that something is going to happen while I'm away."

"Did you ever have these doubts and fears before?" she asked, trying to hold his gaze. Arthur's eyes darted to the floor to avoid her eyes. He paused for a few moments wondering if there ever was a time he felt so insecure.

"No," he finally answered, bringing his eyes back up to meet hers.

"Then what's the big deal? Think of it as if someone is watching over your house. Because that's what I'll be doing. I'll be keeping an eye on the ranch while you're away and you'll come back to see everything is as it should be."

"I know you think you can handle yourself," Arthur started. Sophie immediately narrowed her gaze and crossed her arms over her lap.

"And you think I can't."

"No I think you can, but I want a little more security for you."

"Security? Like what?" Sophie asked. Arthur could see the hair on the back of her arms raise as if his words struck a chord.

"Well, for starters, I want you to learn how to shoot a gun. That way you can keep it by the door and if something happens, you'll have it to protect yourself."

For a moment silence filled the room. Arthur could hear his heart pounding in his ears as he waited for Sophie's response. Suddenly laughter peeled from her lips as she rocked on the couch.

"You're joking right? You want me to learn how to use a gun?"

"Yes," Arthur said matter of factly. "I will show you how and it will give me some peace of mind that you can use it while I'm gone. I don't want to come back home to find I've lost you."

"You can't live your life in fear. You can't always think the worst will happen. I promise I'll be fine."

"I know you will and I'm just going to help you a little bit by showing you how to use the rifle."

"Is that really necessary? I've seen you use it. It'll knock me to the ground."

"That's why I will be right there beside you to give you pointers. I'd rather have it knock you back and come out of it alive than to not use it and end up..." Arthur couldn't finish. Flashes of his family in Texas filled his mind as he looked at Sophie. Suddenly his heart felt like granite free falling from the sky.

His throat closed up as his blood pressure shot up. Every nerve in his body fired off as he clenched his mug. The sound of it shattering in his hand startled Sophie. She jumped back at the noise before realizing what had happened.

"Arthur, your hand," she said, jumping to her feet. She was in the kitchen before he could turn in his seat. The shards of ceramic fell to the ground as he opened his hand. To his surprise there wasn't the gash he had expected. Only minor cuts sliced through his fingers.

"I'm fine," he said as Sophie rushed back to him with a wet towel.

"Let me look at that," she said, taking his hand into hers as carefully and tenderly as she possibly could. Arthur kept his eyes on her as she worked to clean his hands off.

"See, I'm fine."

"What were you thinking?"

Silence filled the room as he swallowed hard and glanced down. "My family."

"Arthur, I'm not going to end up like your parents."

"You don't know that."

"You're right, I don't know but I have faith that everything will be fine. You're only going to be gone a few days."

"And I was gone only a few hours last time and he took everything from me."

"What are you going to do then? Stay here with me? You can't. You need to make sure everything runs smoothly. And what of those men who were giving you a headache last month? Don't you want to make sure there are no troubles on the trail? The only way to do that is if you are there to squash the rumors and issues as they arise."

Arthur shook his head as Sophie dropped to her knees and placed the shards of the mug in the towel.

"You're right. I can't stay. But I can leave the gun with you. I won't need both of the rifles on the trail. Please," Arthur pleaded as he leaned down and pulled Sophie up by her shoulders.

"Please let me teach you how to use the gun. If for no other reason than to please me," he said, staring deeply into her eyes. He watched as her shoulders dropped with her eyes.

"Fine," she relented. "But it's not because I can't handle myself."

A smile played at the corner of his mouth as she rose. He couldn't believe the woman standing before him. She wasn't the meek girl he'd married. She had changed and grown into a self-resilient woman capable of anything.

* * *

"You are standing wrong," Arthur said as he pulled Sophie's shoulders back. "You don't want to be hunched over when you pull the trigger. It's the reason why the butt keeps hurting you. Now stand up straight and hold it tight."

Arthur stepped behind Sophie, forcing her body straight. "You feel that? Feel how tight your arms are right now? The strain in your core, that's how you need to be."

Sophie sucked in shallow breaths as Arthur placed his hands on her stomach forcing her to stand straighter. She knew she was there to learn to shoot but he was such a distraction. It didn't matter to her that she hadn't hit a single glass bottle he'd set up on the log ten paces away from her. It didn't matter that each time she pulled that trigger the gun would kick up and practically knock her off her feet. All that she cared about was how close Arthur stood next to her. His breath tickled her neck as he spoke, sending chills racing up her arm.

"I don't think you are concentrating," Arthur said as he stepped back. "You don't have your feet in the right spot."

"I would say I'm sorry but I'm not," Sophie said playfully as she turned to find Arthur scowling at her.

"This isn't a game," he said, crossing his arms. "You can't treat this like some joke. That rifle has the power to kill someone. One misfire and you could hurt me or yourself."

Sophie straightened her shoulders back and planted her feet. She turned her hips and glared down the barrel of the gun, trying to remember to keep both eyes open.

"Good, now squeeze the trigger," Arthur said quickly stepping behind her. Sophie sucked in a slow steady breath before placing her finger on the trigger. The sun bore down on her as she counted in her head. With Arthur further away from her and not so much of a distraction, she placed her finger on the trigger and tightened her grip.

The explosion of the gun firing caused her ears to ring. But unlike the other fifty times, she didn't blink. Her eyes were locked on the target as the bullet expelled from the barrel and hurtled towards the brown glass bottle. It was only a second before the sound of glass shattering replaced the ringing, but it seemed like forever.

"You did it   !" Arthur clapped as Sophie lowered the gun. Her heart fluttered as she saw what she had done. The brown bottle she'd been concentrating on for what seemed like forever was no more.

"That was amazing," Arthur said coming up beside her. He stood there briefly with his arms open ready to pull her into a hug before he quickly dropped them awkwardly.

"Now, let's do it again," Arthur prompted as he grabbed the gun from Sophie.

"Again?" Discouragement filled her as she watched Arthur move to the log and replace the brown bottle with a slender green one.

"I need to know you can hit a smaller target," he said, looking at her over his shoulder. Sophie threw her arms up in the air and turned around in frustration.

"Wasn't the brown one enough?"

"No," Arthur answered as he walked back to her. "We don't know what kind of dangers may be coming. It could be a copperhead or a cottonmouth on the front porch. You need to be able to hit it without blowing holes all over our porch because you missed."

"I wouldn't do that," Sophie glared at him.

"I know, because you're going to be able to kill it with one shot," he said handing her the rifle.

"Now try again. And do precisely what you did with the brown bottle. Concentrate, breath, and squeeze."

She lifted the gun up to her shoulder and made sure the butt was secure and tight to her shoulder. Planting her feet with her hips turned, she breathed in slowly.

"Good," Arthur said, stepping up closer to her. Sophie could feel his body heat coming off him in waves. She knew exactly how far away he was from her and it thrilled her.

"What if I hit this? What happens then?" Sophie asked, dropping the gun, and turning to face Arthur.

"You're stalling," he scolded.

"No, I want to make a little wager," Sophie said with a crooked grin. "If I hit this target the first time, let's say you milk the cow for a week when you get back from the cattle drive."

"And when you don't?" Arthur asked raising his eyebrow with the same crooked grin to match Sophie's.

"Well, what do you want? It's not like I don't already clean, cook, and milk the cow."

"I want you to make me that roasted duck again," Arthur said.

"Seriously?" Sophie chuckled. "That's what you want?"

Arthur nodded his head once before answering with his chin up. "That's what I want."

"That dish takes all day," Sophie said in a mock grumble.

"Well then, you better not miss then huh?" Arthur teased as Sophie took her stance.

Don't mess this up. Breathe. Slow and steady that's how you got the other one. Think about it. A whole week of extra sleep if you hit this, plus my hands will finally get a break from the squeezing. Concentrate. Just hit the target.

Sophie checked her sights, ensured her feet where planted just so, she breathed in deep, and held her breath as she squeezed the trigger.

"Oh," Arthur shouted, throwing his hands up.

"Looks like someone is milking the cow for a week," Sophie said with a big smile as she turned to face Arthur. The green little bottle rested in pieces with the brown shards.

"Alright little miss sharpshooter," Arthur growled. "Let's see you hit something important."

"Oh no, not going to do that," Sophie said. "I'm already ahead and if my father taught me anything, it's quit while you're ahead."

Arthur laughed as Sophie dropped the barrel of the gun to the ground and held it securely in her forearm.

"I think you're ready," Arthur said begrudgingly as he reached for the rifle.

"For?" Sophie asked with a huge smile.

"To be left alone at the ranch," he said, pressing his lips together.

"Arthur," Sophie rested her hand on his shoulder and smiled. "I can do this. Even without the rifle. But now, you've given me the tools to survive alone. So thank you." Sophie paused and stared at him.

Arthur nodded as Sophie pointed to the glass on the ground. "But you got to admit, that was a pretty good shot."

"Honestly, I didn't think you'd be able to do it," Arthur said as he walked to the horses.

"Can I confess something to you?" Sophie asked as she leaned against the tree and watched Arthur place the rifle in the back of the buckboard.

"Go on," he said, turning his attention to her. She paused as her lips curled up at the corners. "You already won."

"What do you mean?"

"I've had a duck roasting all morning. I wanted to give you the best dish I could before you left. Something to remember me by and all." Sophie's cheeks burned as she spoke. She knew it was a bit cheesy, but it was the truth. She knew her cooking was bar none and Arthur always seemed so impressed by it.

"Really?" Arthur's surprise spread across his face as Sophie nodded. She could feel her cheeks aching as her smile grew wider. It surprised her that she was able to keep it a secret from him. But then again, they weren't at the homestead where he could smell it cooking.

"Well, maybe next time I'll have to think of something else a bit more challenging," Arthur teased as he flashed Sophie a wink.

"You can try," Sophie quipped, climbing up onto the seat and settling herself. She brushed the dirt from her skirt as she propped her feet up on the wooden plank. Her arms went behind her head as if she'd just catch the biggest fish in five counties.

"But you'll just surprise me with that accomplishment too, huh?" Arthur said, climbing in next to her.

"Yeah, probably."

Chapter 16

Sophie wrapped her smock around her shoulders as she stood outside on the front porch. She knew it wasn't the weather that caused her to feel slightly chilly, but the realization that Arthur was saddling his horse for the cattle drive. Her heart thudded unevenly in her chest as she battled conflicting emotions. On one hand, she wanted to prove to him all would be well and that she could handle herself in his absence. But there was the nagging insecure siren in her gut warning her not to let him leave.

She pulled in a deep breath of the morning air. It was crisper and light. She looked over the tips of the trees to find that the sun's rays were barely peeking over the mountains.

"Do you have everything?" Sophie asked as she turned her attention back to Arthur. He didn't turn to look at her. All she got was a bit of a grunt as he pulled up the cinch under the horse and secured the buckle.

"Want me to make you a bite before you go?" Sophie asked, trying to stall him. She knew there was no way he'd say yes, but she had to at least try to keep him around a few more moments.

"You know I don't have time for that, the boys are probably already waiting for me," he said securing a pouch around the horn of the saddle.

"I can make you a cup of coffee really quick, it won't take but a minute or two," Sophie said as she could feel the emotions cutting off her air supply.

Just breath, you can't break down now. He'll never leave you alone then and that's not how you want to live. Keep your chin up and your shoulders back. This is your life now, you're a rancher's wife and he's going to have to go every year like this, so you might as well get used to it now.

Sophie forced the lump in her throat down as she watched Arthur attach his rollup to the back of the saddle. Seeing all the pieces fit like a puzzle made her wish he didn't have to go at all. She could feel a tight squeeze as if some unseen hand clenched around her heart making it difficult for her to get enough air.

"I won't be gone long," Arthur promised as he turned to face her. Sophie locked her eyes on his taking in their deep marble gray color. It was as if they were made from the sky. She looked up and smiled, noticing the resemblance.

"I know," she said as he took the stairs two at a time. Her arms dropped as he stood inches from her. With each breath, she prayed for him to take her in his arms and press his lips to hers. Every second they stood on the porch staring at each other, she longed to be in the warmth of his embrace.

"You know what to do if anything happens," Arthur spoke slowly and nodded as his eyes shifted to the front door.

"Shoot a round into the sky and wait for Garner," She answered.

"That's right," Arthur said approvingly. He cupped his hand around her oval shaped face. Sophie leaned into his hand, absorbing the warmth from the palm of his hand. She closed her eyes as she swallowed to quench her dry throat.

"He knows to keep an ear open for you. And if all else fails, they are more than happy to have you for a few days," he said as she opened her eyes.

"I don't need a babysitter," Sophie said.

"No, I don't suppose you do."

Butterflies fluttered about her stomach as she held onto Arthur's hand cupping her face. She noticed the twitch of his lips as he stared at her. For a brief moment, she wondered if he'd lean down and kiss her. She wanted nothing more than for him to take her into his loving embrace and give her a reason to look forward to his return.

Disappointment stabbed her longing and killed her desires as Arthur slowly slipped his hand out of her grasp and stepped back. He stood on the first step for a heartbeat more before turning. Sophie's heart shattered as she watched him mount his steed.

"Take care," Arthur said as he settled on his horse.

"Be careful," Sophie said, trying to keep him there with her a bit longer. The rooster crowed and before Sophie could tell the thing to shut it, Arthur was charging down the dirt road.

Please come back safely.

Regret squeezed the air out of her as she wondered why she didn't take what she wanted right then and there. There was no denying the facts any longer. Watching Arthur ride away broke her in ways she never thought possible. Although she knew he'd come back in a few days, there was no denying those days would be lonely.

You have to come back Arthur Soul because... I love you.

Instinctively, she covered her mouth with her hand as the realization sunk in. There was no denying the truth any longer. She longed for Arthur, craved to be near him. Even the small things like his laugh were something she wanted to keep just for herself.

Sophie held to the post of the porch and stood in the cool morning air until she couldn't see Arthur any longer. Her heart ached as she wished she knew the words to keep him there with her. As she chewed on her lower lip, she waited and hoped he'd stop at the edge of their property and wave goodbye.

The moments ticked by and Arthur steadily moved closer and closer to the edge. Then as if he had remembered something he forgot, he pulled the reins of his horse. Sophie's heart took flight as she watched him throw one hand into the sky as he turned.

Goodbye my love and take care.

Sophie pressed her fingertips to her mouth and crushed her lips to them. By the time she opened her eyes once more, Arthur was gone. Her heart sank as she curled the shawl around her arms and exhaled slowly.

"Now comes the hard part," Sophie said to the empty space. She looked around the ranch. She had seen the view a million times, but Arthur's absence made it stark. It was as if the ranch and all the animals knew he had left them too.

Sophie looked up to the sky that reminded her of the marble gray color of Arthur's eyes. A tear spilled down her cheek as she tried to come to terms with his departure. Although it was something that had been expected for many months, she never thought she would feel this much agony over it.

Then again, you never loved him before. Now you do. That's what's changed. That's why this goodbye is so hard.

Sophie turned and wandered back into the house. The creaks and moans of the wood settling seemed louder than before. The rooms appeared bigger and more daunting without Arthur there to fill up the space.

Sophie knew these next few days were going to be long as she looked about the empty room. But she also knew it was something she was committed to. After all, she'd known Arthur's plans long before she agreed to marry him. He spoke of the cattle drive often in his letters to her. Yet, she didn't realize the impact of his absence until right then.

"As my stepmother always used to say, the best medicine is work," Sophie said, tossing off her smock. She knew there was no point in lingering and wishing for Arthur to come back as she moved into the kitchen.

Although there weren't a pile of dishes in the sink, she tidied up the area and dusted the shelves that hadn't been touched in a while. She worked her way around the house, finding odd jobs to keep her hands and mind busy.

"There," she said, dusting the palm of her hands on her apron. It seemed as if every nook and cranny in the kitchen and living room had been touched up. Pursing her lips together she crossed her arms and dropped her shoulders.

At this pace I'll have the whole house cleaned. I have to leave something for tomorrow, or I'll go out of my mind thinking about him.

Pulling in a deep breath, she made her way to her room and shut the door behind her. Scanning the room, she looked around for laundry or any other chore that could take her all day. But since she had to do Arthur's clothes for the drive, she didn't have any left to do. For a split moment she wondered if she could go back to sleep. A look at her already made bed made her think better of it. After all, she was far too wired to try and sleep anyway.

Sophie scrambled about the house and paused at Arthur's bedroom door. Her heart raced as she wondered if his pillows would smell like him. Carefully, she reached for the doorknob. Despite the fact that she was completely home alone, she couldn't help but glance over her shoulder towards the front door.

"Just a little peek," she told herself as she turned the knob.

A big boom on the front door startled her and she quickly released the doorknob without ever opening up the bedroom door.

"Coming," she said loudly. Her voice seemed to bounce off the walls of the hallway as she straightened her skirt and tried not to look so suspicious. Sophie's heart raced as she made her way towards the front door. Her eyes flickered to the rifle leaning against the nook between the door and the wall but thought better of it.

Slowly she opened the door and peaked out. "Hello?"

"Hello Mrs. Sophie."

"Sam, what are you doing here? Aren't you supposed to be helping with the cattle drive?" Sophie stared befuddled at the ranch hand standing on the front porch.

Sam lowered his hat and dipped his head down. "Yes ma'am, Arthur told me to stick around here this year to keep an eye on things."

Sophie pressed her hand to her chest as she scanned the area before letting her eyes shift back to Sam.

"I didn't startle you now, did I?"

"No of course not," Sophie said with a smile as she opened the door wider. "What can I do for you?"

"Actually, I was just letting you know I was here ma'am. Arthur wanted me to stick around on the ranch, something about an extra set of eyes and hands to help out."

Sophie nodded as she pushed back the loose strands of hair that seemed to be sticking out in every direction. "Of course he did," Sophie mumbled as she tried to put on a good face.

"Excuse me ma'am?" Sam said with a pensive look.

"It's nothing Sam, thank you for stopping by. And if you'd like some lunch later you let me know. It'll be strange only making food for one these next couple of days."

"Oh no ma'am I couldn't," Sam said, dropping his eyes to the wooden planks of the porch.

"Well, suit yourself," Sophie said as Sam nodded and turned. The panic she felt drifted as she watched Sam walk down the steps and head into the barn. It was a nice feeling to know she wasn't completely alone, but at the same time a pang of frustration stabbed at her.

One of these days Arthur, you'll see I can take care of myself.

Chapter 17

Long shadows drifted across the living room floor as Sophie finished dusting. She plopped down on the couch and looked about the room. It was a strange sensation being the only person in the house. Although she'd been living here for some time, she'd never really been in the place alone. The creeks and moans of the house settling sounded like thunder in her ears.

A low rapping on the front door startled her. She jumped up from the couch and made her way to the door. Pulling in a deep breath, she tried to steady her nerves.

It's probably just Sam.

Shaking off her insecurities, Sophie pulled the door open and flashed a brilliant smile. The instant she realized the man standing before her wasn't Sam; she closed the door a bit and hid behind it.

"Can I help you?" she asked as her gaze drifted over the strange man with dark shaggy hair. She couldn't help but notice his stunning blue eyes and charming smile.

"I'm terribly sorry to be bothering you ma'am," he said, pulling his hat from his head. Sophie kept her distance from him using the door as a shield. Her heart fluttered in her chest as flashes of the men from town drifted into her mind. Swiftly her eyes darted to the barn. Deep within her she had hoped to see Sam. Just a glimpse of her husband's ranch hand would ease her troubled mind.

"My name is Clay Thorn." The tension in Sophie's shoulders eased a bit as Clay flashed a bigger smile. He wasn't anything like the men she'd seen in town just a few days ago. Clay showed no signs of wear and tear from the road. His face was clean shaved, and his clothes looked pressed.

Sophie dared to step out from behind the front door as she pulled in a long deep breath.

Maybe he's lost? Or perhaps he is selling something?

"What can I do for you Mr. Thorn?"

"Well ma'am, I was wondering if a man by the name of Arthur Soul lived at this residency." Clay kept his head down, but his eyes locked on Sophie while he played with his black hat.

"And what is your business with my husband?" Sophie asked as she swallowed the lump of fear in her throat.

"Actually ma'am, I am an old friend of the family and heard he lived out here," Clay said. "I simply wanted to come by and say hello. Is he here?"

"My husband will be back later," Sophie said, lifting her head up as she scanned around the ranch. She couldn't help but feel something was off about Clay. Although he looked presentable, there was something in his gaze that chilled her.

"Mind if I stick around a bit for his return? I'm certain he wouldn't mind," Clay said, stealing a step closer. Instinctively, Sophie pulled the door to cut off Clay's attempt to get into the house.

"I'm sorry, but I can't allow you into the house," Sophie said, clinging to the door to hide her trembling hands.

"Of course not ma'am," Clay said with a wink. "Would you mind though if I wait out here for him then?"

"Perhaps it is best if you come back another time."

"I did not mean to offend ma'am," Clay said, lowering his head. "I just thought I'd talk to Arthur a bit about his family in Texas. It was a real shame about what happened to them, don't you think?"

The pang of suspicion eased from Sophie's chest as she stood before Clay.

He knows about Arthur's parents? What if he was a neighbor or some other relative that Arthur hasn't told me about? Should I let him in? I would hate to be an inhospitable host to an old friend of the family.

Stealing a glimpse over his shoulder, Sophie noticed Sam working with the horses corralled in the yard along with the black stallion that seemed content eating the long grass near the barn. Seeing Sam gave her a sense of relief and she knew all she had to do was scream if she needed any help, and of course she could always use the gun in the nook by the door.

"Forgive me," Sophie said with a timid smile. "I didn't realize you knew Arthur so well. Won't you come in for some tea?"

"That's mighty kind of you ma'am. I am a bit peaked."

"I'm sorry for being so distant, Mr. Thorn. But it would seem you can't be too sure of people these days."

"It's only right you keep your guard up with strangers. But I promise you, your husband and I go way back."

Sophie tried to smile as she stepped aside allowing Clay into the house. He paused in the living room and shook his head. Sophie watched as he scanned the room. Sure, there were the large bookshelves that had a variety of books on them, and an old vase with wildflowers that needed to be replaced, but nothing of value. Still, it was a large room with high vaulted ceiling that made the whole room appear bigger than it really was. The way Arthur designed the house was one of the things she loved about it.

"This is some place you have here. It's so open." Clay said, setting his hat down on the small table.

"Thank you. So how do you know Arthur?"

Sophie moved towards the kitchen trying to think of what she'd do if Clay turned on her. She glanced towards the nook by the front door. There resting against the wall was the loaded gun Arthur left for her. For a split second she wondered how fast she could get to it. But Clay seemed too concern with the nick knacks in the living room.

"Old friends. We used to play together if you can believe it," Clay said with a chuckle. Sophie moved swiftly to the pitcher of tea on the counter and filled the shortest glass she could find.

"You don't say," Sophie said, coming back into the living room with the full glass. "Arthur has never mentioned you to me."

"And you've known Arthur long?" Clay asked before downing every last drop of tea from his glass.

"Long enough," Sophie answered as Clay extended the glass to her. Sophie quickly swiped it from his hand and turned on her heels.

"Might I ask where you came from?" Sophie could feel Clay's eyes on her as she returned to the kitchen.

"Did you grow up around these parts?"

"No actually. I moved out this way a while ago."

"Is that so? About how long ago?" Mr. Thorn asked as he pulled the glass to his lips and kept his eyes locked on her.

Don't answer that. A strange voice in the back of Sophie's head whispered to her. Her skin tingled as the room seemed to drop in temperature. Swallowing hard, Sophie tried to steady her nerves despite Mr. Thorn's attempts to frazzle her.

"How was the tea? Do you think it needs more sugar?" Sophie turned to ask.

Sophie could feel an uneasy pang of self-preservation stabbing her. It was almost as if she could hear Nadine's voice whispering in her ear as she returned with a full glass of tea for Clay.

"It was just fine," Mr. Thorn answered as his lips curled at the corners. "If I offended you, I am sorry. It's just been so long since I spoke with Arthur. I was just trying to catch up with him and his life is all."

"I was born in Alexandria, Virginia," Sophie answered, extending the glass. Clay's fingers curled around Sophie's as he took the glass from her and she felt their raw callused strength. A spark of uncertainty shot through her at being alone with such a powerful man. Never in all her life had she felt so unnerved.

"My, you have come a long way, haven't you?" Clay said, lifting the glass to Sophie before bringing it to his lips. Sophie tried not to notice Clay's eyes locked on her as he gulped down the liquid.

"I must say ma'am, this is the best sweet tea I've ever tasted."

"Thank you," Sophie said as she noticed a dark shadow shifting from the corner of her eye. Fear gripped her as panic hit every nerve in her body. With her heart racing, she couldn't help but wonder who was coming around the house.

The front door jerked open causing Sophie to gasp. With wide eyes she stared at Sam. Relief flooded her and drowned the terror.

"Everything alright in here Ms. Sophie?" Sam asked as he turned to face Clay.

"Fine, Sam, thank you."

"Ms. Sophie?" Clay turned and flashed a crooked little smile that rattled her. Sophie had been so careful not to disclose her name and in a single moment that small advantage she had was gone and she knew it.

"That is a very lovely name," Clay said still smirking. Sophie quickly shook her head as her eyes darted to Sam who opened his mouth to interject. Sam clamped his mouth shut as Clay moved around the couch to collect his hat.

"Well," Clay said, shifting his hat on his head. "If you'll excuse me, I'll be on my way. It's clear that Arthur won't be home anytime soon, and I don't want to keep you any longer. I do thank you for the tea."

"I'll inform Mr. Soul you stopped by," Sophie said as she escorted Clay to the front door. Sam stepped back and allowed Clay room to pass before flashing a concern gaze at Sophie.

"Thank you much and you have a lovely day," Clay said as he moved down the steps. Sophie and Sam stayed on the porch, watching Clay mount his horse. With the tip of his hat, Clay tugged the reins and rode off down the way.

"Who was that?" Sam asked turning to Sophie.

"He said he knew Arthur's family from Texas."

"Strange he'd show up out of the blue like this, don't you think?" Sam asked as a cold chill raced down Sophie's spine. She nodded as she tried to calm her frantic heart.

"Stay close tonight, will you Sam?" Sophie asked, looking Sam. His head bobbed as he cleared his throat.

"Arthur told me to look out for you Ms. Sophie, and that is precisely what I intend to do. Even if it means staying in the barn for the week."

"There was just something off about that man, don't you think?"

"Don't know for sure, I wasn't here. But if you say so," Sam said, stepping away from the front door.

"It was just odd how fast he left once he thought I wasn't Arthur's wife."

"Why did you say that?" Sam's frowned as he stared at Sophie.

"Honestly," Sophie crossed her arms over her chest and scanned the dirt road. "It seemed like the right thing to do at the time."

"Well Ms. Sophie, if you need me, just holler."

"Will do Sam and thank you."

Sophie stepped back into the house and scanned the living room. She couldn't help but wonder if Clay had taken anything from the shelves. After giving the room a once over, she realized nothing was missing. Still, the odd and uncomfortable feeling in her stomach remained. She shook her head trying to shake the feeling, but it lingered like bad perfume.

Oh Arthur, please come home soon. I miss you terribly.

* * *

Arthur lifted his eyes to the horizon. The dark purple clouds drifted by the bright orange sun dipping below the horizon. His heart ached as he watched the sun set. Although he sincerely wished that he was back at his ranch with Sophie, he knew he had to be out here in the wilderness with his men.

"Hey boss." Arthur turned as Dave walked up beside him and handed him a tin bowl. "Grub."

"Thanks," Arthur said staring into the bowl. His stomach turned with hunger but after a week of the same beef stew over and over again, he was ready to be back at home with one of Sophie's meals.

"Don't look so glum, we'll be headed back soon enough," Dave said, patting Arthur hard on the back. Arthur bobbed his head as he lifted up the spoon to watch the slop drop back down into the silver container.

"Do you ever get sick of the same food day in and day out?" Arthur asked Dave with his eyebrows raised.

"Never one to complain," Dave said shrugging. "But then again, if I had a pretty lady back home waiting for me who knew how to cook, I'd probably be thinking the same way you are now."

"Is it that obvious?" Arthur asked leaning over the bowl to breathe in the hearty aroma of beef stew.

"Let's just say you've changed since you've gotten married. Last year you could care less what was in that bowl as long as you could eat it."

"And now I'm grumbling about it," Arthur said digging his spoon into the grub.

"It's not that I'm not grateful for the food, I am." He continued.

"Yeah, we get it boss," Dave said. "But does she?"

"What are you talking about?" Arthur asked as he shoved the bland beef stew into his mouth.

"This whole trip you've been expecting something to happen. Almost as if that woman of yours put thoughts into your head that weren't there before. But then we realized that you weren't really concerned about us, but about what's going on back home."

"This is our first round up," Arthur spoke between bites. "She's never had to take care of the ranch alone before."

"And you're worried there may not be a ranch to come home to?" Dave chuckled as he slapped his knee.

"Not quite," Arthur said. "I'm sure everything is just fine."

"Look boss, we all know this is your life. We realize that things have changed for you. But for many of us, things are the same as they have always been. With that being said," Dave looked at his boots before rolling his shoulders back and clearing his throat.

"You said some things to Glenn on the trail today," Dave glanced over his shoulder. Arthur couldn't help but follow his gaze too. His chest tightened as he spied Glenn striking the flint to the fire. Instantly the orange glow from the flames shot up.

"Yeah," Arthur said, shoveling another bite into his mouth.

"You know we are all out here for one reason, to get the cattle to the market so we can feed our families for another year. We do it because we have to, you do it because you love it. That passion though can be intimidating for the newer guys."

"I hear you," Arthur said as he lowered his bowl of stew and nodded.

"Thanks boss," Dave replied as he patted Arthur on the back. Arthur stared out at the herd sipping up the crystal-clear waters of the brook. The sunset made the water look as if it were on fire. Arthur couldn't help but think of Sophie and the first time she lit the stove in the kitchen.

Arthur turned to his cowboys scattered about the area. Some seemed content playing cards while others were cleaning their rifles. He sighed deeply as he looked at them.

"Alright boys," Arthur said moving to the center of their encampment. "Gather around will ya."

The grumbles and chatter didn't go unnoticed as he sat his bowl down on a rock and put his hands on his hips. His men gathered close to him. Arthur's lips pulled up into a crooked grin as he spied Matthew in the middle of shaving, with half a face of hair.

"I'll get to the point since most of you have other things to do right now," Arthur said, clearing his throat.

"Now I know you all have given me all you have. And so far this drive has been successful. Come tomorrow we should have this herd to the buyer, and it will be a grand pay day."

The boys around Arthur cheered and howled at the news. No doubt even Arthur was pleased to know that his trip was nearly over.

"I just want to say thank you all for your hard work this season. We made fast time getting here and I couldn't have done it without each and every one of you." Arthur's eyes lingered on Glenn's for a moment.

"I know I may have been a bit tough on some of you when I shouldn't have been. For that I'm sorry. I don't want y'all to go back home after this season and pray that next year I don't call you." Arthur kept his eyes locked on Glenn as he spoke.

"I should have had more confidence in you as I did previous years. As you all know I've gotten married this year," Arthur said as the boys hollered and hooted around him.

"My fears weren't justified. I'm sorry my mind was on the Mrs. and I took out my frustrations on you."

"We get it boss, you had other things on your mind," Tony said laughing as he nudged Dave with his elbow.

"Still, that shouldn't have been a reason for me to be so harsh," Arthur said. "I promise next year, if you'll ride with me, it will be like all the other years we've taken this trail together. What do you say? Can I count on you for next year too?"

A long pause filled the space and for a moment panic gripped Arthur's heart. He studied his men as each stared at him as if they all kept the same secret.

"Of course you big softy," Dave shouted as he came up to Arthur and patted him on the shoulder. "We're here for you."

"You know you could make me the cattle driver," Glenn said coming up to Arthur and shaking his hand. "That way you can stay home with the little lady."

Arthur shook his head as Glenn batted his eyes to make fun of the women who stayed back. Nodding and trying not to laugh, Arthur bobbed his head.

"I'll consider it," Arthur conceded as the men laughed and cheered before drifting back to their activities.

"You aren't seriously considering Glenn cattle master are you?" Dave asked with wide eyes.

"Are you kidding me?" Arthur said laughing. "If anyone is to be cattle master it's going to be Henry."

Dave and Arthur turned their attention to the thinnest and youngest man to join Arthur's team. Dave slapped Arthur on the back hard enough to drive Arthur forward as he laughed.

"You make my son cattle master and I swear I'll revolt," Dave said.

"Then I guess I'll have to make his father the driver next year," Arthur said, staring at Dave. "After all, it was Henry's father who pulled that calf out of the muck and mire three days ago. We almost lost him, but you were quick and pulled it out just in time."

"Shucks boss," Dave said, lifting his head up. "You'd have done the same."

"That's why I'd consider you for the job," Arthur said with a smile. "You know how to handle the herd and the men."

Dave nodded as he puffed his chest up. "Thanks boss."

Arthur nodded as he turned to catch the last bit of sun dipping below the horizon. The thought of staying home with Sophie filled him with such glee that he felt as if his heart would explode.

I wish you could see this Sophie. I wish you were right here with me so that I could tell you I love you and that I'm not going away ever again.

Arthur's heart fluttered as he realized just how much he missed his wife. It was a longing he had never felt before, one that went beyond a good meal and a kind gesture. It was a feeling that had blossomed into admiration and love.

Arthur closed his eyes as his mind drifted to Sophie's tender oval face. How he longed to press his lips to hers.

You should have kissed her. She was right there on your front porch. You should have taken her in your arms and expressed how you felt right then and there.

Arthur chewed on his lower lip as he kept his eyes locked on the horizon. He didn't care about the men behind him or the cattle resting by the brook. All he could think about was Sophie and how badly he wanted to see her again.

I'm going to do it. The moment I get back I'm going to tell her how much she means to me. I'm going to take her in my arms and lay it all out on the line. It will be her call on whether she wants this marriage to be something more. But I can't do this anymore. I can't pretend that my heart doesn't want her, because I do and it's about time I let her know.

Chapter 18

Arthur's heart drummed in his ears as the ranch came into view. He couldn't believe he'd only been gone a short time, yet it felt like forever. Although his back side ached and he stunk to high heavens, the only thing he wanted to do was see Sophie.

"Come on," Arthur said nudging his spurs into his horse's side. The horse charged forward as he galloped down the dirt road. The log house he'd built with his own two hands slowly drew closer. But once the roof of the barn could be seen over the small mound, Arthur forced his horse to pick up the pace.

"You get me there faster and I'll see to it that you get oats for a month!" Arthur promised as he noticed Sophie beating the rugs as she always did on Tuesday. His heart sputtered and leapt. For a brief moment he wanted to pull back on the reins and hold this moment in his heart.

The sun drifted through the white fluffy clouds and for some reason the entire ranch seemed as if it were cleaner. The grass was a brighter green, the wooden porch looked as if it had just been laid, and there she was in the yard, wiping the sweat from her brow.

"Arthur?" Sophie gasped as she noticed him coming over the hill barreling towards her. She dropped the stick and rushed to the corral. Arthur yanked back on the reins the instant the horse entered the corral and slipped off his horse.

"You're home early," she said as she stepped closer to him. Arthur reached out for her and Sophie moved in closer only to quickly step back. Her nose wrinkled and she tried not to look repulsed by the stench coming off him.

"I know," he said. "I need to clean up."

"Did you not take a bath the entire trip?" Sophie asked as a small giggle escaped her lips.

"When you're out there with a bunch of men, it doesn't really matter," Arthur said.

"I suppose it doesn't," Sophie looked down as a smile played at the corner of her lips.

"I'm sorry," she quickly said, bringing her attention to him. "If I'd had known you'd be home today I would have made your favorite."

"Don't worry, anything you cook will be better than the slop I endured while I was gone."

"You're just saying that."

"No," Arthur shook his head as he looked over at his horse. "I really mean it. I missed your cooking."

Sophie's cheeks turned a brighter red. She looked down to dust her hands on her apron before rolling her shoulders back and lifting her head up.

"I take it everything went fine here while I was gone?" Arthur asked. His arms ached to hold her, but he wanted their reunion to be memorable, and not in a bad way. He moved around her to ensure he stood downwind as they moved towards the house.

"Everything was..."

She hesitated. Why did she hesitate? Did something happen here while I was gone, and she doesn't want to say?

"Let's just say, I didn't have to call on the Davidson's if that's what you were wondering. And with Sam being around, there was no need to ask for help."

"I had forgotten I left him here with you," Arthur said with a quick hesitant smile.

Maybe something didn't happen. I could be paranoid. But she isn't normally so tense. Or maybe I'm the one who is tense? Perhaps I'm reading into her crinkled brow and it's nothing more than the sunlight straining her eyes. Then again, maybe something did happen. Just ask, ask her, and get it out there.

"So nothing out of the ordinary happened then?"

Sophie shook her head and smiled. "No. Although you did receive a visitor while you were gone."

Arthur's heart sank as he stopped at the front door and turned to face Sophie directly.

"A visitor? Did they give you a name?"

"Of course," Sophie said as she reached for the front door and pulled it open. "Clay Thorn. He stated he knew you and your family back in Texas."

Arthur's face crinkled as he wracked his brain to place the name. Out of all the people his path had crossed over the years, he couldn't for the life of him remember a Clay Thorn. He glanced back at Sophie as she walked into the house. Arthur followed and closed the door.

A strong hint of lavender drifted through the house taking Arthur by surprise.

Had it always smelled like this and I just didn't notice? Or was this her doing?

A smile drifted over Arthur's lips as the sound of his boots clapping the hard wood floor filled the silence. He cleared his throat as he looked about the tidy living room. It appeared cleaner than before. The books seemed straighter and the vases were filled with fresh flowers.

"You certain that was his name?" Arthur asked.

"Oh yes," Sophie answered as she moved to the kitchen. For a brief moment she vanished from Arthur's sight and his heart plummeted. Of all the weeks he spent on the trail, he couldn't shake his feelings for her. And now that he saw her, he didn't want to miss a moment.

Before Arthur could step into the kitchen, Sophie emerged with a tall glass of tea and a beautiful smile that lit up the room.

"I have a confession," Sophie said, handing him the glass. "I allowed Clay into the house. He said he was an old friend and I didn't want to be rude. Was that okay?"

Arthur pulled a long deep gulp and shook his head. Between seeing Sophie, and coming home to find someone visited, Arthur wasn't sure how to feel. His emotions were scattered like grains to the wind.

"Maybe if you told me how this man looked like, it might jog my memory," Arthur said as he moved around the couch and leaned against the kitchen door frame. Although he wanted to sit beside Sophie, he'd been in the saddle for so long, it hurt just to think about sitting.

"Well," Sophie said as she took a seat on the couch. Arthur watched as she brushed out the wrinkles in her skirt before meeting his gaze. "He had shaggy black hair that came to about his chin. Long sideburns." Arthur watched as Sophie brushed her fingertips down the side of her face as she described him.

"Mr. Thorn had a thick lower lip, but a thin upper lip and his face was clean shaved. He looked very respectable in his blue buttoned shirt. But what really stood out were his eyes."

Arthur could feel his blood draining from his body as he stared at Sophie.

Don't say blue, please, don't say blue.

"They were a stark blue. Almost like the way water looks when it freezes on a lake," Sophie said as Arthur straightened up and rushed to the window.

"Are you alright?" Sophie asked as she watched her husband dart about the room.

"He was here?" Arthur gasped before whipping his head back to Sophie.

"Yes," Sophie said, rising to her feet. "Do you know him? Was it wrong of me to let him in?"

"Yes," Arthur snapped before shaking his head. "No. You didn't know."

How could she know? I have kept the truth from her to protect her from my past, but it is chasing her down just as surely as it has been chasing me.

"Did he want anything?" Arthur asked, setting the glass down on the table before he rushed to Sophie's side. She shook her head.

"No. He didn't even leave a message for you. Although, it was a strange visit."

"Why?" Arthur's eyes widened as he tried to find any clues in Sophie's expression as to what happened while he was gone.

"He showed up out of nowhere and started asking questions that seemed random. He wanted to know where I came from and how long I had been here. Then Sam came to check in on me and the instant he learned my name, he left. It was a very strange visit."

"Was there anything else that happened?"

"No," Sophie said glancing down. Arthur could see the regret and shame in her eyes as she pressed her lips into a tight line.

"I shouldn't have let him in. But I didn't want to be rude."

"Don't," Arthur said holding her. "You did the right thing, and nothing happened right? So what is there to worry about?"

"He made me feel awkward, like he was trying to pry news from me that was none of his business."

"Sophie," Arthur held her by the shoulders and forced her eyes to meet his. "You did the right thing. Better than having to fire the gun in fact." Arthur forced a smile on his face as he stared at his wife.

"You never fail to amaze me," he said, fighting every instinct to lean down and press his lips to hers.

"Arthur," Sophie tried to smile back at him as she wrinkled her nose. "As much as I appreciate your kind words, you really do smell. Perhaps we can talk more after you've freshened up a bit?"

Arthur released his grip on Sophie and nodded. "Of course."

Sophie stood in the middle of the living room as Arthur headed towards the kitchen. His heart sputtered as his nerves rattled.

Surely it can't be a coincidence he'd show up while I was gone. What if he was scoping out my house to find a way in? He's made the first move, now I have to be ready for the next one.

Arthur's heart sank as he pulled in quick ragged breaths. His mouth went dry as he thought of Randal in his house. Every step he took felt heavy as scenarios played in his head.

He could have killed her. What if she had told him she was my wife? Would I have come home to...

Arthur dropped his head as he fought back the urge to scream. He couldn't think about the what ifs. All he could think of was how clever his wife was to misdirect the stranger and keep herself distant from him as much as possible.

Chewing on his lower lip, Arthur turned as he heard the door close. He moved slowly to the window to see Sophie heading to the pump with a bucket in her hand.

You really are the most loyal person I've ever known.

Arthur watched as she pumped the water and filled up the bucket. He pushed all negative thoughts from his mind and stole a moment to enjoy her. For the past few weeks she had been the only thing on his mind, the only reason he rode so hard to get back.

I can't lose you. I won't. I'll protect you, I swear it. But if Randal was here, he's up to something and I need to know what game he is playing.

*   *   *

Dear Diary,

I have to admit, I was thrilled to see Arthur today. He'd returned a day early which was a blessing if you ask me. These past few weeks have been hard as you well know. My mind has been wrought with worry about him. I've heard the tales of cowboys dying on these kinds of things and each day my heart ached a bit more.

But I don't have to worry about those things anymore, for he's come home, and my heart is overflowing with happiness. I never knew how much I missed him until he was gone.

He looked different today. The hard line in his forehead that I've been accustomed to seeing was gone. It was as if all his worries vanished the instant he returned home. I can't help but wonder if he was concerned for me while he was away. He did after all leave Sam behind to watch over things as well as leave his best rifle at the door. Still, I saw the relief in his eyes when he saw me and I have to admit, I felt the same for him.

It was a strange reunion though. The electricity between us feels more potent than ever before. I found myself fighting every second not to take him into my arms and kiss him. My lips yearned to touch his and my hands twitched to reach out and feel him. For a moment I wondered if what I was seeing wasn't an illusion when he first came home.

But then when his fingers curled around my shoulders and held me close, every part of me jumped for joy. I shouldn't want him like this. I shouldn't crave such things, but I do. I love my husband, but how can I say that to him when he expects something so different from me?

Ever since the attack in town, I've found myself gravitating towards him. And although the cattle drive separated us for a moment, I feel we are closer than ever before. So why do I feel so ashamed?

Perhaps I shouldn't have confessed to him of my betrayal to his family friend. Still, there was a warning in my gut that I couldn't ignore or shake. Arthur swears to me that I did the right thing by lying, but how can telling a lie be the right thing to do?

There was no denying the fact Arthur looked rather disturbed by Mr. Thorn's arrival. Why, his face turned as white as the sheets I had hanging to dry. There was something about the concern in Arthur's eyes and the tightness of his fingers in my arms that still worries me. Should I have not said what I did?

It is one of those things that -

Sophie glanced up from her small desk and immediately dropped her pen. Her heart sank into her stomach as a scream roared out of her open mouth, "FIRE!"

Sophie raced from her desk to the bedroom door and threw it open. There was no time to think about her modesty. She flew down the hallway and out the front door in her night gown.

"Arthur quick!" she shouted as she grabbed the bucket and scrambled to get to the watering pump. It seemed as if it took forever for the water to start flowing into the bucket. Only when she had the first bucket filled did she notice Arthur at the barn doors.

Where was Sam? Please don't let him be in the barn too.

A huge billow of black smoke poured out of the barn as the animals trapped inside pleaded to get out. Sophie's heart drummed and banged around in her chest as she pushed down on the pump once more and grabbed the bucket of water.

"You just keep pumping the water," Arthur demanded, collecting the bucket from her as she went to toss the water on the flames.

"Don't stop till we get this put out, do you understand?" Arthur's voice was quick and stern, but Sophie wasn't about to argue. She darted back to the watering pump and forced a second bucket under the spout to fill it up.

"What's going on?" Sam asked, rushing from around the house. Sophie looked over her shoulder to see his eyes widen at the sight of the fire licking the barn. Relief slammed against her as she tossed a bucket to Sam's eager arms.

"Quick, get the animals to the corral," Arthur said as he exchanged an empty bucket for Sophie's full one.

Sophie's heart pounded as she focused on her job of pumping the water.

Just keep pumping the water.

Her arms burned from the exertion, but she wasn't about to stop. Their livelihood depended on getting control of the fire and she wouldn't be the weak link. Sophie pushed down on the pump and watched the water flow into the bucket.

The crackle of the wood burning up frightened her. She couldn't help but worry about the roof coming down on Arthur as he pulled the last horse from the smoky barn.

"That's all the animals," Arthur noted, grabbing the bucket from under the spout. Sophie pulled in deep breaths as she brushed her arm over her forehead. Arthur pulled back the bucket and let it fly through the air. The water crashed against the flames, extinguishing them.

"Is everyone alright?" Arthur inquired turning to look at Sophie. She nodded as she dropped to the ground, spent.

"How did this happen?" Sam asked, plunging his bucket into the stock tank at the corral. Arthur shook his head and shrugged.

"Did we leave a lamp on and one of the animals kicked it?" Arthur asked as Sophie stared at her black hands.

"Don't think so boss," Sam said.

Arthur moved to Sophie and leaned down to help her to her feet. "Are you alright?"

"I think so," Sophie said as she instinctively threw her arms around his neck and held him close. The fear that swelled in her released as Arthur curled his arms around her body. The comfort she felt was more than she expected.

Suddenly, what she was wearing dawned on her and she pulled away from him. Her cheeks turned crimson as she turned her head in embarrassment.

"I should," Sophie said as she tried to cover herself with her arms.

"Yes, of course," Arthur cleared his throat and turned his head to glare at Sam.

A lump formed in Sophie's throat as she straightened her shoulders back and turned towards the house. In the shadows of the trees near the barn, she couldn't help but notice a dark figure lurking between the shadows and the light. Her heart stopped as did she.

"Arthur," Sophie whispered, hoping her voice was still loud enough for him to hear.

Arthur turned his head to her. Just as his mouth opened to speak, Sophie lost sight of the shadowy figure and stepped back.

"I thought," Sophie said, pointing to the house. "There is someone there."

"What? Where?" Arthur moved to her side immediately and curled his hands around her shoulders.

"Just over there, next to the house. I swear I saw something," Sophie said, trying to keep her voice down so as not to give away any suspicion.

"Sam," Arthur's voice was scratchy and low but it was enough to cause Sam's head to pop up. Arthur tossed a pitchfork to Sam and pointed to the opposite side of the house. Sophie watched Sam nod once and take off towards the shadows.

"Get inside," Arthur said. "And don't come out until I say so, do you understand?"

Sophie's could feel every panicked heartbeat throughout her body as she hurried to the house. Chewing on her lower lip and with her eyes peeled she prayed for Arthur's safety.

This can't be happening. I just got him back.

She stood by the window holding her breath. Every second felt like an eternity. Only when she noticed Arthur coming back around the other side with Sam did she exhale. Although Arthur didn't give her all clear, she knew there was no way she would stay in the dark house alone. She needed to be next to Arthur.

"Anything?" Sophie asked, stepping out onto the porch.

"Get back inside," Arthur ordered, pointing to her as if she was a child that needed to be scolded. "I don't know if it's safe for you to be out here."

"But," Sophie said as the horses started to neigh and whinny in the corral. Sophie cupped her hands to her mouth as the lot of them reared up and barreled out of the gate.

"Stop them," Arthur shouted to Sam as the herd stomped and stampeded out of the gated corral.

Sam darted to the left as Arthur took to the right of the corral. By the time the men met up, half the herd was racing down the way. To Sophie's eyes they looked like black shadows against the dark horizon.

Before anymore horses could escape, Sam slammed the gate close trapping the rest of the herd. With her nerves rattling and her mind racing, Sophie tried to keep her wits about her.

"Who opened the gate?" Sophie asked

"It doesn't matter right now. We need to get the other horses back before they reach the Davidson's," Arthur said as he jumped over the fence and mounted the black mare trapped in the corral.

"Open the gate," Arthur ordered as Sophie's eyes, watching him take off after the horses.

"Sophie, get yourself inside and arm yourself. The gun is still loaded in the corner by the door. I want you to get it and have it ready just in case," Arthur said as Sam ran to the side of the house and came back with a rope.

"Something awfully strange is going on here and I wouldn't want to see you hurt," he said. Sophie pressed her lips into a tight line and nodded as she tried to find Arthur on the horizon. Just as Sophie pulled open the front door to step inside, Sam had disappeared into the night on foot.

Suddenly Sophie didn't feel so secure and safe. Not even the darkness seemed to cloak her insecurities. Racing to the front door, she slid inside and grabbed the gun. Racking a bullet into the barrel, she strained her eyes to see through the veil of night. Although she couldn't see the shadowy figure, she knew whoever it was, was still out there somewhere in the darkness. Instantly, her mind drifted to Arthur. With her heart pounding in her ears, she prayed.

Please be okay. Please.

She waited by the window and peered out into the night. Her heart drummed in her ears as she kept a keen eye out for Arthur. With her palms getting moist and her knees feeling as if they were about to buckle, she spied Arthur coming up over the hill.

Thank God.

Sophie rushed to the door and pried it open. The night air kissed her face as she wrapped her arms around her body. All the events of the evening had her on edge, but seeing Arthur relaxed the stress building in her shoulders. Lowering the barrel to the floor, she stepped out of the house and down the steps. She paused at the fence of the corral, straining her eyes to see better.

"Where are the horses? Do you need help?" she called out.

"Funny, I was going to ask you the same thing."

That's not Arthur.

Panic swept through Sophie as she stepped back, hoping to make it back inside before Clay approached. But it was too late, his black hair and icy blue eyes startled her.

"Mr. Thorn," Sophie said trying to swallow the fear that lumped in her throat. The gun in her hands seemed heavier and slick from her sweaty palms. "What brings you to these parts so late?"

"Well ma'am, I saw the smoke and thought of you being out here all by your lonesome. Wanted to make sure you were alright," Clay said with a wicked grin stretching across his face.

"I'm fine thank you," Sophie said, squeezing her arms a bit tighter around her body.

"As I can see," Clay said, looking at the blackened part of the barn.

"Arthur will be back momentarily," Sophie told him, stealing a step back towards the open door. She watched as Clay slipped off his horse and moved towards her swiftly.

"I do hope so," he said, pulling his hat off his head. "There are things he and I need to discuss."

Chapter 19

Wiping the sweat from his forehead, he double and triple checked the lock on the fence as Sam drove the horses back into the corral. Swiftly, he closed off the fence and exhaled. He couldn't believe everything had gone wrong in one night.

"Good work," Arthur said, dipping his head to Sam. "You were quick on your feet and even faster with that to rope the horses. We sure did miss you on the cattle drive this year."

"Arthur." Sophie's voice was barely a whisper and so soft that for a moment Arthur wondered if he had heard her at all.

"Arthur," her voice was a bit louder making it impossible for Arthur not to notice the panic behind the syllables. He turned his head to the direction of Sophie's voice. Instantly his eyes popped as he slipped off his horse and threw his hands up.

"Sophie, step away from him," Arthur said, keeping his eyes locked on the tall man standing near the steps beside his wife and holding her gun.

"I don't think so." In a flash, the man's fingers curled around Sophie's arm holding her beside him. Panic gripped Arthur's heart as he noticed the terror in Sophie's eyes.

"What are you doing here Randal?" Arthur asked, moving slowly towards the porch.

"And here I thought you'd forgotten all about little old me," Randal said with a crooked grin. Sophie's eyes widened as she looked at Randal. Her mouth dropped and she shook her head.

"What do you want?" Arthur asked as he kept his eyes locked on the man holding his wife hostage.

"You never wrote, you never stopped by to say hi. So, I thought I'd come out here and see how you were doing. We are after all old pals, are we not?" Randal pulled Sophie to his body. Arthur could see her revulsion as Sophie tried to free herself but couldn't.

A lump formed in the back of Arthur's throat as he contemplated the different scenarios. No doubt Randal could kill Sophie right then and there and never think twice about it. But by the way Randal's eye twitched, Arthur realized there was something more the outlaw wanted.

"Let my wife go and we can sit down and chat," Arthur said, holding his hands up to show he was unarmed.

"Don't think so," Randal said. "You see, my boys were talking, and they told me you got yourself a little wife." Randal leaned in closer to Sophie and for a split second took his eyes off Arthur to scan Sophie's tiny frame. Suddenly it became very clear what Sophie was wearing and it pained him to see her under Randal's hold.

Stay calm Sophie. Just stay calm. I'm right here. I swear I'll ram him into the window before I let him do anything to you.

"So, I thought I'd come out here to see for myself if the rumors were true." Randal rattled Sophie like a rag doll as he spoke. "I have to say though, I'm impressed with you Arthur. I had expected the fire to consume more than what it did."

"You set the fire?" Sophie gasped, looking at Randal with shock all over her face.

"Oh honey, it was the least I could do," Randal drawled, reaching up to squeeze her cheeks together.

"Honestly, I expected it to burn completely to the ground. But you know what? Arthur here is a really good carpenter.

Turns out he built himself a pretty stable barn. I can only imagine that the house will be constructed just as good."

A sadistic grin shifted over Randal's lips as his eyes widened. Arthur had seen the look plastered on Randal's face many times, always before he executed a plan.

"Is that what you're going to do then?" Arthur asked, trying to inch his way closer to the porch to get in reach of Sophie. "You going to set my house on fire?"

Randal laughed as he shook his head and scratched his chin with his free hand. "You know, I did think about that. In fact, I thought of a lot of ways I'd kill you if I ever got a chance. You know what I came to realize though?"

Arthur shook his head as he looked at Sophie. He could feel knots tying him up in the pit of his stomach. This was all his fault. His worst nightmare was happening right now and there wasn't a thing he could do.

"Killing you would be far too easy. You put me through hell, Arthur," Randal said as he grabbed Sophie's face with one hand. "I figured it would be best to give you back what you gave me. An eye for an eye and all."

"And just how are you going to do that?" Arthur asked as he felt the prick of terror enter him. All Arthur could see was Sophie's lifeless body in Randal's arms. The mere thought of it made him cold.

"I'm going to take everything from you," Randal said. "Every little thing you value in this life, I'm going to snatch it out from under you. Every bit of happiness you've built for yourself, I'm going to turn it into mire. Your life will be the hell that I had."

"You can try," Arthur said, locking his eyes on Sophie. Terror filled her eyes, but there was something else Arthur noticed in the dead of night that sparkled. Sophie raised her knee into the air and slammed the heel of her boot into Randal's foot. Instantly Randal's grip on her loosened and she bolted to Arthur.

"You're going to pay for that," Randal hissed as he stepped back.

"I'm sure I am," Arthur said as he wrapped his arms around Sophie and held her to him.

"Don't think I haven't noticed the kind of life you've built for yourself here in Tennessee. It's almost identical to the one you had in Texas," Randal taunted as he paced the length of the porch.

"I'd be careful what you say next," Arthur warned as he clung to Sophie.

"Or what? You think that doofus of a ranch hand is going to help you?" Randal laughed. Arthur and Sophie's heads whipped around as the laughter echoed behind them.

Sophie gasped as she noticed two men holding Sam by the arms.

"That's the men from town. The ones who..." Sophie curled her head into Arthur's shoulder trying not to look at them. It didn't take Arthur long to put two and two together. Those were the men that caused his wife all those restless nights.

"You'd think I hit a nerve," Randal said, skipping down the steps. "But I must say Arthur," Randal stopped inches from Arthur and glared at him.

"You have me envious. Turns out you have everything I ever wanted. You have the young wife, countless cattle, a nice homestead, yep, everything I ever wanted. I bet you're even respected in town, aren't you?" Randal said, glaring into Arthur's eyes.

"I wonder how the townsfolk would see you if they knew you rode with me. Huh, I bet they wouldn't be so keen on you. Chances are people wouldn't want to buy your livestock anymore either seeing as how they could all be stolen."

"Don't listen to him," Sophie said as she looked at Arthur. "He doesn't know this town like we do."

"Oh darling, you'd put your faith in people? You really are naive," Randal said as he leaned in fast, startling her. Arthur could feel her jump in his arms as Randal moved back and laughed at her.

"Just like you huh?" Arthur countered as he rolled his shoulders back. "You did after all let someone like me into your gang. Turns out you were just as gullible and naive."

"Not anymore," Randal snapped. Arthur sucked in a quick breath as Randal ran his fingers through his hair and shook his body as if he'd stepped into spider webs.

"That does pose a question though," Randal said as his lips twitched. "Why did you want to be in my gang? You and me, we were close. Yet, you betrayed me, why?"

"Does it matter?" Arthur asked as his eyes drifted from Randal to Sam and back again.

"Tell me why you did it," Randal said, lifting his hand up. Sam's eyes widened as Randal's men drew their blades from their sides and rested the sharp knife to Sam's throat.

"Seven years ago you were in Texas, were you not?" Arthur asked as he spat the words at Randal.

"Possibly," Randal said as he circled Arthur and Sophie.

"You raided a ranch in El Paso," Arthur continued as he tried to keep his distance from Randal.

"What of it? I've pulled off many raids and heists," Randal confessed as he stopped circling and picked at his teeth unamused.

"That ranch you raided belonged to my parents," Arthur said lifting his chin up. "You slaughtered them as if they were animals and left them there for the vultures. I had to come back to find them like you left them," Arthur could feel his voice quaking as he spoke. If Sophie wasn't in his arms, he knew his body would be trembling.

It took all he had not to tackle Randal right then and there. But Arthur knew Sam's life was at stake and he wasn't about to have Sam's blood on his hands, not when he still could save him.

Randal's eyes widened as his mouth popped open. Slowly he cocked his head to the left and stared at Arthur dumbstruck. Even Arthur was surprised by Randal's expression. But as quickly as the awe came, it was gone.

"I rode with you so that I could one day kill you," Arthur said, allowing the words to come out like venom.

"But you didn't," Randal sneered with his lips twitching. "You don't have the spine for it."

"You have no idea what I'm capable of doing," Arthur said as he released Sophie and stepped between her and Randal. "If you really want to find out whether or not I got what it takes to put you six feet under, stick around."

"You're bluffing," Randal laughed as he shook his head.

"You really want to find out?" Arthur said with such conviction that the words startled him.

"I think you're just as yellow now as you were then," Randal drawled as his eyes flickered to the two men by the corral holding Sam back. With a single flick of his head, the men dropped Sam.

"What is it you want Randal?" Arthur asked. "You want my cattle? My land? What?"

"Revenge," Randal said through clenched teeth. "I know you sold me out. It was because of you I couldn't take care of my mother. My mother died while I was locked up. She may not have, if I'd been around to take care of her. So here we are, thanks to a stack of cash and Bergen's confession. We now have something in common seeing as how we've both lost people precious to us," Randal paused to wink at Sophie. She stepped behind Arthur and clung to him.

"But mark my words, I'm here to take all that I can from you," Randal said. "Bit by bit, what's yours will soon be mine."

"You can try," Arthur said.

"Oh, I don't need to try," Randal said, glaring maliciously at Sophie. "You won't even know I'm gunning for you until it's too late. But I suggest if you want me to steer clear of that pretty little wife of yours and keep your secret, you'll leave the law out of this."

"And if I don't?" Arthur challenged as he watched Randal snap his fingers.

"Let's just say I can get pretty creative with a blade, if you remember," Randal said laughing as he walked to the tree line.

Arthur couldn't feel anything but cold. Every fiber in his body trembled as he watched Randal mount the dark steed lurking in the shadows. Quickly he turned to Sophie and cupped his hands to her face.

"Are you alright?" he asked, holding her gaze. Tears filled her eyes as she reached up and placed her hands on his.

"Don't you worry," Arthur reassured her as he pressed his forehead to hers. "I won't let anything happen."

"Nor will I Miss Sophie," Sam added, coming up next to them. "That man has just messed with the wrong ranch."

"No," Arthur said, shaking his head and looking at Sam. "Don't do anything. I don't want to provoke him. He's dangerous and there's no telling what he has up his sleeve."

*   *   *

"Let's get you inside."

Sophie couldn't stop her body from trembling as Arthur guided her back into the house. Every muscle in her body strained and tightened as she glanced over her shoulder to the road.

"He's here," Sophie managed to say as they stepped into the comfort of their living room.

"Yes," Arthur said as he brought her to the couch. Looking at her hands, Sophie tried to feel them, but she couldn't. They trembled like the last leaf on the maple tree before the frost.

"What are we going to do?" Sophie asked as she watched Arthur pull the blanket out of the closet and rush to throw it over her shoulders.

"Nothing," Arthur said. "We can't do anything. Randal is sick and demented. If he suspects we've gone to the authorities, all hell will break loose and I can't let that happen."

"Am I in danger?" Sophie asked, pulling the blanket over her shoulders, and bundling into it.

"We all are if we don't play his game."

"Arthur." Sophie's head whipped to the door as her eyes widened with fright. Relief crashed against her as she noticed Sam standing in the doorway.

"Sophie," Arthur grabbed her by the hands and cocked his head to force her to look at him. "I will be right outside."

Sophie nodded as she tried to wrap her head around all that had happened in such a short time. Swallowing hard she kept her eyes locked on Arthur as he stepped out of the house to speak to Sam.

You're fine. Everything will be fine. There is nothing to worry about. Arthur will come up with some plan, some way to keep Randal in check.

Sophie nodded as she looked about the house. Fear and panic stole her nerves.

I let him into the house. He was in my home. He stood right there.

Sophie scrambled to get up as if some part of Randal remained in her home. Shoving the blanket off her shoulders, she rushed to the kitchen. The urge to clean consumed her as she grabbed a bucket and the rag. Quickly she bolted from the kitchen to the front and pulled open the door with the bucket in hand.

"Sophie?" Arthur's voice was strained as she walked past him.

"What are you doing?"

"He was in our house," Sophie said with wild eyes. "I have to clean. I have to make sure every scrap of him is gone."

"Sophie," Arthur raced to her side and grabbed her by the arms. "Randal is gone. You watched him leave."

"No, he's here," Sophie said as waves of panic pounded against her. She whipped her head to the watering pump and tried to free herself from Arthur's grasp.

"Let her go," Sam said, grabbing Arthur's shoulder. "She needs to cope in her own way."

Suddenly she was free. No one held her back. Sophie scrambled to the watering pump and pumped the lever frantically. The water splashed into the bucket. Tears swelled in her eyes as she grabbed the handle and moved back to the porch with determination where Randal held her captive.

Sophie paused and scanned the area. Her heart felt heavier than it ever had before. Dropping to her knees, she plunged her hands into the bucket and pulled out the rag. The water splashed about the floor as she scrubbed until her hands were raw.

"Sophie?" Arthur's voice startled her as she glanced over her shoulder. His hands were raised in the air as he moved to her side so slowly.

"He was right here," Sophie said, scrubbing with all she had.

"But he's not there anymore," Arthur said, lowering himself to her side. Arthur looked at Sam briefly. Sam nodded and stepped away slowly before turning and walking away to give them privacy.

"I'm scared," Sophie said, allowing the tears to spill down her cheeks.

"I know," Arthur agreed, reaching his hand out to hers and gently stopping her from cleaning. "This is my fault, my past coming back to haunt us. For that I am sorry. Maybe we should get you on the next train. Get you as far from here as possible. I couldn't live with myself if Randal ever did anything to you."

"I'm not leaving you," Sophie scowled. "What kind of person would that make me if I left my husband when he needed me the most?"

"I can't lose you, Sophie," Arthur said, squeezing her fingers. "If Randal did anything to you it would be on me."

"And if I left you to take care of him alone? He could kill you."

"He won't. You heard him. He wants to take everything from me and that includes you." Arthur's hand slipped off Sophie's and rested on his knee.

"Arthur, he tracked you here," Sophie said. "What makes you think he won't try and find me if I left? He has men who could follow me. And then what? I'm off in some other place away from you and you'd never know they got to me. Is that how you want to live?"

"No," Arthur agreed, shaking his head. "But I don't want you going into town alone anymore. At least not while Randal is here."

"Fair enough," Sophie said. Her eyes drifted to the puddle of water on the floor. She knew it was a funny thing to think she could clean away the grime that stained her from the events, but she had to try.

"Leave it," Arthur said as if he already knew what she was thinking. "We'll clean tomorrow."

"But," Sophie started to protest. She looked at Arthur who shook his head and cupped his arms around her frail body. Sophie curled her arms around his neck as he hoisted her off the ground.

"Tomorrow," Arthur said, carrying her into the hallway.

Sophie kept her eyes locked on him as he moved into her bedroom and sat her carefully on the bed. The wood moaned under her weight but the blanket and pillows felt like a dream.

"Please don't go," Sophie said, reaching for Arthur as he turned his back to her. "I'm afraid when I close my eyes I'll see them. Stay with me tonight?"

The silence in the room weighed heavily on Sophie. All she could see was Arthur's back as his hands balled into little fists before releasing. He turned and glanced over his shoulder. A soft tender smile tugged at the corner of his lips as he nodded.

"Please try and get some sleep," he pleaded, moving to the sitting chair in the corner of her room.

"I will if you will," Sophie answered, trying to mimic the smile that she saw on his face.

"You've been through a lot tonight," Arthur said, pulling the chair closer to the bed before sitting.

"Thank you," Sophie said, pulling back the blankets and shoving her legs between the mattress and the sheets.

"It's because of me you're in this mess," Arthur sadly shook his head.

"Don't do that," Sophie whispered, smoothing out the blanket. "You don't get to take the blame for Randal tormenting us tonight."

Arthur's jaw tightened and his eyes shifted to the floor. Sophie snuggled down into the pillows and tried to calm her frantic mind. Just knowing Arthur was next to her seemed to ease her fears, but in the back of her subconscious she knew the nightmares would stab at her.

Slowly sleep over came her. Flashes of Randal and his men drifted between the darkness of her dreams. In the vastness of her sleep, glimmers of Nadine interrupted her nightmare. Sophie shot out of bed gasping for air.

"Sophie?" Arthur's voice was distant and hoarse.

"Just a dream," she answered, searching the dark room for his face.

Sophie reached through the space. Arthur's rough callous hands curled around hers easing her fears. She didn't hesitate to pull him towards her. Only when she felt his body beside hers did she exhale.

Arthur ran his hand over the top of her head as she nestled into the nook of his arm. "Rest, I've got you."

Chapter 20

The gentle chirping aroused Arthur. His eyes fluttered open to find Sophie still nuzzled into his chest sound asleep. A gentle smile drifted over his lips.

You are so beautiful. I have to be the luckiest man on the planet to have you. How I wish I could tell you just how much you mean to me.

Arthur carefully leaned down and pressed his lips to her forehead. Sophie moaned and snuggled deeper into his embrace. The sunlight poured into the room causing her hair to look as if it were made of gold. He breathed in deeply. Arthur's fingers brushed through Sophie's hair and he couldn't help but feel overwhelmed in the moment.

I wish I could wake up like this with you all the time. And I know you said you wanted a marriage of convenience, but can't you see what you are doing to me? Don't you know how much I want to make you happy and be with you always?

I'm sorry my love for everything I've put you through. Randal is my responsibility, not yours. Yet, here you are. Still beside me.

Arthur's heart trembled and quaked in his chest as the last brick he'd placed around his heart tumbled and crashed. There was nothing left for him to hold on to and he knew it.

"I love you Sophie." His voice was barely a whisper but there it was out in the open. Arthur couldn't believe the pressure and weight of the words that drifted out of his mouth. Exhaling, he stared at Sophie still fast asleep in his arms and held her tighter.

Slowly, Sophie began to stir as the light drifted to her eyes and pulled her out of her slumber. Arthur smiled at her as he watched her rub the sleep from her eyes.

"Morning," she mumbled with a yawn. She stretched out, letting all her aches and worries slip off her.

"Good morning," Arthur said. Sophie shot up out of bed with wild eyes. For a brief moment Arthur noticed the panic in her gaze.

"You're fine," he said, scooting to the head board. "There's no one here but you and me."

"The chores," Sophie said glancing down to see her nightgown covered in soot. Quickly she pulled the covers up to her chest, shocked to find Arthur in her bed beside her.

"I figured you and I could sleep in today. We had quite the night wouldn't you say?" Arthur smiled at her as the shock on her face slowly faded.

"It wasn't a dream?" Sophie's lower lip trembled. Arthur reached out for her and pulled her into his arms.

"I'm afraid it wasn't."

"And the barn?"

"As far as I know it's still standing. I am going to have to go into town to pick up supplies to get it fixed."

"I was afraid of that," Sophie said, feeling the tension in her shoulders.

"You don't have to go with me if you don't want to," Arthur said, holding her tighter. He couldn't help but wonder if he would be able to leave her here alone ever again. With no way of knowing if Randal was waiting for him to leave, Arthur couldn't take the chance.

"Then again, maybe it would be best if we stuck together," Arthur said back tracking. "I don't want to leave you alone."

"And I don't want to be alone. I don't care if the rifle is loaded by the door or not," Sophie said. "But can't you send someone else to go in your stead? Sam, I'm sure, wouldn't mind and then you can stay here with me."

"Sophie, I know you're frightened. By the dreams you had last night -"

"What did you hear?" Sophie gasped, looking up at him with wild fearful eyes.

"You were mumbling about the men from town and a bit about your sister," Arthur answered, keeping a tight grip on Sophie. "Those things were to be expected after the night we had. But we can't let Randal keep us prisoners in our own home. We have to show him that we aren't scared of him."

"Arthur," Sophie pulled the covers up and shook her head. "I don't know if I can do that."

"I will be right here with you the whole time. There is no way I am ever going to let that man touch you again."

Sophie's head bobbed and her gaze drifted further and further away like she was reaching for a thought that wouldn't come to her. Arthur studied her as her chest rose and then fell.

"You're right," she said finally. "We can't live in fear. We can't let him get to us. The best thing for us to do is fix the barn and move on with our lives."

"I will be right beside you," Arthur promised. He gave her one last squeeze around the shoulders before throwing his feet over the edge of the bed.

"Arthur," Sophie's voice was small and faint, but he paused to look at her. "Thank you for sleeping with me last night."

Anytime. Of course, don't you know I'd do anything for you?

He knew the words would never escape his lips. After all, she had only come out West because she needed a home, not because she needed him. Yet, here he was, head over heels for her and unable to tell her how he really felt about her.

Just tell her how you feel. If there was a time to do it, now would be it.

With a faint smile, he bobbed his head. Arthur reached down and grabbed his boots from beside her bed. The floorboards moaned as he walked to the door.

"Get yourself ready," he said over his shoulder. "We'll head out when you're dressed."

"What of breakfast?" Sophie asked.

"I'll just have a bit of bread, you don't need to do anything fancy for me today."

Arthur pulled open the door and stepped out into the hallway. His heart ached and fluttered as he closed the door behind him. It took all his strength to leave her alone in the room, but he knew if he was going to move on with his life, it would mean giving Sophie her space.

"If you need me," Arthur said in a loud voice. "Just holler."

"Will do," came the muffled reply as he made his way to his bedroom to change. The smell of smoke still lingered on his clothes reminding him of the disaster waiting for him outside.

Arthur reached his bedroom door and paused. *No sense in changing if I'm just going to get dirty again. Might as well see the damage first.*

Arthur pivoted on his heels and strolled back down the hallway. He moved to the front door and pulled it open. Closing his eyes he sucked in a deep breath. The morning air was crisp and clean with no hint of smoke. Slowly, he opened his eyes and stared at the mess before him.

"Not as bad as I thought," he said out loud. The side of the barn was pitch black from the ground to the roof. But the damage was only in one spot.

He shook his head and put his hands on his hips. *Thank God for Sophie. If she hadn't seen it when she did, it could have been a heck of a lot worse.*

Arthur moved down the steps as the horses and goats welcomed him. For a moment he wondered if he should count the animals. A faint suspicion that Randal had stolen some of them last night flickered through his mind but was quickly gone as he did a head count.

"Not too bad eh boss?" Sam's voice was welcoming. Arthur turned to find his ranch hand propped against the oak tree on the side of the house. Sam stood and moved to Arthur's side.

"I took the liberty of sticking around last night just in case they decided to come back," Sam said as he slipped his knife into the holster at his side.

"Thanks Sam," Arthur said, patting him on the shoulder. "Looks like we got our work cut out for us today, doesn't it?"

"Sure does boss," Sam said pressing his lips into a tight line. "But honestly, I'm more concerned with Miss Sophie. How's she holding up?"

"I think she'll be just fine," Arthur said as he allowed his mind and his eyes to drift to her bedroom window.

"You sure about that?" Sam asked, keeping his attention on the barn.

"Only time will tell," Arthur said. "For now, we just got to focus on the little things we do have control over. Like fixing the barn and getting this place back to the way it was."

"Yes sir," Sam nodded. Arthur turned his head to the animals in the corral and to the barn. It wouldn't take them long to fix the place up again, but Arthur couldn't help but wonder if Sophie would ever be the same again. Deep down, Arthur knew no matter what, he'd be right there with her the whole time, just as she was for him. And no matter what happened, he would never leave her side.

* * *

Sophie pulled off her night gown and formed it into a ball. She didn't want to think about the events of last night. All she wanted to do was forget the whole thing had ever happened. Still, she couldn't help but be grateful, after all, if it wasn't for the terrors of last night, Arthur would have just gone to bed alone.

A smile played on Sophie's lips. Thoughts of Arthur's arms around her, comforting her, made her heart flutter and her cheeks burn. There was no denying the fact that she wished she could stay that way forever.

"Sophie?" the rapping on the door startled her. She scrambled to put on her clothes and look presentable for Arthur. Carefully, she moved towards the door as she inhaled and exhaled slowly to steady her nerves.

"Are you about ready?" Arthur's voice was muffled but it still made her heart flutter like hummingbird wings. She pressed her hand to the door knowing fully well Arthur was just on the other side of it waiting for her.

"I'll be out in a moment," Sophie answered hoping her voice didn't sound too excited.

He'll probably just think you're nervous. Or maybe even still afraid. And of course I'm afraid. Arthur told me about him, but never gave details as to what he looked like. How was I supposed to know? I should have never let him in.

Sophie shook her head trying to shake out the memory of Randal Munger in her house, drinking her tea, and lying to her. Suddenly Sophie didn't feel well. She could feel her face getting flushed as her mouth went dry. Even her palms started to sweat a bit. It seemed as if each breath she pulled in was short and not nearly enough to keep her head from being dizzy.

She rushed to the bed and sat down. Her chest rose and fell quickly as her body trembled.

Calm down. You have to get a grip on yourself. You can't let Arthur see you like this, he'll never let you out of his sight again. And you just got him to leave you alone for the cattle drive.

Relax. Breathe in.

Sophie pulled in a long deep breath and held it for a moment. The swaying of the room seemed to stabilize. Slowly and deliberately, she exhaled as her fingers dug into the fabric of the blanket.

Sophie looked at the bedroom door and rose to her feet. If it wasn't for Arthur waiting for her on the other side of the door, she wasn't sure she'd be able to get up. She mustered every ounce of her courage to move towards the door.

"You alright in there?" Arthur asked through the door. Sophie shook her head and arms to get the jitters out of her before clearing her throat.

"I'm fine," she said, pulling open the door. "Are you ready to go?"

"Only if you are," Arthur said smiling.

Keep calm and don't think about Randal or his men. Just stay focused on the here and now.

Sophie swallowed the lump forming in her throat. She didn't dare look at the living room where Randal had stood but instead moved swiftly to the door.

"I think I'll need material for a new nightgown if it's all the same to you," Sophie said, pulling the shawl off the hook by the door and wrapping it around her shoulders.

"Of course," Arthur said keeping a close eye on her. Sophie knew he was waiting for her to break, but she wasn't going to. If anything, she was more resolved in keeping Randal out of her mind at all costs.

"Let's go then," Sophie said, reaching for the door. Arthur moved swiftly to her side and held open the door for her. From the corner of her eye, she spied Arthur reaching down and snagging the rifle by the door.

Sophie paused to look at the damaged barn. It was the first time she'd seen it and she couldn't believe how small it was compared to the damage she'd seen in her nightmares.

"Are you sure you're alright?" Arthur asked, holding out his arm for her. Sophie nodded and took his arm. A strange sensation washed over her as she noticed the gun resting against his shoulder.

"Arthur, I'm not as fragile as you think I am," she said, trying to convince herself more than she was trying to impress Arthur.

"I know," he said as he walked around to the buckboard. Arthur shoved the rifle under the seat before helping her up. Sophie's heart fluttered as his fingers curled around her waist to hoist her up. She sat down and straightened her back as Arthur moved around the horses and climbed up beside her. He reached down and grabbed the reins.

"You've proved to me time and again that you are more than capable of taking care of yourself. But you know this is bigger and Randal -"

"No," Sophie shook her head and pressed her fingers to Arthur's lips. "I don't want to hear that name around here. At least not today. Let us go to town and get what we need to fix up our home. I want to put this all behind us," Sophie said.

"You know he'll be in town though, right?"

"We don't know that," Sophie replied.

"Sophie," Arthur said, cracking the reins to get the horses going.

"Arthur," Sophie mimicked Arthur's serious tone. "Just for today. Come tomorrow we can discuss what we are going to do. Just give me today."

Arthur nodded and sucked in a deep breath. "And what if we see him in town?"

"We will cross that bridge when we get to it."

Chapter 21

Sophie's heart raced as the small town of Oakbury came into view. Just seeing the rising smoke from the blacksmith caused her palms to get sweaty. Rolling her shoulders back she sat taller in the seat and tried to remember how to breathe.

"You don't have to do this," Arthur said glancing at her. Sophie shook her head and cleared her throat. It was a kind gesture, but she knew deep down that unless she wanted to live in fear her whole life, she had to be there.

"I can drop you off at the Boyel's and go to town for supplies and the lumberyard for the wood alone."

"No. I want to go. I'm not comfortable with that idea," Sophie answered. Her voice was ragged, and her heart pounded in her ears. "I'll be fine."

"You sure? You know we have to cut through the town to get to the lumberyard."

"I'll be fine," Sophie reassured him, trying to keep calm as she stared at Arthur.

"I promise, we will be in and out of town quickly. And we can even take the long way to avoid going through town to get back home if that makes you feel better," he said. Sophie nodded and straightened her skirt. She knew she didn't want to go to town, but she wasn't about to stay at home by herself either or have the Boyel's watching over her.

Every fiber in her body screamed at her to turn around. She pressed her lips into a tight line and breathed in deeply to steady her nerves as the steeple of the church grew closer. It didn't take long before they were riding down the main street headed right for the grocer's.

"Do you think..." Sophie started to ask. She couldn't bring herself to finish her thought. All she could think about was the rough riders she'd seen before. Their dark set eyes and dirty faces still haunted her as she scanned the faces of those walking down the street.

In the pit of her stomach she couldn't shake the fact that they were Randal's men. Pulling in a deep breath she tried to steady her nerves as Arthur moved around the buckboard and extended his arms out to her. Carefully, she slipped down. The simple feeling of having Arthur's fingers around her waist calmed her down a bit. But the feeling slipped away the instant Arthur's hands left her sides.

"Mr. and Mrs. Soul," Mr. Wickman greeted them as they walked up the step to his store. "What can I do for you today?"

"We are here for supplies," Arthur said, looking over his shoulder. Three men were around the corner of the barber shop. Sophie could feel their gaze on her as she tried not to let her fear overcome her.

Swallowing hard, Sophie stole a glimpse over her shoulder to find the three men leaning against the barber shop. The taller of the three smirked and licked his lips as he looked at her. Sophie quickly made her way to Arthur's side feeling panicked by their presence.

"And what exactly can I get for you today?" Mr. Wickman asked as Arthur held out his arm to Sophie. She didn't hesitate to take it and pulled closer to Arthur.

"Well, seeing as how your family runs the lumberyard too, I thought I'd ask if you have any lumber in stock before heading out that way. Also, we need flour and a few other things for the homestead," Arthur said loudly than normal conversation allowed. For a moment Sophie wondered why he was speaking so loud. In the reflection of the grocer's shop, she noticed the three men chuckling as they stood upright. There was malice in their glares as if daring Arthur to say another word.

"Well, the flour and rice I have, but you'll have to talk to Billy about the lumber," Mr. Wickman's voice faded into the background. Sophie could feel her heart fluttering as she wondered how long they'd be in town. The sooner they were back on the road headed to the lumberyard the better.

But I suggest if you want me to steer clear of that pretty little wife of yours and keep your secret, you'll leave the law out of this. Randal's words played back in Sophie's mind as she tightened her grip around Arthur's arm.

Pulling in a deep breath, she turned her attention to Arthur. He patted her hand and nodded. The calm collected look in his gaze reassured Sophie he had no intentions of getting Noonen involved either.

"Planning on extending the house, are we?" The grocer smiled as his gaze fell on Sophie's stomach as if he suspected she was with child. Her heart fluttered and she quickly shook her head as Arthur choked and coughed.

"No, just a small accident," Arthur said once he gathered his senses. "We need a few boards to mend the barn."

Sophie could see the three men behind them standing straighter as if waiting for Arthur to make a mistake. She could feel the tension growing behind her as she forced the lump of fear in her throat down.

"A few of our horses got a bit wild the other night and kicked a hole right through the barn walls," Arthur said louder than Sophie expected. The three men standing across the way seemed to relax on hearing Arthur's explanation.

"Well, I think we might have something in the back if you will follow me," Mr. Wickman said with a pressed smile. Sophie couldn't help but notice the grocer's eyes locked on the men across the way.

"You alright Mr. Wickman?" Sophie asked, moving past him, and entering his store.

"Of course," he answered as he exchanged a look with Arthur. The instant the three of them were in the store, Mr. Wickman closed his doors and exhaled.

"You look whiter than a sheet," Sophie said, turning to find Mr. Wickman panting like a dog in the summer sun.

"It's those rough necks," a woman by the fabric said. Sophie looked to find Mrs. Hazel, the town's seamstress fiddling with the tassel of one of the newer fabrics. Sophie nodded the moment she recognized her.

"They've been causing all sorts of trouble around these parts the last few days."

"Excuse me?" Arthur turned to look at Mrs. Hazel. His eyes were wide with fright. Mrs. Hazel moved swiftly to his side keeping her eyes locked on the window and the men across the street. She leaned in closer to Arthur.

"Those men aren't like the others that come through here," she said with her eyes flickering between the window and Sophie. "Usually we can handle a few strangers passing by. But these men don't seem to want to go anywhere. You know Mr. Boyel, the tailor and Mr. Hastings, the teacher have each had issues with them getting a bit rowdy."

Sophie gasped as she turned to Arthur. Every ounce of her body felt like a live wire sparking and firing off. She wondered what was going on.

"What do they want?" Sophie asked Arthur.

"Some folks have overheard them say how they are just looking for a good time. But we aren't that kind of town. We've tried to tell them they'd be better off in Nashville, but they refuse to move on." Mrs. Hazel's eyes widened as the small bell on the door rang causing Sophie's head to whip around.

"Morning Mr. Wickman," Eddie greeted as he waltzed into the grocer's store. Sophie exhaled the moment she saw him.

Eddie scanned the store and stopped the instant he noticed Sophie hiding behind one of the shelves.

"Mrs. Soul?" Eddie gasped and quickly walked over to her. He smiled and nodded to Arthur.

"It is a surprise and a blessing seeing you here today," Eddie said shaking Arthur's hand. "In all honesty I didn't expect you'd be coming around so soon."

"Why?" Mrs. Hazel inquired, stepping in closer to Sophie.

"You didn't hear?" Eddie asked, turning his attention to Mrs. Hazel. For a split second, Eddie's eyes shifted to Sophie. She bobbed her head and pulled in a deep breath.

"I was attacked in town," Sophie answered. Eddie pressed his lips into a tight line as Arthur squeezed Sophie's arm tighter.

"It's alright," Sophie said, trying to hold her head up high. "What's done is done. No sense in living in the past."

"My word," Mrs. Hazel said, drawing her hand up to her chest. "Aren't you a brave girl."

"Mae was with me," Sophie answered. Her heart quickened as she recalled the event in her mind.

"Did they ever find the men who attacked you?" Eddie asked.

"Yes and no," Sophie said in hushed tones. Although the door to the grocer was closed, she couldn't help but feel the three men across the street could somehow still hear her.

"Are you saying they are here?" Mrs. Hazel gasped, whipping her head around to see the three men across the street huddled close together.

"I'm not comfortable talking about it," Sophie said. Arthur patted her hand.

"Let's just get what we came to get, and go home," Arthur said.

"Well," Mr. Wickman said, coming around the corner. "I do happen to have the wood in stock. If I could have a hand loading it we can get you on your way."

"Much obliged," Arthur said. Sophie's stomach twisted up in knots as Arthur slipped his arm out from hers.

"I have to help him," Arthur explained. Pressing her lips into a tight line she nodded.

"I know," she whispered. Even though Sophie was with Mrs. Hazel and Eddie, she still felt alone and isolated.

"Please hurry," she said to Arthur as her heart broke watching him walk away from her.

"Don't you worry dear," Mrs. Hazel said patting Sophie on the arm. "Those men will find this town too small and too dull. They'll move on soon enough."

"Better sooner rather than later," Eddie said, turning to look out the window.

"What in the world?" Mrs. Hazel's eyes widened. Sophie turned to find the barber being tossed out of his shop by his belt.

"Stay inside," Eddie said, stopping Sophie and Mrs. Hazel from heading to the door. Sophie cupped her hand over her mouth as she watched two men walking out of the barber shop, hands on their guns looking for an excuse to fire.

"Mrs. Hazel, Mrs. Soul you two need to head to the back," Eddie shouted over his shoulder. Sophie grabbed Mrs. Hazel and dragged her to the corner of the shop. She pushed the fragile woman down to the ground and craned her head.

Arthur. God, where is Arthur?

Fear stabbed and poked Sophie. Every second dragged on as the shouting outside got louder and louder. Not even the closed door could muffle the cursing that came from the rough necks.

From the corner of her eyes, she spied a distorted figure coming around the corner of the shop. He was tall with broad shoulders and short hair. Sophie's heart dropped to her stomach.

No. Arthur.

Arthur stood outside the grocer's store next to Eddie and Mr. Wickman. Sophie could feel her blood pressure rising as Mrs. Hazel ducked down to cover her head with her hands.

"We are going to die," Mrs. Hazel whimpered alone in the corner as Sophie stood by the window watching the scene unfold. The men's voices outside grew louder and louder as they spat cursed words at the barber cowering on the ground at their feet.

"No, we are not," Sophie said, keeping her eyes locked on Arthur as the three men across the street moved towards barber.

"You have no right to be beating on that man." Arthur's voice rose higher than the rough necks beating on the barber.

"And who are you to say what we can or can't do?" One of the men hissed. Sophie's heart had stopped the instant she heard Arthur's voice.

"You heard the man," Eddie shouted and stood taller. Sophie watched from the corner of the grocer's store. Each second dragged on and Mrs. Hazel's cries filled Sophie's ears.

"We'll be okay," Sophie said, stroking Mrs. Hazel's head.

"Our boys aren't like those men out there," Mrs. Hazel said to Sophie between her sobs. "They are going to get themselves killed."

"And so you'd rather have Mr. Jenkins the barber die instead?"

"Of course not," Mrs. Hazel said gripping onto Sophie's arms.

"You will leave that man alone," Arthur warned, drawing Sophie's attention to the tussle outside.

"Or what? What will you do? From what I've heard, you don't have what it takes to kill a man," the rough neck said before spitting his chew at the barber's head.

"You want to find out?" Arthur asked as Sophie closed her eyes. She wasn't about to watch her husband die in front of her. Fear, terror, rage all boiled inside her. Slowly she opened her eyes and peeled herself off Mrs. Hazel.

"Where are you doing?" Mrs. Hazel asked, trying to reach for Sophie.

"Defending my husband," Sophie answered. She rushed to the counter and scanned the area. Tucked under the countertop, she spotted the rifle and pulled it from its hiding spot.

"Don't," Mrs. Hazel gasped. "You'll get us all killed."

"I won't live in fear," Sophie said as she loaded the gun. With her head held high, Sophie charged towards the double doors of the grocer's shop.

*   *   *

Arthur found his nerves firing off in every direction. He held his position on the boardwalk staring down Randal's men.

"Arthur." Sophie's voice startled him, but he didn't dare jump. He knew any sign of weakness and the bullets would start flying.

"Look what we have here," the men in the street laughed. It was an odd sound and the last thing Arthur expected to hear. "I'd get a handle on that girlie if I were you."

"Sophie what are you doing?" Arthur asked, turning back to find Sophie with a rifle on her shoulder. The determination in her eyes gave Arthur strength.

"You will leave that man alone," Sophie ordered, stepping out from behind Arthur. In the corner of his eye, he could see her arms shaking as she aimed the gun at the men in the street.

"You ain't gonna shoot us little miss. You ain't got what it takes," the man with a long wiry gray beard said with a gleam in his eyes.

"If you think I won't do it," Sophie said stealing another step forward, "then it is you who is sorely mistaken."

The crack of gun fire echoed and bounced through the street. Arthur's heart stopped briefly as the smoke swirled around Sophie.

No.

Panic coursed through him as his heart started beating once again. Without warning, his hand shot out to the barrel of the gun and pulled it down.

"What are you doing?" Arthur hissed as he yanked the rifle out of Sophie's hands.

"I'm not going to let them hurt you," Sophie said as the men in the street scanned to see what Sophie had hit. When it was clear she hadn't injured any of them the street filled with their laughter once again.

"Seems we were mistaken," the old man said between chuckles. "She will fire the gun. Whether or not she hits something is entirely different."

"Come on, let her have the gun again. We could use a good laugh," another teased as he drew his leg back and rammed it into the barber's side.

"You best keep that girl locked up," the third man with thin lanky arms said as he stood straight and glared daggers at Sophie. "She's going to get herself killed one of these days."

"Or I'll just kill you," Sophie said charging towards him. Arthur reached his arm out and grabbed her before she could reach the steps.

"Enough." Randal's voice blasted over the commotion in the street causing everyone to stop and take notice. "Just what is going on here?"

Arthur's heart plummeted into his stomach as he watched Randal push through the double doors of the saloon and step out into the sun light. Arthur kept his eyes locked on the outlaw as Randal moved to the center of the street.

"Who are you?" Randal asked, pulling a cigar from his pocket. Randal leaned down with a match in hand and struck the end across the barber's rough face. Arthur's chin went up and his palms grew sweaty. He had seen Randal do that very same thing to countless people before killing them.

"Michael Blake, the barber."

"Well, mmm Michael Blake," Randal said, purposefully stuttering the same way the barber had as he lit his cigar. "What's the commotion about?"

"He tried to kill me." Randal's head popped up as one of his men with a half shaven face stepped forward.

"Andrew," Randal rose and turned to face him. "Show me."

Andrew lifted his head back. Arthur squinted his eyes to see the nick on Andrew's neck where he claimed Michael had sliced him.

"That is something," Randal said, raising one eyebrow. "You certain he did it on purpose?" Randal looked back at the barber cowering on the ground. Michael trembled and shook his head trying not to whimper too loudly.

"He did," Andrew said. "And now look at me. My pretty face is all messed up."

"I can see that," Randal said as Arthur's grasp around the rifle tightened.

Randal slowly turned his attention to Arthur and Sophie standing on the boardwalk. He shook his head ever so slightly as he pulled a drag from his cigar, daring Arthur to use the weapon in his hand.

"Aren't you going to do something about it?" Andrew asked, stepping forward. "He made me look ugly."

"You always looked that way Andrew," Randal said, causing the men around him to laugh. "But I suppose we should make an example of him."

"Please no," Michael said as the gang pulled him to his feet. "I have a family."

"You should have thought of that before you tried to slice my throat," Andrew spat.

"I didn't... I didn't mean to," Michael stuttered. Randal's head dropped as Arthur's hoisted the rifle to his shoulder.

"You'll learn one way or another," Randal said and for a moment Arthur couldn't tell if Randal was speaking to him or the barber.

Chewing on his lower lip, Arthur drew the rifle up and aimed it. His heart drummed in his ears as Randal lifted up his head and glared at him. With a snap of Randal's fingers, the men took turns pounding their fists into Michael.

"Stop that." Sophie screamed as she cupped her hands to her mouth. The men laughed as they each took turns beating the barber on the ground.

"Make an example out of those who would cross us," Randal said to his men all the while keeping his gaze locked on Arthur. Arthur inched his way closer to his buckboard and slipped his hand under the seat where he'd stashed his rifle. The hard-cool metal tingled the tips of his fingers as he quickly jerked the gun from under the seat and held it at the ready.

The men laughed and turned on their heels. Arthur wasn't about to lower his gun from Randal. He knew all he had to do was squeeze the trigger. But then what would happen was anyone's guess.

Would Randal have a plan b? Do his men have orders to kill me if I fire?

Arthur wasn't too keen on dying. He sucked in a deep breath as Randal's men gathered in the saloon and came back out with glass bottles.

"No," Sophie cried out. She moved towards the stairs. Arthur's heart dropped and so did the rifle in his hands as he reached out to stop her.

"We can't let them do this," she cried out as the rough riders moved swiftly towards the barber's shop and tossed their liquor bottles at the wooden building. Randal moved slowly to the wooden building and flicked his cigar at it. It didn't take long before the side of the building was covered in flames.

"Get water!" Mr. Wickman cried. Arthur dropped his arm, releasing Sophie. She scrambled down the steps to the trough and grabbed the bucket on the side before plunging it into the water.

"Quickly, before the whole town goes up," Eddie cried out, helping to get more buckets. Arthur rushed to Sophie's side to help her. He glanced over his shoulder to find Randal and his men walking casually down the street to the herd of horses tied off by the saloon.

"Get water on that," Sophie cried out, rushing to the burning building, and throwing her water on it before darting back to the trough.

"Best you remember who's in charge here," Randal said before mounting his horse. "Would hate for anyone else to get hurt."

"Arthur," Sophie gasped and pointed to Michael still unconscious in the center of the street.

Arthur dropped his pail and rushed to the barber's side as Randal's men charged down the street. Arthur knew Randal wasn't ready to kill him just yet. But feeling the breeze of the horses rushing by him caused him to wonder how much longer Randal would keep him alive.

"Thank you," Michael gasped and reached out to Arthur. Glancing down at the barber, Arthur nodded and helped him to his feet.

"My shop," Michael said through slanted swollen eyes. The flames licked the wooden planks and reached the windowpanes. Luckily with the townsfolk working together, they managed to get the fire under control quickly. Still, Randal had made his point very clear.

"The fire is out," Sophie said coming up to Arthur and Michael. "We can all chip in to help rebuild it."

"Won't do any good if that gang continues to torment us," Eddie said, dropping his pail in defeat.

"There isn't anything we can do about it," Mrs. Hazel agreed, coming out of the grocer's shop. Sophie turned to stare at the older woman who appeared untouched and unaffected by the event.

"Says you," Sophie snapped as it dawned on her what she and the town needed to do. "If we all stayed hidden with our tails tucked in, then there won't be anything left of this place. I don't know about you, but we can't just sit by and let this happen."

"Sophie," Arthur's eyebrows rose as he looked at his wife. She was covered in soot and dirt, but in his eyes she never looked more beautiful.

"No Arthur," Sophie shook her head. "We can't just sit by and let that gang have their way with us. We have to stand up."

"And what do you suppose we do, Mrs. Soul?" Mr. Wickman asked as he picked up his rifle from the side of the trough.

"I don't know," Sophie said shaking her head. Arthur kept his eyes on her as she moved to the steps and sat down. "But we can't keep living like this. This is our home."

"I know," Arthur said, moving to her side and sitting beside her. She rested her head on his shoulder. He scanned the faces of his friends surrounding him and sighed.

She is right. We can't keep this up. This town is my family and I can't do this to them.

Arthur curled his arm around Sophie's body and pulled her closer to him. His heart raced and pounded in his rib cage as he contemplated telling everyone his secret right then and there.

"I'm tired of this," Sophie said, looking up at him.

"I know" Arthur said, glancing down at her. It was clear she was in the same boat as he was, both at their wits end.

"Mr. Wickman," Arthur called to the grocer as he helped Michael to the boardwalk and sat him down carefully on the wooden planks. "Think we can finish loading up?"

"Absolutely," Mr. Wickman said, patting the barber on the shoulder.

"Let me finish loading up the supplies and we'll head to the lumberyard okay? Then we'll head on home," Arthur said rising to his feet. Sophie nodded her head. Her blank stare caused his heart to sink.

"Let's hope and pray we still have a home to go back to."

Chapter 22

The sight of the burnt spot on the barn stood out like a sore thumb. Sophie couldn't help but stare at it every so often while she made the table ready for dinner. There was no doubt that the mark was stark and black, a blemish to their perfect life on the ranch. It was a symbol that Randal wanted to leave with them, to taunt them each night. Even when Arthur fixed it, the color would be offset, forever marking the night Randal came back into Arthur's life.

"Dinner is ready," Sophie said lifting her eyes from the burnt spot to Arthur. He turned slowly looking defeated and spent. Sophie wanted nothing more than to comfort her husband, to cheer him up and let him know everything would be okay. But how was she to say such things when she didn't know if they were true or not?

"Arthur," Sophie called for him just as he turned back to stare at the burnt area.

"Dinner time," Sophie said pulling out his seat and looking at the empty chair. "Come and sit down. Stop looking at that. We'll get it fixed tomorrow, right now you just need to enjoy the meal I prepared for you."

"And then what?" Arthur looked at her with his deep-set eyes.

"Don't worry about what comes after," Sophie said. "We'll figure that part out when we get to it."

"Why are you so calm about all this? Most women in this town would be terrified of Randal. But not you," Arthur said moving to the dinner table. "You took him on like he was a gnat."

Arthur held Sophie in his sights as she took her seat at the other end of the table. Sophie didn't have an answer for him. She shrugged her shoulders back and shook her head as her lips flattened.

"I don't know what came over me today," she said. "I'm sorry. I should have taken your lead and stayed in the grocer's store."

"No, please, you were great today. You stood up for what was right," Arthur said smiling. "It was more than a lot of the men in that town did today. In fact, I'm almost certain that a lot of the folks that hid inside their shops and homes were shocked and inspired by you today."

Sophie could feel heat in her cheeks, "I don't know about that."

"You gave me goosebumps today. Of course, they were probably because I was certain I was going to lose you today," Arthur's voice dropped lower and lower to the point Sophie could barely hear him.

"What?" she asked leaning over the edge of the table to catch his eye.

"Sophie you have to know what you mean to me," Arthur said pushing his shoulders back. "It terrified me to see you with the gun on your shoulder. But I was so proud to see you like that. You didn't back down."

"And what about you?" Sophie asked reaching for his plate. She filled it up with food and handed it back to him. His fingers brushed against hers as he took the plate sending a warm tingle up her arm.

"You stood there ready to do whatever it took to make him stop," Sophie said smiling. "I saw you there with the grocer and the blacksmith thinking I may not see you again."

"What they did to the barber though," Arthur shook his head as he pushed the food around on his plate. "Barbaric."

"What if they do that to everyone in town?" Sophie asked as she realized this was just the beginning. Her heart fluttered to think of all the damage Randal's gang could do to the town.

"If we don't do something, they'll burn this place to the ground and no one will be around to stop it from happening," Arthur said.

"We can't keep everyone safe," Sophie said. "This isn't the way to live, in fear all the time. You saw Mrs. Hazel in the store today. I think she may have just been in there to stay off the streets."

"I noticed when we stopped at the grocer's there wasn't the same amount of people walking about." Arthur stabbed the meat on his plate and shoved it quickly into his mouth.

"What if that's the way it is now? What if the people in town are too scared to stick around or stand up? I don't know about you," Sophie pulled in a deep breath and exhaled slowly, "but I love this little town of ours."

She looked at Arthur bashfully. She was just as shocked to hear the words coming from her lips as he was to hear them.

"Do you really mean that? Do you really see Oakbury as your home?"

Sophie pressed her lips into a tight line and bobbed her head. "I do. I don't want to see it ruined all because of Randal Munger."

"There isn't a whole lot we can do about that," Arthur said pushing his plate away from him. Sophie looked at the full plate of food understanding his frustration and lack of appetite.

"Let's get out of here and not think about this right now," Sophie said moving her plate away from her too.

"What did you have in mind?"

"Let's go for a walk," Sophie said with a hint of a smile. "We can leave everything right here and come back for it later."

"You really want to leave the house this late?"

"It's a nice night," Sophie said rising to her feet. "Let's just walk around the ranch and enjoy the stars. Forget everything that is going on in town and with Randal and just be together for a few moments."

Arthur stared at Sophie. She could see the wheels in his head spinning as he thought about what she was asking. Sophie's heart fluttered in her chest as her hands felt clammy and wet. It was a strange feeling asking Arthur to walk with her. Since they had been married, she never thought to ask him to be with her. Yet, here she was, eager to be alone under the light of the moon with her husband.

"Alright," Arthur said nodding and placing his napkin on the table beside the full plate of food. "If that is what you want to do."

Sophie's smile widened as she moved around the table and took Arthur's hand. She pulled him to her and cleared her throat trying not to be so eager to get going. Arthur couldn't help but chuckle at her playfulness and innocence.

"Are you ready then?" he asked, walking her to the door. She reached out and grabbed her shawl. Arthur stopped and pulled it over her shoulders. She couldn't help but notice how much time was passing as they stood there staring into each other's eyes.

"After you Mrs. Soul," Arthur said, stepping back and reaching for the door.

Sophie's heart fluttered. The warm night air kissed her cheeks the instant she stepped out onto the porch. Small little lights flickered and flashed between the trees as the soft breeze played with the leaves. The gentle song of the crickets filled the night air. The sounds swirled around her. Sophie sucked in the sweet smells around her.

Arthur closed the door behind him and held out his arm.

"Shall we?"

Turning, she took Arthur's arm and walked with him down the steps. She forced herself not to look at the barn as they moved past the corral. But she knew the blemish was there. Just as she knew Arthur was trying his hardest to put the events of the day behind him.

"Sophie," Arthur squeezed her hand as they strolled down the road. "What would you do if we didn't have any of this anymore? What if one day we didn't have the ranch, the house, all of this," Arthur waved his arm around the space before them.

"I don't know," Sophie confessed. "I suppose as long as I have you it doesn't matter."

"Are you saying you would have married me without the land?"

"Where is this going?" Sophie asked, stopping at the fence that surrounded their property. "What are you asking?"

"How would you feel if we just left here?"

"No." Sophie shook her head and cleared her throat. "We aren't going to run. There are far too many people who would get hurt because of us. Think of what Randal would do if he discovered we up and left. Think of Mae and Garner, the grocer, and Eddie. They would pay for our mistake. I can't do that."

"I know," Arthur said, shaking his head.

"Do you want to leave?" Sophie took Arthur by the shoulders and looked at him carefully.

"No," Arthur said. "It was just a question."

"You've lived here far longer than I have," Sophie said, pulling in a deep breath. She squeezed his hands and looked up to the starry sky. "But I can't see myself living anywhere else. What you've built for yourself here is worth fighting for, you have to know that."

"I do," Arthur said and pursed his lips together.

"So don't you give up on them Arthur Soul, because I'm not going to give up on you. We will figure out what to do about Randal. You'll see. But right now, we just have to steal these moments and be together."

Sophie stared at the brave, kind, honorable, and trustworthy man before her. He was everything she had ever wanted in a man but was afraid to ask for. A smile played at the corner of her lips as the worry on Arthur's face faded away.

"I'll fight for this town," Sophie said lifting her head up. "If you will."

* * *

Arthur stared deeply into Sophie's eyes. There was so much understanding and love that looked back at him that he could feel the wall around his heart shattering.

"Sophie, not everyone in town is like you," he said. "Not everyone would be so understanding to what I've done."

"You don't know that," Sophie said. He could see the hope and innocence in her gaze. It filled him with optimism.

She's wrong. There's no way the townsfolk will accept me if they knew the truth.

"What are you so scared of?" Sophie asked trying to force him to look at her. He knew he had been dodging her eyes as they stood in the warm summer evening.

"I know you are hiding something, Arthur Soul. It's the same look you had on your face when you told me about your involvement with Randal. The same wrinkle appeared then as it has now," Sophie said reaching up to his forehead. Arthur could feel her fingertip graze his skin.

"People in town don't know what I used to do. They don't know I ran with that very same gang. If they found out, they'd shun me. My life here would be over."

"I think you should give the people of this town a bit more credit. If you explain it to them the way you explained it to me, they'll see you had no choice."

"Why are you always so optimistic? Isn't it exhausting to be so hopeful all the time?" Arthur leaned down and pressed his forehead to hers. Despite the fact he wanted to run, he couldn't help but see life the way she did. He wanted to hope all would work out.

"Every day Sophie, you show me that I can be so much more than what I think I am. Every single day you encourage me to be more and for that I am grateful." Arthur pulled back and stared into his wife's eyes.

Say it. Just say it. Tell her how you really feel. Let her know before it's too late. Randal could come tonight and take her away from you and then what? You really want to be that guy who regrets not telling the woman they love the truth?

"Sophie, when I was on the cattle drive," Arthur cupped his hands around her oval shaped face and gazed into her eyes. The tiny light from the stars sparkled back at him as his heart took flight within his chest.

"All I could think of was you. I should have kissed you before I left," he mumbled as his throat went dry.

"I..." Arthur pulled in a deep breath as his body trembled. "How is it that I'm more scared in this moment right here than I was facing down Randal's gang today?"

Sophie shook her head and looked up at him.

"I love you Sophie," Arthur blurted out. "I need you to know that before it's too late. I love you with all that I am. I know you want a marriage of convenience, and I will give you whatever life you want. But you need to know how I feel about you."

Before Sophie could say a single word, Arthur leaned down and pressed his lips to hers.

Chapter 23

How could I be so lucky?

The silvery light of the moon beamed down on the waving fields and tall grass. Sophie stared into Arthur's eyes and found her world completed. Arthur's lips curled at the corners as he smiled at her and ran his fingers through her hair. He held her gaze as they stood in the open field with the warm night air kissing their skin.

"Don't you think it's time for us to get back home? It is getting late after all," Sophie said looking at Arthur and wondering if she would ever be able to keep this moment. It seemed that time was not on their side. In the back of her mind she knew that there was always a threat lingering.

"Sophie, I meant what I said," Arthur grabbed her hands and brought her fingers up to his lips. He pressed his mouth to her fingertips and held her gaze.

"I wish I could give you everything that you wanted. I wish I could give you the kind of life that you deserve; one that doesn't have so many dangers and uncertainties to it. And I know that you wanted a marriage of convenience, but I can't help but want more. You've shown me kindness that no one else has ever shown me before. And I can't thank you enough for everything you've done for me and standing by my side through all of this mess."

Sophie slipped her hand out of Arthur's grasp and cupped his face holding his gaze as the soft breeze played with the hem of her dress. The sweet aroma of lavender and rosemary drifted on the wind.

Do you really mean what you say? That you want more from me?

Sophie's heart fluttered in her chest. It felt like a million birds taking flight and every bit of her body was anxious. Arthur brushed his fingertips over her cheeks causing her skin to rise and his touch stroked a desire that burn with in her.

"I want to give you whatever it is that you want," Arthur said keeping his eyes locked on her. "Right now it may not be much, but it's all I have and it's yours."

"Arthur Soul, don't you understand this is more than enough?" Sophie rose to her tiptoes and gently pressed her lips to his cheek. She wrapped her arms around his neck as he embraced her and pulled her closer to him.

Is this really happening? Is this the love that Nadine had always wanted for me? Truth be told I can feel her smiling down upon me and my heart feels like it's grown three sizes.

"I do think it's best that we get back now," he said. Although in her heart she didn't want this night to end but she knew it had to eventually.

Turning slowly she began walking back to the homestead and she couldn't help but feel a burning desire to hold on to every ounce of happiness that she could. She knew better than anyone how quickly things could change. One minute she could have everything and be blissfully happy, and in the next minute have it all taken away.

Sophie knew that her sister Nadine would have wanted her to be as happy as possible. After all, it was the whole reason Nadine sent out letters to make Sophie a mail order bride. But never in her wildest dreams did she think she would have feelings for her husband. Yet, here she was with a desire to be more than just a helper on Arthur's farm. Sophie realized she would fight for every second that she could just to spend just one more moment with Arthur in this happiness.

As Sophie stared at the homestead against the silvery backdrop of night, she felt a pang of uncertainty.

"Is everything all right?" Arthur asked coming up behind her. Sophie turned to see him standing tall with his broad shoulders back, looking majestic under the twinkling lights of the stars.

"I'm fine," Sophie said as the rumbling of a wagon caught her attention. Both Sophie and Arthur's head whipped around to find the Davidson's rushing towards them in their wagon.

"What's going on?" Arthur asked as Garner pulled the reins causing the horses to slow and then stop.

"Town folks are getting harassed by the gang that's come to town. There's been a town meeting called to figure out what to do about them. They said we need to get to town quickly, everyone's meeting at the church."

Arthur's eyes widened with fright as he turned his attention from Sophie to Garner. In the depths of her being, she knew that something wasn't right.

"Where are your children?" Sophie asked, stepping closer to the wagon.

"We left the kids with my mother-in-law back at home," Mae said in a hurry. "You two can ride with us. Come on, climb in, we need to get going now."

Sophie flashed Arthur a quick glance before turning her attention back to Garner and Mae. There was no hiding the fearful expressions on their faces. Sophie knew it had to do with Randal's gang. After all, she'd seen how they were acting in town trying to cause fires and havoc and chaos wherever they went. She could only imagine what he would do if he stayed longer.

"I'll get the wagon hitched up and we will follow you into town," Arthur said.

"Best if we ride together, safety in numbers and all," Garner said as he looked around in a paranoid fashion that set Sophie on edge.

Sophie moved to the back of the wagon as Arthur moved with her and helped her up. She quickly sat down and ran her hands over her lap.

"Should I be getting a gun?" Arthur asked as he hoisted himself up into the back of the wagon and situated himself next to Sophie.

"No need, we got a couple underneath the boards if anything were to happen," Garner said as he flicked the reins causing the horses to start. Sophie's body jerked as the carriage started moving and she nearly toppled into Arthur's lap. He curled his arms around her waist and held her close to him as they drove down the dark road towards town.

Sophie had no clue what was coming, but she knew whatever happened at the town meeting wasn't going to be pleasant. Her heart skipped and raced as they rocked in the back of the wagon headed towards town.

* * *

Arthur locked his arms around Sophie as the sounds of voices filled the small church. It seemed as if every single resident of Oakbury was in the small room. For a moment Arthur couldn't believe all that he was hearing. It seemed as if every single person had something to complain about.

Small and large families around him whispered about various occurrences that were happening to them.

"That gang came through and stole my steeds," one man complained. His voice rose louder than the murmurs that filled the church.

"Well they slaughtered two of my cows," another man said pounding his fist on the pew in front of him.

"Settle down now, settle down," Mayor Locke warned as he rose from his seat in the front row and moved to the podium in the center of the room. The mayor lifted his hands up and waited as he tried to get the people to calm down and listen to him.

"You all know why we're here," the Mayor said scanning the room. Arthur couldn't help but feel as if the Mayor's eyes lingered on him longer than the other people in town.

"We all know that we have a certain situation here," the Mayor said as he cleared his throat and clung to the podium as if it was his lifeline. "We are gathered here to discuss the terms and conditions for which these people have moved into our town. Now granted, there are some of you who have had grander issues with Randal and his men and there are some of you who have been blessed by not knowing who they are at all. No matter which side of the situation you happen to be on, we are all here to come to an understanding."

Arthur shook his head as he listened to the Mayor. He knew that he was speaking in a bid to appease everybody. But what the townsfolk didn't know was that Arthur knew Randal Munger better than anyone in that room. In his gut he also knew that this poor town didn't deserve what was happening to them.

Concern washed through Sophie's face as she turned to look at him. He wondered if she understood the weight of the situation and how responsible he felt for everything that was going on. A lump of regret sank into his stomach causing it to turn sour. Arthur looked around the room only to find that the walls seemed to be closing in on him and he knew that there was no way he was going to be able to keep up the ruse and pretend that he didn't know what was going on or why this was happening to their small little town.

"Sheriff if you'd be obliged to come up here and tell us your story," the Mayor said stepping away from the podium.

A collective hush fell over the crowd as their eyes darted to the center of the room. Sheriff Noonen rose to his feet and slowly made his way to the podium. The sound of the sheriff's boots dragging across the wooden planks of the floor flooded Arthur's ears. For a moment he couldn't understand where the sound was coming from. It wasn't until the sheriff turned and he saw for himself what had happened to Noonen.

The instant Sheriff Noonen turned to face the crowd Arthur heard Sophie gasp. Arthur's heart crumbled into a million pieces as he stared at his poor battered friend. Noonen stood at the front with bruises and cuts from his brow to his chin. His arm was held in a sling as his body looked as if it would crumble any second. To Arthur's eyes, it looked as if the sheriff had been tied to the back of a horse and lead down the town's main street.

"Many of you know me. I come to your houses sometimes for dinner. I made a promise to protect the town and I do what I can to help everybody here make this place a safe and wonderful place to live. Two nights ago though, Mr. Henderson saloon was being overrun by the gang. I stepped in to fix it and this is what they did to me. Now, I know some of you may be scared, but don't be. We are here to figure out how to handle this situation and get our town back," Noonen said trying not to let his voice crack.

"We should leave," a man shouted as he stood quickly. Fear and anger dominated his face and no one in the room could blame him for it.

"If we leave, who's to say they won't go somewhere else? We can't push them off onto some other town," Noonen said. His words were followed by several cheers.

Arthur's grip around Sophie's tiny body tightened as he watched the sheriff struggle for breath. No doubt Randal had broken several of the sheriff's ribs and only left him alive for this purpose - to speak in front of the town and get the town even more scared.

The sheriff scanned the room with his one good eye until it fell upon the Arthur. Every ounce of Arthur's body tensed, every muscle tightened. Even his heart seemed to turn to stone as he stared at his friend who was trying to stand tall. Anger, revenge, hatred, all the emotions boiled to the surface as Arthur was reminded of what Randal had done to his family so long ago. The memory of finding his family on their farm in Texas flashed before his eyes. Once again Arthur felt the helplessness and the dread of the uncertainty swirled around him. He felt as if he was caught up in a tornado.

"I know some of you think that it would be safer to leave this town and start fresh and new somewhere else but I'm here to tell you that that is not a good idea. We need to stick together," the sheriff said as voices rose in the church. Arthur couldn't blame him now; he understood fully well from seeing the battered town sheriff that this would be no place to raise a family, and many of the folks in this church had children. Arthur glanced over at Gardner and Mae who seemed just as concerned as the other folks around them.

Gardner stood and cleared his throat, "And just what would you expect us to do? Some of us have had places burned to the ground. Who's to say that those folks won't cause more problems? It seems to me that if this gang is determined to burn buildings and steal, cattle then nobody is safe here."

The people in the church erupted. Arthur felt as if the room was spinning and with every moment he remained seated, he felt the air getting smaller and a little more pressure in his chest. He looked over at Sophie and squeezed her hand, "I've got to get some fresh air."

Without another word, he rose to his feet and moved down the aisle to the back of the church and stepped into the fresh air. Panic swirled around him as he thought about all that Randal was capable of doing. He couldn't believe that Noonen would be beaten as badly or that the townsfolk would have to be picking up his mess. Balling his fingers into a tight little fist, Arthur tried not to let the rage consume him. At the moment all he wanted to do was go after Randal and finish what he had started so long ago.

If only I had killed him when I had the chance none of this would've happened. I should have slit his throat when he was sleeping. Or maybe put a bullet in him the first chance I got. But no, I had to be all noble and let him go on living. Now look what's going on. I should never let this happen and what about Sophie? She's just as innocent as the rest of the town.

"Arthur are you okay?" Sophie asked as she came out of the church. Arthur turned on his heel and stared at her for a brief moment before releasing the tension in his hands and dropping his head.

"I don't know what to do. I cannot let him continue to terrorize this town that we love so much," Arthur said as the sounds from the townsfolk inside the church erupted once again. Neither Sophie nor Arthur knew what was going on inside but by the sound of it, it was still chaos and confusion. Families started pouring out of the church, some of them grumbling, some of them saddened but the expressions on each of their faces were the same, fear had stolen their livelihood and their happiness, and it was all Arthur's fault.

"I can't do this alone," Arthur said to Sophie as she stepped closer to him and pressed her hands to his chest.

"You aren't alone. You have me and you have these townspeople too if you just give them a chance."

"Look at them, they are all too scared to face Randal," Arthur said.

"What we do with that fear will determine whether or not we stay in this little town. Sure we can run, and we can pick up and move someplace else but who's to say that he's not gonna follow us? We cannot let him get away with this. We have to be here for our friends."

"I can't sit here and watch Randal tear this town apart, it's become very clear that he is going to stop at nothing to get what he wants, even if that means burning this town to ashes."

Chapter 24

"Can you believe what happened to Sheriff Noonen?" Mae asked as she looked over her shoulder to stare at Sophie. Sophie nodded silently, her eyes flickering back to Arthur. She could see something was brewing within him, but she didn't quite know what.

For once, Sophie was thrilled that Mae was so talkative. If Mae wasn't constantly giving her two cents, it would have been a very quiet ride back to the homestead. Sophie looked over at Arthur and squeezed his hand hoping to convey in that single gesture that she was with him always and that she cared deeply for him. Arthur kept his eyes locked on the scenery and on the shadows around them. It wasn't until they reached the homestead and he helped her out of the wagon did she realize the full extent of what was going on inside Arthur's head.

As Sophie stayed on the porch saying goodbye to her friends, Arthur stormed inside the house mumbling something under his breath. Sophie waited until her friends were out of sight before stepping inside. She was surprised to find Arthur pacing around with his face growing redder and redder with every passing moment.

"You're not planning on doing anything reckless, are you?" Sophie asked as she stole a step forward in an attempt to get him to stop moving around so they could talk. But it was clear that Arthur was too wired and that he was looking for action.

"You heard the town talking. If I hadn't moved here, this never would've happened. If I hadn't tried to settle down here, these people would be okay, and they wouldn't have their livestock stolen. They wouldn't have their barns burned down," Arthur slammed his fists on the dining room table startling Sophie.

"Don't you see? They wouldn't have their businesses ruined if I wasn't here. This is my fault." Arthur's shoulders dropped as he finally calmed down and sank into the armchair near the fireplace. Sophie moved swiftly to the fireplace and grabbed the matches on top of the mantle. Striking one, she watched the little light flicker before she moved to the hearth.

"Don't do that, I need to go to sleep. I have a big day ahead of me tomorrow," Arthur said as he rubbed his temples with his fingers. Before Sophie could say a word she watched Arthur rise to his feet and walk down the hall into his room. The door shutting behind him sounded so final and absolute that its broke Sophia's heart. She had no clue what to do to help her husband nor did she have any idea of what to do about the townsfolk; all she could do is pray.

Sophie placed the box of matches back on the mantle and looked around the quiet little house. She knew she had come here in hopes of finding a home, but she realized that a home was more than just four walls; it was filled with love and understanding and companionship. All the things that she held dear to her heart.

Slowly Sophie moved towards the hallway and tried not to make a sound as she pushed open her bedroom door. She moved to the lantern and turned it on. The soft glow filled the room and although she knew that her husband would not be consoled tonight, she couldn't help but worry about him. Sophie moved her small desk and sat down. Opening her journal, she breathed in deep and finally put pen to paper.

Dear diary,

I find it kind of strange how one minute the world can seem right as rain and the next moment it's turned upside down. I seem to have fallen in love with my husband this evening as we strolled through the tall grass. The stars were twinkling high in the sky and I found myself falling not only into his embrace but into his eyes as well.

And yet things turned sour so quickly that it made my head spin. We went to the town meeting tonight that was called only to discover that poor Sheriff Noonen had been severely beaten by Randal and his gang and he isn't the only one who's been terrorized. The owner of the saloon nearly lost his life when he tried to stop the gang from cheating at poker. And then there's the poor grocer Mr. Wickman and his lovely wife and family who have decided that it's not worth staying here anymore because of the violence going around.

I honestly don't know what to do. I don't even know if Nadine would know what to do. So often I would think that she would have the answers but I'm starting to think that maybe she wouldn't. Either way it would be nice to have somebody to talk to about this.

I do have a confession to make though, a part of me wants to pack up and leave and disappear. But I know there's no place that we can go that Randal and his gang won't find. Which makes me wonder if we should just stay and fight. I know we can't let Randal continue doing what he's doing.

Still I'm not sure which way to go. I know no matter what, I will stick with my husband for I love him. Arthur has been so good to me in so many ways. He's provided me with the life that I have to say is full of excitement and adventure, but it's also very scary with so many uncertainties.

Above all else, I know that I can't lose Arthur. I can't imagine seeing him the way the sheriff was tonight. I don't think there was a clear spot on that man's body. Every inch of him was covered in black and blue splotches and my heart breaks thinking that one day I will see Arthur like that, only worse.

I know I can't stop Arthur from doing what he's going to do and by the crazy gaze in his eyes tonight after the town meeting I know he's concocting something. I just don't know what. I pray to God that he's not going to be reckless. I don't know what to do if I ever lost him, for I think I love him.

* * *

Arthur laid in his bed with his eyes wide open staring at the ceiling as he ran through different scenarios in his mind on how to handle Randal. Each time Arthur tried to close his eyes he saw Sheriff Noonen and couldn't help but wonder when it would be his turn.

Chewing on his bottom lip, Arthur tried to come up with some kind of solution that didn't end in a bloodbath or the destruction of his town. And as the hours ticked by, he realized there was only one thing that he could do. Only one path for him to take that didn't require him coming clean with the townspeople. He was going to have to talk to Randall face-to-face and see if there wasn't some way to compromise.

Before the birds started singing, Arthur slipped out of the front door without a sound. Although he didn't know exactly where Randal's gang was located, he knew Randal well enough to know that it wouldn't be someplace too far away. As he pulled out his steed from the stable and saddled it up, he couldn't help but feel a prick of guilt as he glanced over his shoulder and stared at his home.

Hopefully, Sophie was still asleep, slumbering deeply with good dreams and her mind far away from the troubles that had him up all night. And although he tried desperately to make no sounds as he exited the barn, the horse was determined to be as loud as possible.

"Will you be quiet," Arthur scolded as he stroked the horse's nose in an attempt to calm it down. The horse stomped its hoof into the ground one last time to protest getting up so early. Carefully, Arthur hoisted himself up into the saddle and trotted down the road. Only once the house and ranch was out of sight did he dig his heel into the horse's flank and send it running. As Arthur rode, he felt a hunch to head towards the creek.

Randal you're going to stop this right now. I can't have you terrorizing the town's books anymore. This has got to stop. What is it that you want?

He contemplated all the different ways that he would confront the gang leader. He knew the direct approach would probably be the most dangerous, but in the pit of his stomach he also knew that Randal would respect the man that took what he wanted and didn't back down. But no matter which way Arthur played out how he would greet Randal, the ending always seemed to be the same. Either he would be able to walk out of that camp with his life, or not.

Suddenly Arthur's mind shifted to Sophie. He knew in his heart of hearts that he was doing this not only for himself but for her as well. Now that Randal knew her name and her face, there was no escaping him. Arthur's heart pounded in his chest as he thought of Randal going after her next and that was one thing Arthur could not allow to happen.

A sharp crack scattered the birds into the air as Arthur pulled on the reins and leaned back in his saddle to stop. His eyes shifted around, searching the tree line as his ears perked to listen.

In the distance he could hear soft mutterings. He knew that Randal was an early bird and would most likely be awake at this hour. Arthur's heart thumped in his chest as he pulled in a deep breath. The crisp morning air tingled his nose as he forced his horse to trot closer to the creek. A small ribbon of smoke drifted towards the sky from the bonfire that had been raging the night before. Arthur quickly stopped his horse and slid off the saddle. Panic gripped him as he walked through the shrubs and into the clearing by the creek.

"Are you lost little birdie?" A grumpy voice asked, and Arthur turned quickly to find a slender man with wiry whiskers leaning against a dead trunk. The man smiled at him maliciously as Arthur pulled his shoulders back trying to look taller than what he was.

"Where is Randal"? Arthur said in a deep menacing voice. The cowboy shook his head and clicked his tongue to the roof of his mouth.

"What's it to you?" The man asked as he pushed off the dead tree and moved closer to Arthur.

"Is he here or not?" Arthur demanded refusing to budge or show any sign of weakness.

The man's eyes drifted over Arthur as if to size him up and although Arthur hadn't been in a fight in many years, he still knew how to throw a punch. But he wasn't here to scrap with Randal's men, he was here to negotiate.

Just breathe in deep; keep your eyes focused.

Arthur could feel the weight of his six shooter on his hip and it seemed to weigh him down. Out of the corner of his eye, Arthur noticed Randal emerging from the shrubs closest to the water. His heart picked up the pace as he turned his head and stared down his mortal enemy.

Chapter 25

"You know, I'm surprised that you came out here," Randal said as Arthur moved closer to him. Two men stepped forward blocking Arthur from reaching Randal.

"It's all right boys. I don't think he's planning on doing nothing," Randal said as he kept his eyes locked on Arthur. The two brutes stepped back allowing Arthur a clean shot of Randal. The weight of Arthur's gun seemed ten times heavier. For a moment, Arthur wondered if he was fast enough to pull his gun and shoot the villain before him.

You got a chance. Take the shot.

Arthur's eyes shifted to the men standing around Randal. Mortality stabbed him as he realized if he took out Randal, he wouldn't be going back to Sophie. Pulling in a deep breath he steadied his nerves.

Clearing his throat and straightening his shirt, Arthur stared at Randal. "What is it gonna take to get you to leave? You want me dead? Then do it but stop harassing the townsfolk. They don't deserve your wrath," Arthur said, trying to keep his voice stern as he spoke.

"Is that brave of you? Did you really come all the way out here just to get me to stop?" Randal's eyebrow rose as he eyed Arthur.

"You said you wanted to take everything from me, but all you've done so far is take from the townsfolk. So what is it that you really want?"

"Whatever do you mean"? Randal asked as the corner of his lips curled up into a malicious little smile that sent chills running down Arthur spine.

"Tell me what is it gonna take for you to leave and never come back?" Arthur asked, trying to puff up his chest and look bigger than what he was.

"Now that is the question, isn't it?" Randal intoned, kneeling down to wash his hands in the water.

"I told you what I wanted. I also told you what I was going to do to you. You see you have something that I want. You have a beautiful home, a lovely little wife, and more land than I know what to do with. Not to mention the huge head of cattle that would make me a mighty rich man," Randal said as he rose and picked out the dirt between his fingernails.

"You aren't taking Sophie," Arthur said in a near growl.

"Really? Are you trying to threaten me?"

"I won't let you lay another hand on her," Arthur said, lifting his chin to the sky.

"You know," Randal said, holding Arthur's gaze. "I'd love to see you try and stop me from taking everything I want."

"There are other ways of getting those things besides stealing them," Arthur said as Randal began to circle him.

"Where's the fun in that?" Randal asked

Arthur kept his eyes on Randal as he moved around in a wide circle weaving in and out of shrubs and rocks and his men. Arthur's heart sank as he spied the two men that Sophie had described after the attack in the town. Icy cold fingers stole the warmth of his blood as he thought of all the things he wanted to do to them. Grinding his teeth, Arthur tried to remain focus on Randal.

"But, I will settle for your ranch and cattle," Randal said, drawing Arthur's attention once more.

"And if I do handover my ranch to you, then what?" Arthur asked, trying not to let his voice crack with frustration that Randal would surely mistake for fear. "You won't stop with my ranch, you'll go after every single person in town till you have it all, won't you?"

"Whatever do you mean?" Randal said with a little chuckle. "I have no reason to continue harassing these poor folks around these parts. After all, I'll just simply slide into your place and become part of the town just like you did."

"They won't respect you, you know that right? Not after all the things that you've done to them," Arthur said.

"It would be a pity if anyone decided to cross me, but you see, I had thought about just taking your life and putting you out of your poor misery," Randal said with a gleeful smile. "But that would be far too easy now, wouldn't it? It wouldn't be good enough to quench this desire to destroy you."

"All this hatred because I sent you to jail?"

"It wasn't the jail time," Randal hissed. "You killed my mother."

"I didn't kill anyone but if I was going to, it would be you," Arthur said as his hands balled into tight little fists. Every muscle in his body ached and felt like a coil ready to spring forward. It took every ounce of strength for Arthur to stay still instead of doing what he desired.

"Oh, look at that temper of yours. Now I remember why I let you ride with me all those years ago. I saw potential in you. But now, all I see is an old dead man. But you know what? You and I aren't so different. In fact, we are a lot alike," Randal said, finally stopping near the remains of the smoldering bonfire.

"Don't you dare try to compare yourself to me," Arthur growled.

"You're right, I am the better man here, but you see we both lost people that we loved. I killed your family, you took mine. Granted you didn't kill her with your own hands, but she is still gone, nonetheless. If you hadn't had me locked up, she might have lived. It's sort of an eye for an eye so to speak. But did you ever think that maybe I let you live? I don't kill indiscriminately. My men knew where you were, and we let you go."

"You let me live? I think that's the other way around," Arthur said stepping forward. "Do you know how many times I could have slit your throat? Do you have an idea how any times I could just put a bullet in you and ended you, but I didn't? I was the merciful one not you."

"If you had so many chances then it just shows me what a coward you really are. You should've killed me when you had the chance. You could have saved yourself a lot of grief had you done it. Instead you had me rotting in the jail cell and my poor mama couldn't take care of herself. You robbed me of the last three years of my life. I think it's only fair that I take three years to rob you of everything that you have, wouldn't you say?" Randal moved like a snake towards Arthur and stared at him with cold bitterness in his gaze.

Arthur's blood chilled as Randal stood but an inch from him. For a moment, Arthur wondered whether Randal would draw his knife and cut him through right then and there, but he kept his eyes focused and his body alert for any signs of Randal moving towards his blade.

Randal stepped back and chuckled. "You have the life I always dreamed of since I was young boy and you know what, you're going to pay for the life you took from me. You're going to give me your ranch and leave this place with that wife of yours and never come back," Randal said.

"And if I don't?" Arthur asked as his eyes flickered to the men around him.

"I promise things are just gonna get worse here in Oakbury. You saw what I did to that sheriff, you think I couldn't do that to other people? Ones that are a bit closer to you until I am on your doorstep with a gun in your face taking what I want."

Arthur's face flinched as he thought of the Davidson's in the ranch closest to his. He thought of the grocer and the people scattered about Oakbury.

"You're bluffing; you have no clue who my friends are in this town."

"My men know exactly who you call friends and don't think that that little portable wife won't feel the brunt of my wrath as well. Now, I know this is a big decision for you. I'll give you a few days to think this over. But remember, my patience is limited. It would be best if you gave your answer sooner rather than later."

Arthur tried not to show his hands trembling as he stepped back away from the gang and headed back to his horse waiting for him. Arthur's mind raced as he stepped further and further away from Randal without turning. Only when he was shrouded by the bushes, did he turn and race to his horse. Arthur hoisted himself up in to the saddle and rammed his heels into the horse. The horse darted forward and with his heart pounding as sweat dripped down his brow, they rode back the way they came.

"Don't fight me over this. I will get what I want eventually," Arthur heard Randal's voice shout as he raced back towards his homestead.

Chapter 26

Every five minutes, Sophie peeked through the slit in the curtain wondering whether or not she would see Arthur again. Her heart sank each and every time she peeked out to find the way clear. There was no stopping the fantasies that played in her mind.

Where are you? Please be okay. Please come home.

Sophie had woken with the sun as it trickled into her room. She rose with the determination to stand by her man at all cost and to help him with whatever he needed. But when she slipped out of her room and stepped out into the hallway, the house appeared quieter. Sophie could feel the absence of Arthur immediately. Her suspicions were confirmed at breakfast when she called Arthur to come and eat.

"Arthur?" her voice bounced off the walls, making her voice sound far away. It didn't take long for her to put two and two together and she realized that he had slipped away sometime in the wee morning hours. Going mad with anxiety, Sophie tried to keep herself busy throughout the day, but every creak and moan of the house made her jump, wondering whether or not Arthur had returned. And each time she had been met with disappointment.

The sun was rising higher in the mid-morning sky and all Sophie could do was run through the different scenarios of what had happened with Arthur.

Would I even know if he is dead? Would somebody come to the homestead to tell me they found his body on the wayside? Or maybe Randal would drop him in some creek and let his body drift through three counties.

I can't take this anymore. So help me Arthur, if you come back unscathed you are going to be in some deep trouble.

At her wits end, she turned once more towards the window and pulled back the fabric forcefully. She closed her eyes and sucked in a deep breath as she said a little prayer. Slowly she opened her eyes. To her surprise and relief she spotted Arthur galloping at full speed towards the corral. Sophie's heart dropped and the irritation and anger she felt drifted away as she pushed through the front door to greet him.

It felt like an eternity before he finally made it to the corral. She waited impatiently for him with her foot wrapping against the wooden planks and her arms crossed over her chest. Just the sight of him made her want to fall apart.

"Where on God's green earth have you been? You didn't leave a note. You just took off without letting me know. Do you have any idea how worried I've been for you?" She asked as her eyes scanned Arthur from head to toe to ensure he wasn't injured in any shape or form.

"Do you have any idea how nervous and how scared I've been? I thought you had been kidnapped or worse, killed."

"I'm sorry I should have said something to you last night, but I knew you'd try and find a way to talk me out of it," Arthur said as he slipped down from his saddle and drew the horse into the corral.

"What exactly was so important that you had to take off without letting me know?"

"I was hunting Randal," Arthur said in a muffled voice that Sophie barely heard.

"Are you out of your mind? What in the world possessed you to do that? You know how dangerous that man is." Sophie lifted her hand to her chest hoping to quell her frantic heartbeat. All morning she had been thinking the worse, yet here Arthur stood, unharmed.

Arthur's eyes shifted to the ground as his shoulders slumped.

"Well," Sophie exhaled and allowed the stress to escape. "I take it you found his gang then?" Sophie asked as Arthur dropped his head and rested his weary body over the fence. He didn't say a word but nodded his head.

"And? Did you find a way to end this? Is there anything that we can do to make him stop or better yet, go away?"

Once more Arthur was silent, his head shook from side to side as his eyes remained locked on the horse.

"He wants the ranch," Arthur finally said.

"What?"

"Randal, he wants the ranch. He wants the cattle."

"You can't be serious. You told him no, right? Arthur, please tell me you didn't give into his demands," Sophie's heart rattled in her chest as she stared at Arthur with concern. Every ounce of her body tingled as the warmth of her blood vanished.

"Please tell me you're not thinking about giving it to him, are you?" Sophie's heart sank into her stomach and she rushed down the steps. She threw her arms around Arthur's body and squeezed him tightly. He pushed off the fence and turned in her arms.

"What else am I to do? He promised to keep hurting our friends. Randal even threatened you," Arthur said, glancing at Sophie. "I don't know about you, but I can give up this place if it means you live."

"You can't give in to him. He's nothing but a bully. A mean vile bully. You have to know he won't stop with just this ranch right? He has a lust that won't be quenched, and he'll go after every single person that has something he wants. We can't let him do that."

"Think about it," Arthur said, turning in Sophie's arms to face her. "We could start over and we can build all of this again from the ground up and it will be ours."

"And what's going to stop Randal from coming and tracking you down again? Who's to say he won't come back again and again to claim everything you build? He found you here, he can find you someplace else. Even if you happen to change your name again. Don't you see? If we don't stand up to him now, he's going to just keep doing what he's doing. It doesn't matter where we go, he'll find us just like he did this time around. We can't let that happen."

"There's just too many people at stake here Sophie. Don't you understand? There's the Davidson's and the townsfolk. Not to mention Sam and eight other ranch hands that I have to worry about here. Everybody's fate seems to be resting on my shoulders," Arthur said, dropping his head in his hands.

"It doesn't have to be that way. If we just tell people the truth, I'm sure they'll rally to our side. They all see you as a good man Arthur, you just have to have a little faith," Sophie said as Arthur pushed away from her and turned his back to her.

"People aren't as forgiving as you are. And you saw what happened to the sheriff. I can't lose you Sophie."

"I'm not leaving. This is my home and it's not fair that we have to leave because of one man. But we have here and I'm going to fight for it even if you don't."

Arthur shook his head and pursed his lips into a tight line as he drew his eyes up to her. Sophie could see the desperation and hurt mixed with fear in his gaze.

"And what would you have me do?" Arthur's voice was harsh and timid.

"Randal's leverage is that he knows you were once a part of his gang, right? Well, take that away from him. Don't give him any power over you. Go to the sheriff and tell him everything, leave nothing out. Let Noonen and the townsfolk make up their own minds about what to do. You know half of them are ready to fight and are willing. You don't have to face this alone."

"You don't understand, Sheriff Noonen sees the world in terms of black and white. There is no gray when it comes to upholding the law. The sheriff would have every right to throw me in jail if he ever found out that I ran with Randal Munger's gang and then where would that leave you?"

Sophie pulled in a deep breath and stared at her husband. She knew that there was a lot to consider but one thing was for certain, she wasn't going to let her husband down. She would stand by him and do as he asked no matter which decision he made. She knew that it was all on Arthur now.

* * *

The sound of Arthur's footsteps echoed down the hall as he made his way to his bedroom. It had been a rough morning and despite the fact that he knew there were chores to be done he didn't want to do them. All the stress seemed to be piling up one after another and Arthur didn't know how much more he would be able to handle.

Maybe Sophie's right, maybe I should just tell everyone. The guilt is eating me alive. But then, there's the sheriff who would lock me up or worse - hang me if he knew the truth. Then where would that leave Sophie? She'd be a disgrace in town. After all, it's my fault she came out here in the first place. She wouldn't have come had I not asked her to. It's because of me she's gotten entangled in all of this.

Arthur shook his head and cracked his knuckles as he paced his bedroom floor. He ran his fingers through his hair and tried to figure out his next move. But no matter which scenario he came up with, Sophie's words kept on coming back to haunt him. Randal wouldn't stop. Randal would keep on coming after him. It may not be for a year or even two years or decades later, but eventually Randal would find a way to keep making his life a living hell.

Maybe it isn't as bad as it seems. Maybe I can talk to someone and tell them the truth. I mean after all, that is what Randal is dangling over my head like a blade ready to come down. But if I take that away from him, what else does he have on me?

Arthur plopped down on his bed and rubbed his chin as he concocted a way to tell people about his past. He thought of the ramifications of what he had done before moving to Oakbury. In a brilliant spark of inspiration Arthur leapt to his feet and clapped his hands, excited to finally see the light at the end of the tunnel.

Sophie's right. She's been great this whole time. If I take that one thing away, Randal won't have a leg to stand on. He won't be able to blackmail me for the ranch. He won't be able to hurt me. Sure it's going to be painful letting the truth out and I know I am gambling with the fact that my past has come back to bite me. But it can't be any worse than the bite that Randal Munger is trying to take out of me.

With a huge smile stretching across his lips, Arthur raced to the door and threw it open startling Sophie. She whipped her head around as she sat on the couch in the living room.

Arthur's heart broke as he noticed the tears in her eyes, but he knew that her solution to their issue would fix everything.

"You're right," Arthur said, rushing to Sophie. He dropped down to one knee as he looked up at Sophie's red eye. "I need to tell people about my past. But I need to start small. Invite the Davidson's over for dinner and maybe if their reaction isn't as horrible as I think it will be, then I'll go to the sheriff."

Sophie threw her arms around his neck and squeezed him tightly. "I promise everything is going to be just fine, you'll see." She pressed her lips to Arthur's cheek, "You just need a little faith."

"It's not for lack of faith," Arthur said, tucking the loose strand of Sophie's hair behind her ear. He paused to gaze at her as a single tear escaped down her cheek. He brushed his finger over her cheek and smiled tenderly at her.

"You know that when I first moved out here, I didn't know what to expect," Sophie said staring up at her husband. "I didn't know what kind of man you were going to be. Sure you could have put whatever you wanted in those letters you sent to me, but I didn't know. No one ever does until they spend time with the person and get to know them." Sophie cupped her hands around Arthur's face and smiled at him.

"Arthur Soul, you are a decent human being and anyone in this town who doesn't see that is a fool. Every single one of us has a past. Some hide from it, but not you. You are brave enough to face it."

Chapter 27

Sophie pulled in a deep breath and held it for moment as she stared at the empty table in the dining room. With each tick of the clock her heart felt heavy. Of course, she knew what she was feeling was nothing compared to what Arthur was going through.

She shifted her attention from the beautiful dinner she had laid out on the table to Arthur in the living room. His foot rapped against the wooden floors as he squeezed his fingers tightly between each other only to release them again. But the impulsive knocking of his foot made Sophie even more nervous and a bit frightened. She knew they both were.

For Arthur though, it was much worse. After all, he had lived here for several years under the guise of someone else and coming clean to his friends was going to be rough. Sophie knew he had a hard-enough time just trying to explain to her about his past but now that his friends were coming to hear the same story, she knew that his nerves were probably shot.

"It will be fine," Sophie said, trying to reassure him as she walked around the table and squeezed her fingers into his tense shoulders. She massaged the tension from them and heard him exhaling. The hard knocking caused both of them to jump.

"I don't know if I can do this," Arthur said as he squeezed Sophie's hand that rested on his shoulder.

She leaned down and pressed her lips to his cheek, "Everything will be fine."

Clearing her throat, she rose and dusted her skirt before straightening her petticoat to ensure that she looked pristine for her guests. She moved quickly to the door and opened it wide.

"My, my, I always do love coming here," Garner said as he took Sophie's hand and pressed it to his lips. Sophie flashed him a weary smile as she stepped aside, allowing him into the home.

Mae flashed Sophie a brilliant smile that seemed a bit out of place. She looked over at Sophie and frowned.

"Something going on?" Mae asked as she stepped in and gave Sophie a huge hug.

"Welcome," Sophie said. "Won't you come in?"

"Enough," Mae said, glaring at her. "I know you and there is something wrong. You can feel the tension stepping into this house, now out with it."

"We just have a few things we need to discuss," Sophie said trying to keep her voice low so as not to cause Arthur any more distress than what he was already going through.

"If this is about the goats on your property, there isn't anything I can do about it. They are slippery little buggers that don't seem to know where my land starts or ends," Garner started as he turned his attention from Arthur to Sophie and then back again. Arthur slowly rose from the couch to greet his old friend and moved around the furniture to shake hands.

"You two look like someone has died or something, what's going on?" The concern on Mae's face broke Sophie's heart. Although Sophie wanted to explain everything, she knew it wasn't her story to tell.

"Why don't we sit down first and have some dinner before we get into the details of the matter?" Sophie said, lifting her hand up to escort her friends to the dinner table. Confusion mixed with uncertainty flashed across Mae's face as her skirt swished on the wooden floor like a broom as she walked.

"Miss Sophie, I swear you outdo yourself every time we come over here," Garner said, clearly amused by the food on the table. Sophia had made Arthur's favorite foods to ease his mind and comfort his nerves. It was a simple spread with the roast duck and potatoes. A hint of rosemary swirled around the air causing their stomach to crawl with hunger.

"If y'all don't mind," Sophie said as she waited for each person to sit down before she took her seat. Her eyes shifted from Mae to Arthur who sat at the end of the table.

"All right now. I've known you for quite some time and I have never seen anyone so sad as the lot of you. What in the world is going on?" Mae plucked the napkin from the side of her plate and put it onto her lap. Arthur's eyes shifted from the plate to Sophie. She could see perspiration on his brow as he pulled in a deep breath and turned to their friends sitting next to them.

"Honestly, I don't know how to tell you this," Arthur said.

"Out with it", Garner said as he reached for the food that was in front of him and piled his plate high.

"Arthur, why don't you let me explain," Sophie said as she noticed her husband's face scrunching and his eyes turning red.

Arthur didn't have to say a word, he nodded quickly and folded his hands on the table. Sophie watched his shoulders drop as she reached for his hands.

"We know why that gang came into town", Sophie said, looking at her friends across the table. Garner nearly dropped his fork and clamped his mouth shut as he stared at her.

Mae sat back in her chair with an eyebrow lifted, waiting for more.

"And just how do you know these folks?" Mae asked in a tone that caused Sophie to sit straighter. For a moment, Sophie thought she was being scolded by her stepmother.

"Arthur... well," Sophie paused as she struggled with the words to say. The longer she stared at Mae the harder it seemed to get them out and into the open. Sophie swallowed the lump forming in her throat and reached for her glass to quench her parched tongue. Once her mouth was wet and her tongue loose, Sophie began to speak.

"Arthur used to ride with them," Sophie said in a rush of words it seemed almost unintelligible. Garner looked at Sophie with a stern expression before turning his gaze onto Arthur.

"Come again?" Arthur looked back at his friend and nodded with his lips pulled into a tight line.

"What Sophie says is true," Arthur said. "I used to run with the gang, but I have a very good explanation for it that is if you'll hear me out."

It took all of ten minutes for Arthur to explain his past. And when he was done, he sat back in his chair with his head and shoulders dropped, looking completely defeated. Sophie's heart broke at seeing her husband in such distress that she scooted her chair out from the table and walked over to him to show that he was not alone. Even if her friends castrated them, she would not allow her husband to sit there alone.

"Well that certainly is a story," Mae said, her eyes flickering to Garner before turning back to Sophie.

"It's all true. Every word of it," Sophie said, trying not to dig her fingers into Arthur's shoulders as her nerves rattled within her.

"And just so you know, you're the only folks in town who know the story. We didn't know whether or not we should tell anybody else. Arthur felt that it was only right that he shared it with you first," Sophie stared at her friends as her heart pummeled inside her rib cage. Mae was one of Sophie's closest friends since she'd stepped off the train but even Sophie knew there were limits to a friendship. If Mae was going to turn her back on her now, Sophie was prepared for it.

Slowly, Garner shoveled a forkful of food into his mouth and chewed. He didn't say a word; he just ate the food on his plate and tried to keep his eyes off of Sophie and Arthur.

"Aren't you gonna say something?" Arthur asked, expecting the brunt of the reaction to come from Garner.

"Ain't nothing to say," Garner said, "Except perhaps, could you pass the gravy?"

Sophie gazed down at Arthur as he stared up at her completely shocked at Garner's lack of interest about their situation. Although it was a blessing in disguise, Sophie couldn't help but wonder why Garner was being so blasé about it all.

"Look son," Garner said as he finally sat his fork down next to his empty plate and turned his attention to the couple. "Everybody has a past. Every single one of us. But from what I just heard come out of your mouth, you didn't do anything wrong. Sure, you may have joined them, but you never stole anything. You never shot anyone. But there's your reputation that they are trying to drag through the mud. Out here, that's all a man has. For me, you've shown me what kind of man you are. Revenge is a funny thing, but I didn't know you back then. I only know the man here before me. You've been a fine outstanding citizen of this community and if you say you're being terrorized by this here Randal fella, well I support you."

The tears that Arthur had been holding back finally spilled over and raced down his cheeks. He dropped his head into his hands and his shoulders racked back and forth as he wept. Sophie dropped down to her knees and tried to console her husband as he rested his head on her shoulder.

"I told you everything was going to be okay," Sophie whispered to him as he let out all of his stress and regret.

Arthur pulled himself together and cleared his throat. Sophie rose and moved over to her seat and sat down with her hand extended to Arthur for him to take. As Arthur's fingers curled around hers, she knew that they could face everything with their heads held high.

"I honestly don't know what to say. I expected tonight to be completely different and you guys shutting me out of the community," Arthur said as he glanced from Mae to Garner then to Sophie.

"Well, I wouldn't go blathering to Miss Hazel about this but, Lord knows how the rest of the town will take it," Mae said. "But it's like my husband said, we're here for you and will always be here for you. Y'all are family you know."

"Speaking of family, where's the children? Why didn't you bring them around tonight?" Sophie asked.

Mae smiled. "We left them with Nora tonight."

"My mother has been itching to have them to herself for a while now and we thought we'd kill two birds with one stone you know?" Garner said eyeing the food on the table.

Arthur's lips curled up at the corners as Sophie allowed a single tear to spill from her eye. She quickly brushed the moisture away and slipped her hand out from Arthur's to reach for the roast duck.

"Here," she said filling Arthur's plate. "You need to eat. We had a long day and tomorrow will be just as long. If tonight is any indication of how the town will take the news, then you can rest assured that tomorrow is going to be a good day."

Arthur nodded his head as Sophie smiled.

You are as gentle and as honest as them, aren't you? You are my husband and you make me love you more and more every day.

* * *

Arthur curled his arm around Sophie's waist and with his free hand waved goodbye to Mr. and Mrs. Davidson as they drove their wagon back to their home. Arthur turned to Sophie as the cicadas serenaded them with their haunting melody. He looked into Sophie's eyes and smiled.

"I don't know if I would have been able to do that without you by my side," he said cupping his hands around her face and holding her attention.

"You would've done just fine. You are a brave man Arthur Soul, I just wish that one of these days you'd see it for yourself."

"I think you give me too much credit," Arthur said as he leaned down and pressed his lips tenderly to Sophie's.

Releasing her he stepped back and took a look at the moon. The white light shone down on the ranch making everything look pristine.

"I suppose we should head on in," Sophie said, "We do have a big day tomorrow."

"You are coming with me right?" Arthur asked as he pulled open the front door and waited for Sophie to enter the home. Pulling her shawl from her shoulders and hanging on the hook by the door Sophie nodded.

"When are you going to learn that you ain't getting rid of me? I have been by your side since before this madness started. I have stuck by you even though you keep trying to push me away."

"I just don't want to see you get hurt," Arthur said.

"I won't. I'm stuck with you for life."

"Are you certain that is what you really truly want?" Arthur asked as he stared at his wife. Sophie smiled as she bobbed her head up and down.

"I just don't know how you do it, you are so brave and so beautiful and so kind. Why don't you go ahead and turn in," Arthur said, "And I will wake you in the morning so you can get ready to go to town."

Sophie nodded her head and hesitated for a moment. She looked as though she had something to say, some burning question lingering in her eyes. But instead of releasing it, she held it and kept it close to her as she turned on her heels and walked down the hallway. Arthur's heart fluttered as Sophie disappeared into her bedroom.

"I suppose tomorrow really does have its own worries. I just hope I can handle the outcome," Arthur mumbled as he dusted the lamps and move towards his bedroom.

The sweet song of the Blue-jay startled him awake. He sat up in his bed with his eyes wide and scanned the room once over before jumping out of bed. He couldn't shake the feeling that today was going to be the start of the end of his life. He knew that the Davidson's had accepted him for who he was but there was still an uncertainty about the sheriff.

Pulling in a deep breath Arthur got dressed for the day. He fixed himself up in his Sunday best hoping that the sheriff would see him as an upstanding citizen and not a ruffian in disguise.

A light rap on the door startled him as he adjusted his tie.

"Come in," he said. The door squealed as it opened, and Sophie's head popped through the crack.

"I was just making sure that you were awake," she said as she smiled to find him dressed like the fine gentlemen that he hoped to be.

"I've already hitched up the wagon. I'm just waiting for you," Sophie said. Arthur nodded once and followed Sophie down the hall and out the front door. He helped her into the wagon and double checked the horses before climbing up himself.

"Don't look so guilty," Sophie said as she reached for his hand and squeezed tightly.

"I just don't know what is gonna happen".

"Well that's the beauty of life isn't it?" Sophie said with a smile. "All we can do is hope for the best right?"

Hope for the best? Easier said than done.

Arthur's mind raced and his heart sputtered as they made their way into town. He knew that he wasn't much company and allowed Sophie to do most of the talking on the trip, but he wanted to make sure that he was completely prepared for what was about to happen to him. Tugging on the reins to stop the horses in front of the sheriff's building, Arthur swallowed the lump of fear that was in his throat. It seemed as if the building was three times bigger than what it really was, and it towered over them like a giant ready to squash them.

"You ready for this?" Sophie asked with a huge smile on her face as if she knew the future and had seen the outcome. Arthur nodded, slipped off the wagon and moved quickly to her side to help her down. He paused at the door waiting for Sophie.

"What we got going on here?" Sheriff Noonen asked the instant they walked in through the doors. Sophie looked over her shoulder at Arthur causing the fear to bubble up in his stomach.

"You're looking much better," Sophie said, stepping in to hug the sheriff briefly.

"I have always been a quick healer," the sheriff said with a bit of a chuckle as he walked towards Arthur and extended his hand to shake it. Arthur wiped the sweat off onto his slacks and squeezed Noonen's hand tightly.

"Well what can I do for you today?" the sheriff asked. "If it's about them rough riders out by the creek, I'm working on it. I got a few deputies out there trying to keep them corralled so they don't cause no more trouble. But they are a slippery bunch and don't seem to mind tossing my boys around a bit."

"Actually we are here about the gang", Sophie said, looking at Arthur.

"You might want to sit down for this sheriff," Arthur said as he swallowed hard to quench his perched throat.

"I have a story to tell you and only you can tell me how it's all going to end," Arthur said, "Truth be told, I don't know how your gonna take it, but I need to tell you before anyone else gets hurt."

Arthur and Sophie watched the sheriff walk around his desk and take a seat in the wooden chair that seemed to protest the large man's weight. Sophie curled her arm into Arthur's, giving him the courage that he needed.

"It all started several years ago before I even moved here," Arthur stated. It didn't take long for the whole story to come spilling out of Arthur's mouth. Sophie clung to Arthur as Arthur kept his eyes on the sheriff, explaining how Randal killed his parents which caused Arthur to hunt down the gang to get revenge.

As Arthur told the story he studied the sheriff's face and grew nervous as he finished. Unlike Garner and Mae's there was a distinct spark in the sheriff's eyes that caused Arthur to squeeze Sophie's arm tightly.

This is it; he's going to arrest me.

Chapter 28

The sheriff rose slowly to his feet as his eyes remained locked on Arthur. Sophie could feel Arthur's arm squeezing tighter around hers as the sheriff moved around his desk with his hand on his gun. Fear gripped Sophie and she closed her eyes. Never in all her life did she expect the sheriff to be arresting her husband.

"Arthur," Noonen lifted his head up and dropped his hand from his hip. "Tell me one thing."

"Anything," Arthur said, swallowing hard.

"You ever hurt anyone? Maim them in any way?" Noonen asked as he lifted his chin and licked his lips.

"No sir," Arthur said, shaking his head quickly. "Never, and I never would. I swear on my life."

"Relax Arthur, I know you wouldn't hurt a fly," Noonen said chuckling. "We've known each other a long time and I'm a bit insulted that you didn't come to me with this information earlier."

"Look John," Arthur released Sophie's arm and stepped closer to the sheriff. "I'm so sorry. I had no idea the town would be in so much jeopardy because of my connection to Randal. I thought he would just be targeting me, not the whole town."

"Well, now we know just how far he is willing to go, and don't you be blaming yourself for this," the sheriff waved his hand to his bruised and swollen face. "This wasn't your fault. If anyone is to blame, I'd be blaming that no good marshal. All we got is our word and if a man swears to uphold the law and is bribed, well, he don't have no part wearing the badge," Noonen said, patting Arthur on the shoulder.

"No," Sophie said, shaking her head. Relief washed through her as she stared at the two men before her. She had walked into the building believing all would work itself out and here she was, seeing it happen before her very eyes.

She glanced up at Arthur and flashed him a small smile as he scooped her hands up and brought them to his lips. Closing her eyes she let all the stress drift out of her. In the pit of her gut she felt more safe and secure than ever before.

As she opened her eyes, a loud scuffle outside the jail caused her to spin around. She didn't have to be told who was causing the ruckus. One glimpse out the dusty dirty windows gave her a clear view of the rough riders howling down the main strip.

"I can't go out there alone," Noonen said, glancing at Arthur. "Last time I stood up to them, they beat me down like I was a dog."

"We can't let them continue terrorizing this place," Arthur said. "Maybe if we go out together or if you got all your deputies in here we could pick them off one by one. But any of us goes up against them alone, no doubt we'll get beat down," Arthur said stealing a moment to look at Sophie.

Her heart sank like bricks in her stomach as she listened to Noonen and Arthur plot their next move. Pulling away from Arthur, she stared out the window, keeping her eyes locked on the men. A curt little smile played at the corners of her lips as she watched them behind the dingy glass.

"Honestly, they aren't any better than a pack of wild dogs," Noonen's voice drifted into Sophie's ears causing her to turn.

"They work as a pack. Maybe even take orders as a pack would do. Perhaps all we have to do is get Randal alone and we could take down this whole operation and stop them from terrorizing us anymore. I wonder how hard it would be to get Randal alone."

Sophie turned to find Arthur and the sheriff hunched over a map of the county. She could hear Arthur explaining to the sheriff where he last saw Randal, but they all knew the chances of Randal still being there were slim to none.

"Maybe what we need right now is a distraction?" Arthur suggested as the noise outside grew louder. "Something that throws them all for a loop."

"Actually, I have a plan," Sophie said, looking at the men who seemed more concern with what was going on outside than the bigger picture. Sophie cleared her throat and stepped closer to them.

"Arthur," she paused and waited for him to look at her. Arthur straightened up and gazed at her just as a bottle slammed against the outside wall of the jail. Sophie couldn't help but jump at the sound of shattering glass.

"I have a plan," she said a bit louder. "Although, I'm not so certain you'll like it."

* * *

"No," Arthur said flat out as he shook his head. "You don't know Randal the way that I do. He is smart and cunning. The man can spot a trap a mile away not to mention the fact that he's paranoid. You didn't see how many men he had back at his hideout."

"Arthur, you have to trust me. I know that you think you can save me from everything, but you can't. Sooner or later something is going to happen, and you won't be there to help me. At least with this plan we have a shot of ending the terror swiftly."

Arthur's chest felt as if someone was squeezing the life out of him. He stared at her, "It's not about trusting you. It's about what he'll do to you."

"You can't stop him with his gang around him like they are. But if we can lure Randal away from his men under the pretense that I, a woman, want to talk to him, then maybe we will have a shot at capturing him. All we have to do is get as many men gathered as possible," Sophie said with her eyes filled with hope and awe. The way the light trickled through the dirty window made her resemble an avenging angel.

"Arthur," Noonen called, stepping closer and patting him on the shoulder. "Your wife is right. I had that man on the ropes four times and still he managed to slip through my fingers. It was only because of his gang he was able to do the damage to me that he did. We have to give this plan of Sophie's a shot."

"No, this won't be happening. Neither of you know Randal the way I do. You don't know what he's capable of doing," Arthur said as his fear made him shiver. In the back of Arthur's mind, he could see his family's ranch burning and his younger brother sprawled out like a rag doll on the porch. His heart tightened as he blinked to find Sophie in his brother's place.

"Arthur, my plan will work. Randal will be convinced that as your wife, I am concerned for your safety and only your safety. I'll plead with him not to do anything else around town and distract him while you and the sheriff come to my aid."

"It's too risky," Arthur said as the hollering outside died down a bit. For a moment Arthur wondered if the gang had all dropped dead. Carefully, Arthur slipped towards the sheriff's door and peeked out. The street was practically empty. Once upon a time, Oakbury had been a lively town where people would grace the boardwalk with their presence, but now it looked like a ghost town.

Arthur couldn't deny that he missed the way the town once was. He missed the people and all the smiling faces. But now, the only people daring enough to stroll through the streets belonged to Randal's gang. Shaking his head and realizing he was at an impasse with Sophie, he stepped back inside.

"You will carry the rifle I taught you how to shoot with, do you understand?" Sophie pressed her lips into a tight line and bobbed her head. In all the months he'd been with her, never once had he seen such excitement drift over her face. It was as if a new woman stood before him.

"Agreed," Sophie said. "First though, we need to get the word to one of Randal's men that I want to talk. How do you suppose we do that?" Sophie asked, glancing at Noonen.

"Well, that's not as tricky as you might think," Noonen said, lifting his head up. Arthur could see a sense of pride and a tinge of hope sparkling in the sheriff's eyes.

"Those boys have their ears to the ground. A simple little side comment at the grocer's store and I'm almost certain word will get back to Randal. Only problem is, you won't know that Randal got the message," Noonen said as he plopped down in his chair behind his desk.

"You do realize that this plan of yours is twofold right?" Arthur asked, turning his attention to Sophie.

Dear sweet Sophie you have no idea what you're getting yourself into. But you stuck by me, so this is me standing by you. I just wish you would have asked for another way.

"What are you talking about?" Sophie replied. Arthur could see her breathing increasing. She was scared, but there was no way she would admit that in front of the sheriff, not after all the grandeur she just expressed.

"Randal's gang isn't just going to roll over the second Randal is cuffed. Chances are they will lash out and try and escape with their lives. We have to be smarter than they are and split our resources. We'll need two groups. One to be with you as you take down Randal and the other to round up the cowboys that flee."

"But we don't have that many people," Sophie said, her voice cracking with defeat. Arthur watched as she dropped her head.

"Maybe we do," Noonen said. "If there is one thing I've seen above all else in this crazy life is how desperate people do desperate things."

"What are you going on about?" Arthur asked, looking directly at him.

"That marshal you spoke of, think he might be up for a bit of redemption?" Noonen's lips curled up at one corner as he cocked his head. "If the table was reversed, I sure know I would want that chance to make up for my mistakes. Think your buddy might be feeling that way too?"

"I don't know," Arthur said, staring at Sophie. She lifted her head up and smiled at them. Arthur's body sparked as if it had been struck by lightning. He knew their plan was crazy, but it was so far out there that not even Randal would see it changing.

"Didn't he come to warn you a few weeks ago?" Sophie asked with a wide-eyed look.

Arthur's head bobbed up and down dumbstruck that she would remember such a thing. "Actually, he did. The marshal probably isn't very far. He might even be in the next state over."

This will work.

This has to work.

Finally I'll be free of him and be able to live out my days with Sophie. Bless you Sophie.

"Well you send the marshal a telegram and I'll see what I can round up around town. We might just scrape up enough men to get our town back." The sheriff smiled and slammed the palm of his hand down on the desk startling Sophie. She jumped and a slight giggle escaped her lips. Her laugh was like bells to Arthur's ears, bells that he hadn't heard in some time.

"Sophie, you handle the gossip," the sheriff said turning to her. "Remember, all you need to do is start the conversation and it will get to one of Randal's men. As for you Arthur, send the telegram but keep it as secretive as you can. Don't want the wrong people hearing you are trying to contact a marshal. Might start a panic and Randal and his gang might flee before we can trap them. Now, is everyone clear on what needs to be done?"

Arthur bobbed his head as he stepped closer to Sophie. Although he didn't like the fact that she'd be alone with Randal for any given time, she was right. There was no other way to trap Randal.

"Then let's go take down those mutts," the sheriff said slamming his fist on the desk.

Chapter 29

Dear Diary,

It's been two weeks since we spoke with the sheriff and I must admit my nerves have been rattled all the while. It seemed that each day that passed with no news made things so much worse. Arthur appeared to be on constant alert.

I've noticed him looking over his shoulder out in the field. Even at dinner time his shoulders are back as if he's ready to spring to action. Watching him wound up so tightly is painful. But our prayers were answered tonight.

After dinner, just as I was settling, we heard a knock on the door. Of course Arthur shot up and reached for the rifle by the door. The fear in his eyes chilled me, but the instant we opened the door, we were shocked to find the marshal standing there in the dead of night. It would seem that our plea for help was heard and he brought along with him several men of his own.

I honestly cannot believe it. Knowing that we have men on our side ready and willing to fight for our town is more than inspiring. Although I know Randal Munger is a dangerous fellow, the men that showed up seemed to be even more menacing which tells me Arthur is in good, capable hands.

Tomorrow we are riding into town to see the sheriff and I can't help but hold onto the hope that he too will have good news for us. Going over the plan again and again in my mind is starting to make me believe we can accomplish it without any hitches. But still, doubt lingers, and I can't stop myself from thinking that perhaps I am putting too much faith in my own ability to distract Randal. We will all see soon enough though.

Once the sheriff tells us whether or not he has gotten his men ready then it will all come down to my part. Somehow I will have to get the word to Randal's men that I need to talk to their boss. I must say I am nervous about this part of the plan. In theory it sounds solid, but in practice, well, I know I'll find some way to bungle it, I always do.

I know, I must not think like that, especially when so much has gone our way. But still, I would be lying if I said I wasn't a little frightened by all this. With so many lives and homes at stake, there is a sense of responsibility that rests on my shoulders. And what if things go wrong? What if Randal doesn't take the bait? Granted, I'm sure he will since Arthur has made it perfectly clear that Randal wants everything Arthur has. But still, the 'what if' remains and spreads doubt like a weed.

Still, I think it is the waiting that is driving me to the edge. Patience was never a virtue I had and waiting for the sheriff seems to be dragging on forever. I wish this was all said and done so that life could get back to normal.

Sophie sucked in a deep breath and closed her journal. She took a moment to gaze out of her window to the veil of darkness. In her heart she knew that even if they had to sign over the ranch, as long as she and Arthur were together she'd be happy.

Tucking her book into the desk drawer, Sophie moved to the bed and sat down. The soft blankets welcomed her as she nestled down into the pillows. Slowly sleep over came her. Before she could even begin to let the nightmares in, the call of the sparrow on her window seal woke her up. Rubbing the sleep from her eyes, she rose and stretched out the insecurities and doubts that seemed to linger from the night before.

Relax, the sheriff may not be ready just yet. Last time we spoke, he was still getting his pose together. Not to mention we still haven't heard anything from the marshal. All of this is very frustrating. If only we had answers, or a direction to take.

I hate waiting.

Sophie quickly dressed and stepped out of her room. Arthur sat on the couch and looked over his shoulder as she approached him.

"You're up early," Sophie said, tucking the last bit of her hair into the pin at the back of her head.

"Actually, I couldn't sleep. There was too much on my mind," Arthur admitted as he shifted his weight to get a better view of Sophie. She smiled as she walked around the couch and sat down.

"Is what's bothering you the same that is bothering me?" Sophie asked, trying not to look so guilty.

"Perhaps. Sophie," Arthur paused and reached out to take Sophie's hands. He rubbed the tip of his fingers over her knuckles ever so lightly as he spoke. "I don't want you to go through this. If you are going into town today, I should be there with you."

"No," Sophie said, shaking her head. "Randal's men know you. They know that Randal wants what you have. If you go with me they might try and pick a fight and what will that accomplish for us? I have to go alone. Plus, by being alone in town might show Randal that I want this done in secret, behind your back. Randal might be more willing to meet with me then."

"You have no idea how much I wish I could take your place," Arthur said squeezing her hands.

"I know. But there is nothing to worry about. Not yet anyways. As far as we know, Sheriff Noonen doesn't have the men ready yet and I'll be in and out of town in a matter of hours."

"Even that seems to be too long," Arthur said flexing his jaw muscle. Sophie slipped her hand out of his grasp and cupped it to his face. Her eyebrows rose as she forced him to look at her, square in the eyes.

"You are worrying too much," Sophie said. "Let's just get through this morning. I'll go to the jail and talk with the sheriff to see where he stands. He has to know that Bergen upheld his part of this plan and that we are just waiting for him to give the word."

"The way you speak, you make it sound like a list of groceries you have to get," Arthur said shaking his head. Sophie could see the hurt in his eyes as she tried all she could think of to get him to calm down.

"That's precisely how it needs to be," Sophie said after a while. "We need to have this plan packed down so there will be no hitches or bumps along the way. The more prepared we are, the better the outcome will be. Now," Sophie slipped her hand out of Arthur's grasp and rose to her feet.

"I have to get the wagon hitched up and ready to go," Sophie said with a short smile.

"Actually, I've already got that taken care of. Like I said, I've been up for a while." Arthur rose to his feet and pulled down on his shirt, inhaling as deeply as his lungs could allow.

"Thank you," Sophie said. "But please don't worry so much. I'll be back soon enough."

"Are you sure you don't want me coming? I could find something to do in town to keep me busy," Arthur said. "What if Randal's men are causing havoc all over town today? What if something happens like what happened to the barber and you need me there?"

"Arthur," Sophie stepped forward and placed her hand on his chest. "You can't be doing that to yourself. Dwell on the good things not the bad. Everything will be just fine you'll see, and I'll be home for dinner."

"You better be," Arthur's voice dropped as Sophie cocked her head. Her lips curled at the corners as her eyes narrowed in on him.

"Or what?"

"You wouldn't dare make me fix dinner for Bergen and his men alone now, would you?" Arthur asked in such a pleading manner that Sophie couldn't help but laugh.

"I'm sure you'll do just fine. Don't you have this many men on your cattle drives?"

"Yes, but usually I'm not the one cooking for them," Arthur said as he walked Sophie to the front door. She reached for her shawl and he snatched it off the hook before she could.

"Allow me," he said, holding it open for her. Sophie turned and felt Arthur's fingers brush her shoulders as he set the cloth on her.

"Thank you," Sophie said as heat rose into her face. It always amazed her how the simple touches Arthur stole made her heart go into overdrive.

"Come back to me," Arthur said.

"I promise," Sophie answered as she reached for the doorknob and pulled it open. The fresh air kissed her burning cheeks. Sophie was pleased to find the buckboard hitched and ready to go. Although she couldn't help but wonder how long the poor horses had been waiting for her, she didn't have time. There were things that needed to be done.

"Please be careful," Arthur said, stepping out of the house.

"I always am," Sophie replied as she climbed into the seat. Grabbing the reins, she cracked them and startled the horses. Slowly the carriage started moving and Sophie couldn't help but wonder what the day would bring.

Her thoughts shifted as she rode to town. Struggling between racing back home and moving forward, Sophie realized that it was the waiting that was driving her insane. She wanted all this over with and with as little bloodshed as possible. The church steeple slowly came into view and her heart raced in her chest. She pulled up beside the grocer's and looked over her shoulder to the jail.

In the window, she spied Noonen perched against the frame of the window like he had been waiting for something to happen all morning. Keeping her eyes on him, he tipped his hat to her. Sophie found her heart fluttering with excitement. Slowly, Sophie climbed down and cleared her throat as she recalled Noonen's instructions.

"Remember, each item you get at the grocer's will represent the days until the meeting with Randal. So if he tells you to meet him in a week?"

"I'll buy seven items and put them in the wagon."

"That's right. That way you don't even need to step foot inside my building. I'll be keeping an eye on you and what you load into your wagon. To everyone else, you just came to town to buy supplies. The last thing we want is for Randal's men to be suspicious about you or me. If we keep our distance, then maybe they won't think nothing of it. Sound good?"

"What if you don't have your men ready?"

"Don't you worry about that; they'll be ready one way or another."

Sophie climbed the steps of the grocer's and paused. Every fiber in her body felt like it had been kissed by electricity. She couldn't help but feel jittery when Noonen tipped his hat to her.

That's it. That's the sign. Noonen is ready. But am I?

* * *

"Tomorrow? Are you sure?" Arthur's heart sank like a ton of bricks into his stomach as Sophie slipped off the buckboard. He lifted up the bag of flour she had purchased from the grocer and was astonished.

"This can't be right," he said shaking his head. "That means -"

"I know what it means," Sophie said as she walked around the buckboard and placed her hand on his. "It means that the waiting is over. That come tomorrow, Randal Munger will be back where he belongs, behind bars."

"Are you certain? Did you talk to Noonen?" Arthur asked, trying his hardest to find some loophole. The last thing he wanted to do was put Sophie in harm's way.

"I glanced at Noonen twice. He nodded his head and tipped his hat. Arthur, he is ready. We have the men. Tomorrow I will ride out to meet Randal by the old dried up well."

"You can't go, I won't let you," Arthur said grabbing Sophie by the shoulders. He was desperate and uncertain. Suddenly everything about the plan was wrong.

"Don't let fear guide you," Sophie answered, grabbing his hands on her shoulders. "You knew this day would come and what I would have to do when it did. What you need to focus on now is protecting me. You need to be there right on time and without delays or this whole thing will fall through."

"I know," Arthur said, dropping his head. "I just never thought that we'd be standing here like this."

"Trust me, no one thinks that more than I do," Sophie said.

"Tell me again what you're going to say to Randal. We need to make sure that he doesn't leave that area and that you know what to say to keep him as distracted as long as possible."

"Trust me," Sophie said as she pulled away from Arthur and headed towards the house. "I know my part in all this."

"I'm certain you do, it's just that," Arthur paused and stared at her. His heart felt as if she were squeezing the life out of it. He knew he didn't want her to leave and meet with his mortal enemy alone. But there was no other way. It had to be Sophie and they both knew it.

"I know what you are going to say," Sophie said, turning to glance at him over her shoulder. "And I'm not going to back down. Not when everything is ready. The sheriff has his men as does the marshal. Everything has already been set in motion and there is no way of stopping it now. Only tomorrow knows what it has in store for us and we can't back down now."

Arthur nodded. He knew Sophie was right but still, he wondered if he'd be able to let her go tomorrow. Everything was riding on her ability to keep Randal there until they showed up. And Arthur knew better than anyone how quickly things could change.

THE SCARRED RANCHER'S UNFORGETTABLE BRIDE

Chapter 30

Sophie's heart pounded in her chest as she gripped the reins. Glancing down at Arthur she couldn't help but have doubts about what she was doing. After all, Randal Munger was the most violent and dastardly men she had ever known, and she was about to confront him.

"Just keep your head up. Randal is a man who respects power and decisiveness. You show one sign of weakness, bat your lashes the wrong way and he'll be on to you. Make it believable that you're there to negotiate. And most importantly," Marshal Bergen stared up at her as he spoke. "Remember we aren't that far behind. We will have eyes on you at all times."

"Ride true and remember, the moment we show up, you leave. I'll meet you back here when it's all over," Arthur said, grasping Sophie's hand and pressing his lips to her knuckles.

"Promise?" Sophie asked in such hushed tones that Arthur had to lean forward. She could see his desperation and love all squeezed together in the concern that plastered his face. She knew what Arthur was giving up, but she didn't have a choice. This was, in fact, her idea and backing out now would only delay their happiness.

"I promise," Arthur said trying to smile.

"Then I'm ready," she exhaled. All the pressure and stress that had built up in her shoulders seemed to cause her to sink into the saddle. Still, she pushed back as she kicked her heel into the horse's side and took off down the dirt road.

You can do this. Nadine always used to complain about you talking too much. Funny how that's what's going to save you now. Just keep him talking, keep him there and trust in Arthur.

Sophie knew she could trust Arthur to be right behind her. She didn't need to steal a glimpse over her shoulder to know that Arthur would be riding out in a few short moments to the second location. All she had to do was stay on course and all would be well. Pushing her horse through the wee hours of the morning, she finally came across the barren brick well on the outskirts of Arthur's land.

Scanning the area she couldn't help but wonder why, out of all the places, Randal decided on that one. There was nothing special about it. Sure, it once had water, but that well had been dry since before she came out here. And yes, it had a lovely view of the valley that if Sophie squinted her eyes, she could get a glimpse of town. But still, Randal had chosen one strange place to meet up with her.

It's the barren wasteland. Probably symbolic to him or something.

What is wrong with you? Stay focused. No telling if or when he'll show up.

As Sophie's horse wandered around the area she couldn't help but think of Arthur. She knew he was a kind man that didn't deserve the life he had. He deserved a place that was free of worry and strife. Pulling in a deep breath, Sophie couldn't help but wonder about their future together. Sure, it was possible that after today everything would change. But in the back of her mind and in the depths of her being she prayed she would see Arthur again. If for no other reason than to press her lips to his one more time.

The rustling of the leaves behind her, quickened Sophie's heart as she sat on her horse in the middle of nowhere. The sound shifted her eyes to the growing shadows that stretched out towards her. Sweat moistened the palms of her hands despite the sun barely inching over the horizon. She held fast to the reins and breathed in deep to calm her rattled nerves.

Her heart felt like stones in her chest as her eyes narrowed to see through the dark skies.

Stay calm.

"Shh. Everything is alright now. You just stay calm you hear?" she said more to herself than to the horse as she rubbed her hand over the steed's thick neck. The beast under her huffed and stomped its hooves to the ground, unruly and defiant. Sophie realized she shouldn't have been so picky on riding the fastest horse Arthur had. She had forgotten how dominant it was and she didn't want to be bucked from the saddle due to a miscommunication.

"Easy there," she said in a calming voice as she stroked the horse's long neck.

How strange. You almost feel like velvet.

Sophie swallowed the lump forming in her throat as she waited. Every second that ticked by only caused the fear to grow within her. The terror sank its claws into her and squeezed the courage from her veins. For a second, Sophie wondered what had possessed her to come out here alone. Chewing on her bottom lip, she tightened her grip around the reins for some security and stability. Her heart pounded in her chest as she felt exposed, but she knew she had to stay despite every fiber in her being screaming at her to run.

"No," she said defiantly as she straightened her shoulders and back. "You can't back down now. This was your idea. Come hell or high water you will see this through."

She kept her eyes locked on the horizon, waiting nervously for any signs of life to come over the hill. The lonely cry of a hawk startled her as her eyes flickered to the dark blue skies. Clashing against the navy blue was a single speck of black and white. She squinted her eyes as the sun's early light kissed the horizon and scattered the shadows about her.

From the corner of her eye, Sophie noticed the dust cloud forming on the horizon behind her. Relief washed through her as she knew fully well that it was Arthur and Bergen's men riding to meet her. But with the relief also came the panic.

What if Randal saw the dust kicking up from Arthur's horses? What if he sensed someone else was around?

For a moment Sophie wondered if she should throw her hands up and try to get the men to stop and not blow her cover. But the instant she thought of alerting them, the dust cloud faded and to Sophie's eyes she appeared to be absolutely alone in the middle of nowhere.

"Easy there," she said as her horse stomped and grunted. Clearly the beast under her sensed her fear and the dread that had started to swell in her chest. She could feel the tension in the morning air. There was an uncertainty about the morning that she knew her horse could feel. Neither one knew what was coming over the hills, but they understood the significance of it.

Tiny specks emerged on the horizon as the sunlight kissed the hills. Sophie gasped and clung to her saddle. Her heart pounded and rolled around in her chest as she watched the specks grow and come into view.

Here we go. Remember the plan. Just stay calm, this will work.

She tried to keep her hands from trembling, but it was no use. Sophie knew that in a few short moments she'd be face to face with the man who had no issues with his men assaulting her in town. She'd have to look at the man, who had stalked her for weeks, in the eye and lie to him. Sophie knew it all came down to this single moment. The pressure in her chest tightened as she counted three men galloping at breakneck speeds over the hills, heading right towards her.

"Well, what do we have here?" Randal shouted as he rushed towards Sophie. The crackle in his eyes and the shimmer of his rifle caught her off guard. She knew these men were dangerous, but until that very moment she had no clue what she was really up against.

I'm so naive. Of course they'd be armed. Whatever made me believe Randal would come alone?

Sophie tried to pull in a deep breath to steady her nerves, but she soon realized that even her life could be forfeited if this meeting went the wrong way. Swallowing hard, she tried not to think of the rifle at Randal's side or the two men who attacked her in the town riding beside him.

"Ah got to say, I'm impressed. Here I thought you weren't going to come alone." Randal's lip curled up at one corner as his eyes shimmied about the area. Sophie knew what he was looking for; it was the same thing she wanted, a way out, an escape.

"So, do you know what I asked for?" Randal asked as his men came up around her, blocking off all avenues of escape.

"What happened to meeting alone?" Sophie replied, trying not to let her voice crack from fear.

"In all truth? I didn't expect you to be alone, yet here you are," Randal's lips curled at the corners. His smile made her blood run cold as she swallowed the lump forming in her throat.

"Well I did," Sophie said, trying hard to show no fear and to hold her ground.

"So you have," Randal paused and shifted his weight in the saddle as he eyed her. For a brief moment Sophie wanted to shift her eyes to the right in hopes of spying Arthur on the horizon but quickly thought against it. She knew any flinch would give her away and she wasn't about to let Randal, or his men get away, not after all they had done to terrorize her and Arthur.

"What say you?" Randal glared at Sophie as he licked his lips and cocked his head to one side. She closed her eyes for a split second and mustered all the courage she had.

"We aren't giving up the ranch," Sophie said, lifting her head up. She knew those words may end her right then and there, but she let them slip from her lips anyways.

"Is that so?" Randal said leaning over his saddle. His eyes narrowed in on Sophie like she was some kind of prize to be won. Randal gave a short whistle and the men that rode with him closed in on her. She knew her chances of escaping were long gone. All her hope rested on Arthur and the marshal.

"You'd better kill me," Sophie said as she opened her eyes and stared down the villain before her. "Kill me now, because if you don't I promise you, you'll regret it."

"Will I now?" Randal said chuckling.

That's it keep him talking. Keep him distracted at all costs.

"And what exactly is a little thing like you going to do to me? I could easily let my men finish what they started back in town. Maybe that will teach you some respect?"

"The jig is up Randal," Sophie said, trying not to let her voice crack under the strain.

"I don't think so. You see, I'm inclined to keep you as a trophy and make Arthur come find you," Randal said, licking his lips as he stared at Sophie with evil intentions.

"I'll kill myself before I let you touch me."

"Is that so? Or I could do it for you," he said.

"Then do it. Kill me right here and now," Sophie said as she noticed a shimmering light from the corner of her eye. All her thoughts drifted to Arthur.

She thought of the first flowers he gave her, the first touch they shared, the first time she ever saw him. Sophie's mind shifted as her memory of the first time she set eyes on Arthur became crystal clear, almost as if she was reliving the event. He was on the platform at the train station and she was a nervous little bird uncertain of why she even came there. In a heartbeat, the memory and vision were gone. Instead of Arthur's face, she saw Randal's grimacing smile.

"Well now, there's something that I think I can manage," Randal said, making his companions laughed as their horses kicked up dust around her. Sophie's eyes widened as the dark-haired man held her gaze. The rifle at Randal's side slipped from its holster and shimmered in the light of the sun.

"Go on then," Sophie said. She exhaled sharply as her hands trembled. A slight whimper escaped her lips. Randal pulled back the hammer of his rifle with a twisted smile itching at the corner of his lips.

"You know, I take no pleasure in this," Randal said, aiming the gun at Sophie. "But Arthur needs to pay for what he had done."

Sophie closed her eyes and sat very still in the saddle. Holding her breath, she waited for death to come. Suddenly, she found herself jumping with fright as the crack of gunfire filled her ears. Hunching down, Sophie opened her eyes.

"Go, now!" Arthur voice rose above the shots firing and Sophie did precisely as she was told. With a tug of her reins, she jerked to the left and kicked her heel into the horse's side. Instantly the nervous horse took off with her on it. There was no time for Sophie to glance over her shoulder to see what was happening. The wind whizzing through her ears as she pushed her horse faster filled the void and drowned out all other sounds.

Please be okay. Please be okay.

Only when she reached the top of the hill and knew the coast was clear did she ease and sit up. Carefully, she turned her head to find Arthur and the marshal's men surrounding Randal and his men. A smile drifted over her lips. As much as she wished to stop and see what happened next, she promised Arthur she'd go straight home.

"Come on, let's get," she said, forcing the horse to pick up even more speed. Her heart ached as she thought of leaving Arthur alone with Randal and his men, but there was nothing she could do about it now. Even if she turned around and went back, there would be nothing to see and she knew it.

Stick to the plan. Go home. He will meet you there. He promised.

Chapter 31

"It's over Randal," Arthur shouted, flying by Sophie as she fled the area. Arthur's heart raced when he passed her. He wanted to reach out and brush his fingertips to hers just to ensure she was unharmed. But there was no time. Randal had tugged the reins of his horse and was turning to flee.

"Stop right there," Arthur shouted again, firing his rifle into the air as a warning shot. The crack of the shot rang in Arthur's ears as he made his way to Randal's side. The two men Randal came with were fast and managed to flee before Arthur could get to Randal.

"I don't think so," Randal replied, drawing his six shooter, and turning sharply. Randal squinted one eye and took aim. The sound of Randal's gun was sharp. The whistle from the bullet flying by Arthur's head caused him to gasp. For a moment everything slowed as Arthur's mind drifted to Sophie. Whipping his head, Arthur glanced over his shoulder praying the bullet wasn't aimed at her.

His heart thudded in his chest as he kept his eyes locked on Sophie.

Please be a miss. Sophie, please stay true to your course. Keep riding.

Swallowing hard, Arthur waited a moment more before turning his attention back to Randal. With Sophie out of range and the bullet missing her, Arthur could focus on the task at hand. Digging his heels into his horse, Arthur rode harder than ever before trying to catch up to Randal. He pushed himself at breakneck speed until he was riding alongside Randal.

"You missed," Arthur shouted to Randal.

"A mistake that won't happen again," Randal shouted back as Arthur jerked the reins to ram his horse into Randal's. Randal shifted and pulled away to widen the gap between them forcing Arthur to follow.

Arthur followed closely behind Randal, weaving through and around trees. The horses leapt over rocks and other obstacles. No matter what terrain Randal went through, Arthur was right there trying to stop him.

"There's no where you can go that I won't follow," Arthur said as he forced his horse to leap over the fallen tree that blocked the path. "Now stop."

"You're going to have to make me," Randal shouted over his shoulder as Arthur came up on his left. Carefully, Arthur drew his gun and aimed. Taking long steady breaths as the horse charged on, Arthur squeezed the trigger. The crack of the gun shot rumbled like thunder and for a moment, Arthur glanced up at the blue sky.

Quickly, Arthur pulled back on the reins as he watched Randal fall from his saddle and tumble to the ground. Cautiously, Arthur trotted around Randal paying no attention to the frightened horse that had continued running towards the horizon.

"It's over Randal," Arthur moved in a circle as Randal picked himself up off the ground. Blood poured from Randal's left limp arm.

"I'm not going back to that cell," Randal sneered at Arthur.

"Yes, you are."

"What if I made you the same deal I made with that marshal?"

"You are in no position to be negotiating," Arthur said, keeping his rifle at the ready as his horse pranced around Randal cutting in closer and closer.

"Now hear me out," Randal said. "You let me go, and I swear I'll leave your little town alone. No one has to know you and I have history."

"Nice try," Arthur said. "I came clean. Everyone in Oakbury knows of my past and what I did. So if blackmailing is all you have on me, you're going to have to try a bit harder."

Randal's eyes narrowed into slants as his lips curled back over his teeth. Arthur was unmoved by Randal's menacing gaze and remained on his horse, circling the outlaw.

"I know where you live now," Randal said. "You think you'll ever be safe? You won't. My men will come and break me out of that jail cell. Or I'll bribe another marshal and come after you again and again."

"You won't hurt a hair on my head," Arthur said as he shifted his gaze to the horizon where a plume of dust rose up like a cloud of smoke.

"Then I'll just have my men finish what they were doing to that pretty little woman of yours," Randal sneered. "I'm sure they are just dying to get their hands on her again."

"Shut your mouth," Arthur demanded as he jerked the reins back and slipped off his horse. "Listen to me very clearly. You and your men are done. There is no wiggling out of your fate this time, you're finished."

"You really think that the men I brought here are all the men I have? You always were a bit dull. I bet you ten to one that it was Sophie's idea to lure me away from the boys, wasn't it? She's the smart one in your marriage, isn't she?" Randal's lips curled up as he hobbled closer to Arthur.

Arthur balled his fingers into his palms as rage flashed through him like a burning inferno. "Mind your tongue."

Back up is almost here. Just don't lose your cool. Don't get distracted. He can't hurt you.

"What's wrong? Afraid that I'm right? I know what you're thinking," Randal said inching ever closer. "You're thinking about that little wife of yours and if she's going to an empty house, or if I truly have men waiting for her."

Fear flashed through Arthur's body. It pricked him like needles as he glared at Randal who had a wide grin on his face.

"That's right, you don't know do you?"

Sophie.

Glancing over his shoulder, Arthur looked towards his homestead. His heart drummed in his chest as he thought of his wife in danger. Arthur knew better than to think Randal didn't have a second plan in place. In all their planning, neither Sophie nor Arthur had thought that Randal would have more men. Doubt slipped through Arthur's mind like poison clouding his judgment.

In a moment of weakness, Arthur released Randal allowing him to rise to his feet. Dread filled every faucet of Arthur's body as he found Randal inches from his face. Randal's stark blue eyes cut through him like glaciers. Arthur's heart drummed in his ears as he thought of Sophie.

She can handle herself. She'll be fine. Don't let Randal get inside your head. He could be completely bluffing.

"Here's what you're going to do," Randal said raising an eyebrow as he spoke. "You're going to give me your horse and let me ride away. You and your men aren't going to come after me."

"And why do you think I'm going to do that?"

"If you don't, and I don't get back to my men, they have their orders."

"What kind of orders?" Arthur asked, his heart pounding with anxiety at the mere thought of harm coming to Sophie back at the ranch.

"Let's just say that if you kill me, I won't be going alone," Randal said with a twisted smile that caused Arthur's skin to crawl.

"You're lying."

"I know you wish I were, but think about it," Randal said as he started circling around Arthur. Arthur kept his eyes locked on Randal and the bloody mess that was Randal's arm.

"You rode with me once," Randal said. "You know exactly what I'm capable of doing."

Arthur's mind raced to his former years. He knew Randal was meticulous and cunning, so much more than he ever could be. But Randal was a man of his word. If there was a different plan in place to harm Sophie if Randal was killed or captured, Arthur knew he had to choose.

So this is what it boils down to? I either kill my past once and for all and lose my future with Sophie or hold onto my future with Sophie and let my past go.

Swallowing hard, Arthur turned his attention to Randal. The thunder of hooves pounding the ground caused Arthur's heart to quicken.

"Do you hear that?" Randal said. "That's the sound of your life coming to an end."

Before Arthur could turn his head, Randal lunged for him. Suddenly Arthur found himself on the ground as Randal's fists plummeted into his face again and again. The crushing of Randal's knuckles against Arthur's cheekbones caused bright flashes of light to streak through Arthur's vision.

Fight back.

Arthur could hear Sophie's voice in his head. He balled his hands into tight fists and drove back his arm as far as he could. The moment his fist made a connection with Randal's face, Arthur kicked his knee up. Randal fell away from Arthur laughing as Arthur scrambled to his feet.

"Was it worth it?" Randal asked. "Trying to take me down only to have it end like this?"

Through starry and speckled vision Arthur brushed his hand over his upper lip to wipe the blood away. His heart drummed hard in his chest feeling as if it were about to explode. Arthur blinked several times until he regained clear sight and gasped.

Randal stood before him with his limp bloody arm, broken nose, and Arthur's six shooter pointed back at him. Swallowing hard Arthur's thoughts drifted to Sophie. He knew that in a single instant she would be widowed.

"I love you Sophie," Arthur said closing his eyes. The sound of the gun blast startled him. Arthur jumped at the sound and kept his eyes closed for a moment more wondering when the pain of the bullet would strike.

"How?" Randal's voice was ragged and breathless. Arthur forced his eyes open to find Randal on his knees with the light in his steel blue eyes fading.

"Are you alright?" Bergen asked, riding hard and fast towards him.

"Bergen?" Shock flickered across Randal's face before he dropped to the ground, dead.

"We have to get back to the ranch now," Arthur said with the adrenaline still coursing through his veins.

"What's going on? We got him," the marshal said.

"Randal has men around the ranch. They have orders to kill Sophie if Randal doesn't return and I can't let that happen," Arthur said racing to his horse. He paused for a brief moment to steal one last look at Randal lying on the ground. Sucking in a deep breath, Arthur pulled himself up onto his saddle.

"Do we know who?" Bergen asked as Arthur settled into the saddle and turned his horse towards his homestead.

"No, but I'm not going to wait around here," Arthur said and took off.

She's okay. No one knows what happened to Randal - yet.

Arthur rode fast and didn't let up until he crossed into his land. His heart pounded as his nerves rattled. All he could think of was Sophie. Getting to her was his only priority.

"ARTHUR!"

His name was faint, almost ghostly. Arthur pulled back on the reins causing him to nearly get thrown over his horse's neck. Scanning the area, Arthur wondered if what he heard was real or a figment of his imagination. In the distance he spotted a single rider racing out to meet him. For a split second he wondered if it was one of Randal's gang members. But the closer the ride got, the more tense Arthur became.

Something is wrong with Sophie.

"Sam? What are you doing?" Arthur asked as his ranch hand rode up to him. "Is Sophie alright?"

"Your wife is fine," Sam said between gasps of air. "It's the sheriff. Randal's gang has the sheriff and his men pinned down in the ravine. It's a twenty-minute ride from here. Mr. Wickerman managed to break away and came here. He's badly injured and Ms. Sophie is stitching him up inside. But you must go and help," Sam said pointing away from Arthur's home.

"Get back and keep Sophie safe," Arthur said.

"Did Randal escape?" Sam asked, his fear clearly evident on his face.

A prick of guilt stabbed him as he contemplated abandoning the sheriff to see Sophie. All Arthur wanted was to ensure she was safe. But he knew he couldn't do that to the men that came to help him. Arthur nodded and yanked on the reins to guide his horse towards the ravine.

Racing as fast as he could, Arthur couldn't help but wonder if Noonen and his men had caught up with the rest of Randal's men. From what Sam had told him, Randal's men were camping out near the ravine on the east side of town. All Arthur could do was hope that he got there before a bloodbath ensued. If he could convince Randal's men to stand down, then lives would be saved.

After twenty minutes of hard riding, the lush green ravine came into view. Arthur scanned the area swiftly hoping to find some signs of life on either side of the ravine. For a moment, all was still. A flock of birds rushed towards the sky as Arthur rode hard to the boulders and pulled the reins back. His heart stopped as he looked around half expecting to find bodies lying around the water's edge.

It didn't take long before Arthur heard the cracks of gun fire. The ravine caused the sounds to bounce and echo, expanding the horror that Arthur was certain to encounter. As he rode, Arthur spotted the sheriff huddled behind a rock. Small chips of the rock sprayed around the sheriff as the gunshots continued.

"NOONEN!"

The sheriff turned to face Arthur. The expression on his face was of relief and worry.

"Randal's men are on the other side of the gorge. I think there's only a few left," the sheriff said before returning fire.

"Hold up a moment," Arthur said, sliding off his horse and moving towards the sheriff.

"What?" Noonen turned as Arthur lifted his hands up and stepped out from the safety of the rocks.

"I think you should know, Randal Munger is dead," Arthur shouted, hoping his voice projected over the rumbling water.

"There is no place for you to go. Right now the marshal and his men are surrounding us," Arthur glanced over his shoulder towards Noonen. The sheriff's brow scrunched as he watched Arthur step closer to the ravine.

"You lie," a man shouted just before a crack of gunshot echoed around them. A sharp searing pain stabbed Arthur's leg causing him to drop to his knees. Sucking in a deep breath, Arthur tried to hold back from screaming out. He knew if he was going to end this, he'd have to be quick.

As Arthur clamped his leg trying to stop the blood from pouring out of the wound, the area erupted in a blaze of sounds and smoke. Sulfur filled Arthur's nostrils as he ducked down and covered his head with his arms. Just as quickly as the shootout began it ended. With his ears ringing, Arthur lifted his head up to find the marshal once again coming up towards him.

"Did we get them all?" Bergen asked as he scanned the area.

"Over there," one of his men shouted. Arthur's head whipped around to find two men coming out of the shrubs with their hands above their heads. Immediately Arthur's heart pounded frantically in his chest. He wasn't sure if what he was feeling was relief or horror but there stood the two men who had slipped away from Randal's side as Arthur rode to save Sophie.

"It's over then?" Arthur asked more as a question than a statement. After all the months of terror and worry, he felt a huge weight rise up off his chest.

"How bad are you hurt?" Noonen asked as he moved swiftly to Arthur's side and dropped down to inspect the gunshot in Arthur's leg.

"I've been better," Arthur said, still clamping down on the wound.

"We need to get you back to town and have the doc take a look at that," Noonen said. Arthur shook his head.

"I need to get home and see my wife," Arthur replied, reaching for Noonen's hand. "Get the doc to meet me at my house. I have to make sure Sophie is alright."

"You sure you want to wait that long? It would be easier taking you to the doc."

"I don't think this is life threatening," Arthur said. Noonen nodded as he rose to his feet and pulled Arthur to his.

Arthur glanced around the open space to find several men still lying on the ground lifeless. Only two had been spared and they were being tied up.

"I'll see to it these men won't ever see the light of day," Bergen said, walking towards Arthur.

"You sure about that?" Arthur asked, looking at the sheriff before resting his eyes on Bergen.

"There isn't anything they can say or do that will make me walk the path I'd done with Munger," the marshal said.

"And I'll see to it that he stays on the right path," Noonen said patting Bergen on the shoulder. It was an odd feeling for Arthur. Seeing so much death around him, yet there was so much life too.

He pulled in a deep breath and exhaled slowly. Hobbling to his horse, Arthur insisted on climbing up himself. Once settled, he nodded once again to the law enforcement who came to help him and left his past lying there, next to the flowing and shifting waters.

A smile played at the corners of his lips as he charged home. He knew the tension he felt in his chest wouldn't ease until he saw Sophie alive and well with his own two eyes.

Chapter 32

Sophie chewed on her nails as she paced the length of the porch. With her eyes locked on the horizon she prayed for Arthur's safety. She knew Randal was a dangerous man and would go to any and all lengths to get what Arthur had.

Playing back her last moments in her mind, she remembered the desire to reach out her hand to touch Arthur. She saw the same look in his eyes when they passed through the tall waving grass of the clearing. Sucking in a deep breath she wondered where her life had taken her.

"I want you to be happy and find love," Nadine said in a ragged voice. Sophie leaned down over her bedside and pressed her lips to her sister's forehead. There was no pain greater than losing someone. Sophie knew she would trade places with Nadine if she could. But as fate would have it, Sophie was the one sitting beside her sister as she stole her last gulp of air.

Sophie shook her head trying not to think about the pain of losing Arthur or Nadine. Staring at the horizon, she found herself recalling the way the sky had looked as she stepped off the train in Oakbury. It was a pink rose color that stretched on for miles and miles. Her heart had raced as she clung to her umbrella, wondering if Arthur would find her pleasing. Then, there he was stepping through the smoke of the train. He looked almost regal in her eyes. Arthur's broad shoulders were pulled back, his hair parted on one side, and he was dressed in his best. He was stunning and stole her breath that very moment.

"He's fine," she spoke aloud as if somehow the memories would be more potent in her mind. In the depths of her being, she couldn't help but wonder if her flashbacks were fate's way of hinting at Arthur's fate. Pulling in a deep breath she shook her head and swallowed hard.

Brushing her fingertips over her lips, her mind drifted to Arthur's lips pressing deeply on hers. She thought of the way he held her close and made her feel so secure and protected. Even after the attack in the town, Arthur's presence was even more welcomed.

Please come home to me. You aren't dead. You can't be. My love won't allow it.

Falling to her knees, she felt an emptiness seep through her. It was as if a part of her soul was being ripped from her body. Arthur's absence was immediate and permanent. A low rumble vibrated from the core of her body as her mind began to turn black. Instead of the bright and cheery memories she had with Arthur, she started to see the harsh reality that Arthur may not be coming back at all.

Sucking in a deep breath she dropped her head and allowed herself, for one moment, to let go. Tears flowed down her face as she reached for the railing along the porch and squeezed it. She wished with all her might that it was Randal's neck she had a grip on.

"If anything happens to him," Sophie mumbled as the tears flowed down her face, "I will hunt that monster down and kill him. I will show him what a woman scorned really looks like."

Sophie glanced again at the rose-colored sky speckled with clouds. Every fiber of her being wanted to lash out. Quickly she rose to her feet and stared at the horses in the corral.

"I'll go and find him."

Sophie scrambled down the steps while wiping the tears off her cheeks. With swift hands and precision, she saddled a horse, determined to go out and find her husband. If she found him dead, she would hunt Randal to the ends of the earth.

Sophie pulled up on the saddle and looked ahead. She immediately held her breath when she saw something on the horizon. There riding up the road was Arthur. Her heart fluttered and jumped as she dropped off the horse. For a moment she wondered if she was hallucinating.

Please be real.

Is that really you Arthur?

"Sophie!" Arthur's voice cried out and sent Sophie racing towards him as fast as her feet could carry her. As she picked up the hem of her dress to run faster she didn't care that the spiny weeds cut into her ankles.

"Arthur!" Sophie exhaled as he pulled the reins and slipped off his horse. Grunting, he slumped down.

"My god, what happened?" Sophie asked, rushing to her husband's side to aid him. It was at that moment she noticed his blood-soaked pants. Pain and panic shot through her.

"It's a flesh wound," Arthur said in such a reassuring voice that Sophie thought he was in shock.

"We have to get the doctor," Sophie panicked, putting her arm around his body to hold him up.

"He'll be here soon enough," Arthur said, stopping her and grabbing her by the shoulders.

"Sophie, I'm fine, I promise," he reassured her again, catching her attention. A smile that seemed out of place, lingered on his lips. She cocked her head as he leaned down and crushed his lips to hers.

Yes. This is what I needed. Your warmth and love. Thank god you're home. I've missed you Arthur Soul. I've missed you all my life.

Arthur pulled away first leaving Sophie wanting more. She pressed her fingers to her lips as if somehow that would keep the feeling lingering longer.

"He's dead," Arthur said, tucking her hair behind her ears.

"What? Who's dead? Noonen? Bergen? Randal?" Sophie heart went into overdrive as she thought of the brave souls willing to step up and protect their town from the rough riders.

"Randal," Arthur said glancing down.

"Are you sure?" Sophie's heart felt as if it would pound its way out of her chest.

"I saw it with my own eyes. He's gone forever, never to torment us again," Arthur said. Overwhelmed with joy, Sophie threw her arms around Arthur's neck and kissed every inch of his face.

"I thought you'd be pleased," Arthur said as he grabbed her by the hands, causing Sophie to stop and settle down.

"What is it? What's wrong?" She asked, looking at him with such hope and pain that all Arthur could do was shake his head.

"Sophie," he started then stopped. She cocked her head and stared at him with curiosity.

"When all this was happening, do you know what was going through my mind?"

Sophie shook her head as she chewed on her lower lip. Anxiety crashed against the walls of her heart as she moved away from him.

"You. It always drifted back to you. I love you Sophie and I hope that one day I will earn your love in return because there is nothing I want more in this world than you."

"What are you saying?" Sophie said, gulping for air. It seemed like she was struggling to breathe despite the fact that they were in the middle of the open field.

"I want you, Sophie. I love everything about you, and I want you to love me in return. I don't want a marriage of convenience, not with you. I want a marriage and children. I want to make you happy and live out my days as your devoted husband."

Arthur stared at Sophie for some time as Sophie found it difficult to speak. She didn't know if she wanted to cry or laugh. Everything seemed to come to this point and Sophie swallowed hard trying to claim some stake on her heart.

"I love you," Arthur said as he leaned down to press his forehead on Sophie's.

"Arthur I…"

Just say it. You know you want to. You know you feel the same way, so just get it out. Let your heart speak and just say it to him.

"I love you too."

Epilogue

One Year Later

Sophie pulled back the curtain and smiled. She wanted to jump up and down but knew that it would ruin the moment. Glancing over her shoulder, she noticed Arthur sitting on the couch. His leg was propped as he thumbed through a book. The sight of him made her heart flutter.

"Arthur," Sophie called to him. His head darted up to look at her.

"Are you alright?" he asked, shifting his weight on the couch, and looking nervous.

Sophie glanced down at her stomach that seemed to have its own gravitational force. She rubbed her hand over it gently as she nodded. "Everything is fine. But I think Mr. Wickerman is here with our weekly supplies."

Arthur glanced over his right shoulder to the clock on the wall. "He's early today."

"Arthur, do you think maybe you could help me with them today? With my belly the size it's at, I'm feeling a bit unstable."

"Of course," Arthur said hoisting himself up. Sophie watched as he reached for his cane. Although the doctor had managed to pull the bullet from his leg, the accident left him a bit worse for wear. Sophie didn't mind though, she was just grateful to have Arthur by her side alive and kicking.

"Now, don't forget," Sophie said dusting his shoulders as he slowly moved towards her. "The grains need to be separated."

"Yes, yes," Arthur said, bobbing his head. "I know."

Sophie tried with all her might to keep a straight face as Arthur went to the door. The second he yanked the door open, Sophie jumped up.

"Surprise!"

Arthur stumbled back a bit as he glanced around find the Davidson's with their children, Noonen and his wonderful wife, along with the grocer, and what seemed to be every resident of Oakbury in his yard.

"What is this?" Arthur asked, turning his attention to Sophie.

"Well, it's our way of saying thank you for all that you are and everything you've done for this town," Sophie said, throwing her arms around his neck as best as she could.

"I don't understand," Arthur said as the Davidson's rushed up the stairs to shake his hand.

"It's been a year, you old dog," Garner said with a huge smile, rocking Arthur's body with his mighty handshake. "Today is the day you reclaimed our town."

"That's today?" Arthur asked, scanning the faces that were looking up at him.

"We weren't sure you'd be up for a celebration," Mae said trying to push Garner off Arthur so she could hug him. "But Sophie here wanted to show you that you have a place with us here, in this little town."

"I don't know what to say," Arthur said, swallowing the lump forming in his throat. Sophie couldn't contain her happiness when she noticed Arthur fighting tears.

"And with us as well," said a strange voice that was higher than the celebratory cheers. It made Arthur step back and his eyes darted to Sophie as she stepped forward. A tall man with a salt and peppered beard stepped out from the crowd. His lips were curled at the corners and his eyes were just as red as Arthur's.

"Sophie?" Arthur asked, turning quickly to her. She sucked in a deep breath as she stared at the man in the crowd. Arthur knew everyone in town, but this face was new, as was the woman standing next to him.

"Arthur," Sophie said as she moved towards the steps and carefully walked down them. "I'd like you to meet my family. This is my stepmother Lenore and my father," Sophie paused to stare at her father with admiration in her eyes.

"William," Sophie said, squeezing her arms around her father in a loving embrace.

Shock and awe drifted over Arthur's face as he watched his wife curl her arms around the man's neck and peck him on the cheek. The long and sincere embrace warmed Arthur's heart. Glancing over her shoulder, she stared at Arthur with a huge smile which quickly turned sour. Sophie's face crinkled as she grabbed her belly and shot a panicked stare at Arthur.

Arthur bolted from the porch to Sophie's side and grabbed her tenderly around the waist.

"What's wrong?" he asked quickly.

"I think the baby is coming," Sophie said, squishing her face in pain when the contractions began. The townsfolk gasped and stepped back, giving Sophie and Arthur the room they needed to get back inside.

"Leave this to me," Sophie's stepmother said, slipping her hand around Sophie's waistline and helping her back up the steps.

"I'll need a few things," Lenore said, glancing at Arthur and William. The men stood straighter as Lenore prepped them on the items she would need.

"Mae," Sophie gasped in pain. The name barely escaped her lips, but it was clear enough for Mae to step closer.

"I'm right here sugar," Mae said glancing at Lenore. "You tell me what you need, and I'll get it."

Sophie squeezed Mae's hand as her belly tightened with another contraction.

"Breathe," Lenore said in a soothing voice that shocked Sophie. For all the years she had known Lenore, never once had the woman sounded sweet or sincere. Yet, here she was talking in soft soothing tones that Sophie wished she had heard earlier in life.

"This is only temporary," Lenore said. "The pain will pass."

"Slow and steady," Mae said, helping Sophie up the steps and into the house.

"I'm so sorry," Sophie said between her tears. "I didn't mean to ruin this day."

"Ruin this day? Are you Joshing me? You bringing a baby into the world is nothing to be sorry about," Mae said, brushing Sophie's hair to the side.

"I feel like this may have ruined the party," Sophie said between her pants and pangs of pain.

"Nonsense," Lenore retorted, opening the bedroom door. "This is just the cherry on the top."

Carefully, Lenore and Mae helped Sophie to the bed. Arthur gasped and watched helplessly as Mae and Lenore tended to Sophie's needs.

"What can I do?" Arthur asked nearly breathless.

"Pray for a swift delivery," Lenore said without looking at him. Arthur nodded and disappeared into the hallway.

Clinging to the blankets on her bed, Sophie couldn't help but feel overly blessed. Not only were her parents here to experience this moment with her, but so was the entire town. Closing her eyes and clenching the blankets, Sophie brought a new life into the world. And as the baby's cry filled the room, Sophie couldn't help but cry along with it.

"What's her name?" Mae asked, handing Sophie her new baby girl.

"Nadine," Sophie said brushing her fingers over the baby's soft cheek. Sophie looked at Lenore who couldn't help but press her lips into a tight line and nod as she held back the tears.

"That's perfect," Lenore said, glancing at Mae.

"Is that a good name little one?" Sophie asked the baby cradled in her arms. "It was your auntie's name. If it wasn't for her, none of us would be here."

"I have a girl?" Arthur shouted as he popped his head through Sophie's window. Sophie nodded and lifted the girl up for him to see. The love and admiration that filled his features was more than she expected. So much had changed between them and she knew it. Although she came here as a matter of convenience, she found her soul mate in Arthur.

Arthur moved swiftly to Sophie's side and brushed the back of his fingers across the infant's cheek. He stared at the black-haired girl swaddled in Sophie's arms and exhaled. Glancing at him, Sophie noticed that the panic and anxiety that once seemed so dominant in Arthur's eyes had melted. The girl in her arms had broken through all his defenses in a matter of seconds and Sophie couldn't help but smile.

The child cooed and reached out for Arthur. Sophie's eyes lingered on the two of them as Nadine curled her little fingers around Arthur's thick calloused finger and squeezed it.

"I love you," Arthur mouthed as his eyes locked on Sophie.

"And I you."

THE END

Also by Ava Winters

Thank you for reading **"The Scarred Rancher's Unforgettable Bride"**!

I hope you enjoyed it! If you did, here are some of my other books!

Some of my Best-Selling Books

#1 Brave Western Brides [Boxset]

#2 The Courageous Bride's Unexpected Family

#3 Healing the Rancher's Cold Heart

#4 A Redeeming Love in the West

#5 The Rancher's Unexpected Love

#6 A Bounty on Their Scarred Hearts

Also, if you liked this book, you can also check out **my full Amazon Book Catalogue at:**
https://go.avawinters.com/bc-authorpage

Thank you for allowing me to keep doing what I love! ❤

CPSIA information can be obtained
at www.ICGtesting.com
Printed in the USA
LVHW032156040423
743523LV00025B/793